EMMA BLUE

by Beverly Lowry

EMMA BLUE
COME BACK, LOLLY RAY

EMMA BLUE

Beverly Lowry

DOUBLEDAY & COMPANY, INC.

GARDEN CITY, NEW YORK

1978

Library of Congress Cataloging in Publication Data

Lowry, Beverly.
Emma Blue.

I. Title.
PZ4.L923Em   [PS3562.O92]   813'.5'4
        ISBN: 0-385-13135-6
Library of Congress Catalog Card Number: 77-17003

For Moo and Big Daddy,
Henri and David,
The Peach Festival Queen and Santa Claus.
By whatever name. With love.

EMMA BLUE

I

DAMPNESS

It mildewed shoes in closets where they sat, turned crackers to soup, made pages wilt and stick and a starched white shirt to go silk limp yellow. Tree roaches grew long as thumbs, cockroach armies got sassy as cats, salt flowed only if rice was in the shaker, paint wouldn't dry, sheets felt clammy, fresh towels soured, fruit preserves boiled but would not gel. . . .

An in-between season, damp to the bone, a day not one thing or another that you could say, not cold or hot or summer or fall exactly but all of it at once: hot when you're moving, cold when you're standing still, both on top of one another in layers, nothing to do, no way to get comfortable or fix up for it. The sun had made its seasonal pass and declared fall arrived; still summer hung on, and ragweed and dog days persisted and the air was heavy with wetness and pollen and impatience.

Sometimes a thing never knew when to quit.

Never mind it though. Pick them up, lay them down, keep on keeping on . . . once it's begun and got this far, what

else anyway, almost halfway, too late to turn back now, just
go on. Granny says. Just do it. One thing or another, choose
one string, play it out, choose another, go. Sit or stand, walk
or don't but do it, this or that not both at once.

Wood rot ate faster, termites gathered, fleas spawned un-
mercifully: in the rug, on a couch, in your very bed. Lie
down for a nap, watch your ankles turn black. All over town
dogs were scratching; they bit and dug and ate their own
hair, went past fleas down into skin, drawing blood. No rem-
edy but cortisone for the itching, the fleas would die for a
season only when the first freeze came.

Jungle wet, trees dripping not with rain but moisture
from the air, collected and rolled up in drops, running down
branch to branch to fall on the ground in fat heavy drops,
like honey nice and slow.

Like breathing pure water.

Like trying to walk through it. Should have taken a ride.
Had one; should have taken it.

Never mind that though, not now. This far along so what,
shrug it off, don't think about miles, look ahead. Short goals.
One. Another.

Cakes baked up moist but less high, letters went un-
mailed: write one, reach for an envelope it's already glued
shut, licked by the moisture in the air . . . so what, let it go,
tomorrow's soon enough. Fungus thrived, so did snails, and
moss and hay fever and painful sinusitis: sneezes all over, a
rapid-fire morning drill.

People sat in windows looking out. A soft time. Time to
be quiet and think back . . . rehash old stories instead of
making up new.

October. Some October, dragging summer this late into
fall. Some fall. One cold snap only, four days of sweater
weather then back to this. Time to be one or the other, not
both at once. Granny always says, Shit or get off the pot.

But what could you do. Nothing. Only rail against time itself and the year and how seasons sometimes went, too early, too late, overlong, past patience's last thread.

Raising one fist to the heavens, she mumbled a tiny curse and felt better. It did do some good, to rant and rail and fume against gods and time and plots, it did. However useless it seemed, it gave some ease. Especially when you had made such a mistake going out in such jungle-rot no-weather when anybody with any sense knew better. Knew at least to take a ride when it was offered instead of waving the bus on and like a fool walking. Five miles, more than half left to go, one foot in front of the other, keep on. Pick one up, lay it down.

She was coming close to EAT, her midway point, that yellow metal beat-up sign with E-A-T big and bold in blue across the top and, smaller at the bottom, Jesse's Cafe— Downtown Eunola's Choice—Main at the Levee.

She could see a yellow rectangle up ahead through the haze. And some blue: she'd get there.

She wore sandals, jeans, a favorite checked shirt, and went carrying little, going born-again all over again every day, thinking by pure strength of will she could contain it and make it come true: be a girl walking, period, a once-upon-a-time girl—now—with no strings or questions attached, no yesterdays to justify. Start in the middle and call it the beginning, alone and making choices, a girl making it up as she goes. No victim . . . taking care . . . each step her own. One. One.

Her jeans were long and fashionably dragging, covering the tops of her shoes, not conducive to easy walking but so what . . . better than too short, like bus kids' with foolish anklebones sticking out. Nothing was in her pockets or on her arm, no wallet or purse or cards telling her name or how much she weighed, where she was born or lived, none of that. Fifty-five cents lunch money in a shirt pocket was all she had: nothing else extra not even a belt.

Emma.

Her name in fact was Emma but she would not come right out and say, no signs were about her, no announcements giving her away. Instead, like fundamental Baptists born again in water, she would start over every day, on a new road walking, as if newborn down the first hours of a new life. Every day fresh. Now. Once upon, today. People knew old stories enough without her help.

Her head was big and round . . . in front high enough to reflect light and wide enough to span two palms side by side.

High forehead's a good sign, Granny said. High forehead means brains. Means stuffed with brains.

Wouldn't she just. Only because hers was high and wide too; Granny Peavey never gave a thing away free. A Peavey head, she was told: round around and flat on the top. Emma got that head of hers from the Peaveys. They said. And said.

It went first. Her forehead. Out in front in the direction she was going like a blind man's cane tap-tapping the way.

Looks funny the way you walk, Lucille said. Like a string's attached pulling at you. Head juts out by a mile, Lucille told her.

Emma straightened a little, hearing Lucille's complaint. Yes all right okay, Lucille, not so far forward now.

People were in that big round Peavey head, talking and talking, entertaining her journey, making it not so silent and alone. Sometimes herself: a hindsight Emma arguing with another more venturesome and daring self. Other times the others were there, all her people, each in his or her own voice and style, jibber-jabbering their lives away, in easy catch phrases.

Girl I tell you you never know. . . .

The more you do the more they want. . . .

Shit or get off the pot. . . .

Her grandmother Lucille; her great-grandmother Peavey;

people at school; classmates she couldn't get the best of . . .
they all were there. Room enough for everybody in her big
solid head, room for a party, a floating spectacle in her
mind, keeping her company on the road.

Another one too. Her. Every now and then *she* came
along and butted in, in her long-gone silver-whispering
voice . . . every now and then easing into Emma's walking
when Emma least expected or wanted her there. Her. The
Mama. Her. Long gone yet still there. Long gone. Emma's.
Mama.

Not my mother but the. The Mama. Lolly. That famous,
too famous young girl Lolly Ray. Young girl as a mama,
young girl when Emma last saw her, ten years ago going on
eleven this summer. That golden young thing in pictures
spinning dreams, in Emma's mind butting in. The Mama.
Lolly Ray.

The Mama, Emma called her. The long gone Mama.

Not mine however, none of my own, not anymore. Herself
only: what she is and has chosen to be, apart altogether, and
on her own. Not when I never wanted or asked, no. Let her
go. No my-mother in this Emma's life, grandmother and
great- only and they are enough. Set the other one apart,
put her in brackets and call her *The*. And do not above all
say *daughter of* to Emma. Not so she can hear.

Emma plain. Start in the middle and call it the beginning,
set her new and apart from the one they remembered, that
Lolly. Forget daughter: start now, be here, by name and in
the present.

Parasites flourished, new mosquitoes rose like tough thugs
only in packs, birds huddled unsinging. Crickets were quiet
and so were frogs, all the world's noises seemed muffled but
just wait, at dusk there'd be noise enough . . . when locusts
gathered, to lift their wings and sing in the trees. They
made such a shrill screaming every night it seemed the
night itself was in pain. Nothing to do but wait it out: until

the first cold snap it was locust time; until then you might as
well accept them because if you didn't, they'd sing anyway. And once they set up their racket there was no way
to escape it, it went on, loud and unflagging and audacious,
until dark, their volume increasing and diminishing in peaks
and lulls, handed on tree to tree as if conducted, so that the
very trees seemed to swell and contract. After a while the
sound wasn't even sound anymore but only a vibration, ring-
ing like a steel rod whanging between your ears.

After a while you didn't listen anymore. Or most people
did not. Most people said, oh locusts, and went on with their
work. Not Lucille. She heard what she heard no matter
what.

I wish those locusts would *hush!* Lucille said that every
night, and Emma and Granny never responded; they knew
it was Lucille's way.

A dog howled. Emma looked in its direction, off across the
field to her right. It hushed abruptly, as if on command.

Lucille was the same way about a howling dog. Anytime
one cranked up, she opened the door and yelled out, Shut
up.

Emma looked at the sky, all pale, and smiled at herself for
shaking her fist at such a thing, so huge and unblinking. But
she came by it naturally. Weren't they all three fist-shakers?
Granny, Lucille, Emma . . . yelling at dogs and locusts,
baying at shadows, cursing dampness, ranting and railing
and angry, all three. But it helped, it did, it gave some ease.
Sounded crazy but what could you do if it helped but keep
at it.

It had rained the night before, the crowning blow coming
on-again off-again that way, never settling in enough that
you could accurately say it's raining, only drifting in then
steadily back out once again, until morning. In out, out in,
back and forth . . . impossible to get comfortable in your
bed. If you pulled up a sheet to warm up while it rained, the

rain would stop and you'd be hot in the dead stone stillness: kick off the covers entirely and watch what happens. Rain again, and cold. Cold feet.

That had fixed up today all right. Made Monday this way. Wet it down, wrapped it up, put it on a shelf, closed the door, airtight, close.

Some fall.

The highway was on her left, she walked south down its shoulder, a straight line down the center of a perfectly round world. On both sides of the highway there were fields as far as she could see, to the sky. Amazing, that in such a time of manmade so much still came from seeds. But look: to the sky, row after row of stalk after stalk, each topped with a white fire. Cotton. The stalks were dry, brown and leafless, looking at them you'd think the plants were dead. But at the top of each stalk was a full, blooming boll, ripe for picking. The alivest part, the money part, ready and waiting.

The plants had been defoliated: stripped bare of greenness by chemicals to facilitate the harvest. They looked burned from the bottom. Underneath were only sticks, brown and dry, but on top were those cloudlike white balls, waiting.

In the distance, the wheels of a huge red stripping machine straddled the rows. From its air-conditioned cab, the farmer operated the machine, which stripped the plants by drawing clean pure bolls up into itself, one by one . . . zip . . . swooping them up. Without leaves, the cotton fiber was not damaged and no separating was needed. Easier this way. The machine moved slowly but faster than hands: by afternoon the field would be clean.

The field on the other side of the highway had been planted in soybeans and was harvested already. Nothing was left there but leftover rows and some dry stalks and leaves, which soon would be plowed under to rot in the ground and mulch it up more.

Little color was anywhere in her landscape, no playful green, not a cloud or sliver of blue in the pale gray-white sky, no sun to speak of, only a blurred yellow patch across the highway to her left, more like a grease stain in silk than source of light or heat. Below it the earth was black as coffee, rich with nutrients; around it the sky endlessly pale. Yet all three met without notice or distinction and you could hardly tell one from the other the way sky, sun, earth each in its turn simply turned into the other. Without protest or horizon, like water into water simply . . . zip . . . fell in.

A blur.

A peaked day. Seven-something only, past thirty it had to be by now and already it was finished. The rest would be the same as now, pale all day, twelve o'clock, two, four, no sun, no break in the sky or the weather, same day all day, nothing to go toward or look forward to, nothing to mark time by. Flat out the same, hour after hour all day. After more of the same, guess what: still more.

Well but no wonder, should not have walked, should have . . .

HurryEmmayou'llmissthebus!

HurryEmmayou'llmissthebus!

Every morning. No matter what time Emma got up and going either, no matter anything, Lucille said it. *HurryEm-mayou'llmissthebus!* Lucille was not so fickle as to be swayed by changes in schedules and timing, Lucille had it figured out: mornings she said hurry, the bus, late, go on Emma and that kept a morning a morning. As long as she said it she knew what time it was and where she was and the world was the same one more day thank God.

Emma grinned. Thinking of Lucille.

No fad fazed Lucille, she was what she was no matter what, the whole way.

Remember last night? Lucille standing in the living room saying "Some fall" while she dampened her clothes?

"Some fall" she said as her hand went palm-up over a blouse, fingers curled in, dealing out careful doses of water drop by drop across the blouse, dampening, dampening, as patient as a tree, all concentration and intensity and craft, beautiful in it, not satisfied until it was exactly right, an expert. "Some fall." Emma, reading, had looked away from her book to watch. Lucille looked like some kind of Holy-holy giving benediction. Blessing blouses, baptizing pillow-slips, saying amen when it was done then rolling each damp item up in a ball, tight and just so, placing it in a plastic bag and settling it in for an overnight stay in the refrigerator. Cool and stored that way, any overwet spot gave of its abundance to some dry one Lucille might have missed until all of it was evenly supplied. Go for a late-night snack and there they were, staring up at you like weird heads in plastic, between the jelly and cheese and covered leftovers, blouses in plastic sacks saying KEEP AWAY FROM CHIL-DREN*THIS IS NOT A TOY*STA-FRESH SAK.

Like today. Airtight and close. Just like.

Emma wore her clothes straight from the dryer or in a pinch off the end of her bed and as for Granny, who knew. But Lucille's things were always freshly ironed and crisp and smooth and she slept on pressed pillowslips.

Lucille. Wonderful terrible lady, crazy mad housewife Lucille, doing the best she could with what she had. She would yell *HurryEmmayou'llmissthebus* if Emma left at dawn. Before. Middle of the night: Lucille would raise up from her couchbed in the dark and yell it. Emma's high blue eyes brightened, thinking of Lucille. Some crazy. Only keeping it together, how she could.

With other chants too. Such as, anytime anybody mentioned heat, especially on a particularly close kind of day like this one, Lucille said it's not the heat gets you it's the humidity . . . as regular as clockwork. You could bring up heat ten times in one hour, Lucille would simply dish out

the reply she'd come to believe was appropriate and with
conviction too, no irony: it's not the heat gets you it's the
humidity. Lucille believed.

In, Everybody and his brother, for another.

On a holiday you didn't want to go out in the car: everybody and his brother on the highway today, acting a fool.

Clearance sales were out of the question: everybody and
his brother, snatching and grabbing. . . .

Easy for you to say . . .

Girl, you never know, you just . . .

If it's not one thing it's another.

That was her best one. In times of particular exasperation,
or in response to some long-winded tale of endless troubles,
Lucille called it up and it just about summed up her view of
life; that if it wasn't this thing then it probably would be
some other, sooner or later, sooner most likely, one thing or
another.

Chants, like curses, were useful; they warded off danger
and kept things known, summed up situations and made the
world less chaotic, for after all what good did reason ever
do. Like putting down salt before passing it or not telling
dreams before breakfast, like rosaries and rabbits' feet and
praying: do it. For safety's sake. Because one other thing
was certain and that was, you never know. Girl you just
never never know.

True. You didn't. Be prepared for a thing and it didn't
happen. True heat didn't get you but humidity. All true;
clichés always were.

But Emma could not keep that faith and she had not in
fact in spite of Lucille's warnings missed the bus, she had
decided not to take it. She hated the bus, it stank. It and the
kids who rode it, a peculiar smell, nothing she could specify
or tie to causes, not skin color or age, not time of day or
crowdedness, nothing. Even on cold days it stank. Smelled
country was all she'd ever come up with; smelled terrible.

Plus the seats were ragged and torn and the bus itself rattled and bounced and got to school too early: all that time to hang around and wait, nobody to be with but smelly, ankle-sticking-out bus kids. She'd as soon walk and often did. When she went at all.

Her hair stood out from her head in a wild barbed-wire halo from the scalp out. Peavey hair, she was told. The Frankenstein's wife cut, Emma called it: all the rage in horror houses.

Hair was a big topic in their house.

Ought to cut it, Lucille said. Cut, Peavey hair is smooth. Long, mine'd be just like yours.

Should have seen *her* hair, Granny teased, tormented, reminded, reminded, would not let go of or allow to die.

A Peavey she was told. Peavey forehead, Peavey hair, Peavey nature. A Peavey through and through they kept telling her. That while the Mama had not been she was. A natural Peavey, born not made. In her blood, as inseparable as O positive. This familyness, indelibly stamped. Nothing would change it.

Like her hair, going wild . . . long and unruly, in the dampness even frizzier. Nothing to do but cut it.

You *wish.*

Pick them up and lay them down, leave family stuff behind. What I do is what I am. What I choose is me. Step by step, one day, another, across a calendar page, one after another, each square separate from the next. Me today. Once upon today. Choices. Decisions. Making it up. Is me. Is Emma.

EAT.

There: still far-off but plain now, it and the blur of Jesse's Cafe, though Jesse's Cafe had not quite come apart like EAT into letters, but was still a blue fuzz across the bottom of the sign. When she got all the way to it she'd have a small celebration: halfway, an occasion. That was how to do it, how to keep on as Granny called it with the keeping on: by fixing on short goals and not being dragged down by the notion of the whole which was always too long, too hot, too cold, too hard, muddy, full of stickers, whatever. You set short goals and you went for them, when you got to one you set another, like that. Everything in sight, not too far or too close, short hops, small victories.

Keeping *on* with the keeping on. A willed not-stopping that meant no matter how tired you got you did not stop until you got there, wherever it was. That in advance you had set the not-stopping to go a certain distance and then you did it. You simply did. Went on. Step after step, your mind on each one. Picking them up, laying them down. Then if you failed it wasn't so bad, you weren't so downcast and disappointed with yourself, you could handle it.

Her feet were caked and gritty from walking bare-toed through patches of mud and her shirt by now clung tight to her back up and down from shoulder seam to hem. Heat held her breath like one of those NOT A TOY sacks, yet sometimes the first cool turn of winter unexpectedly brushed past her face. When she felt it, just under her skin and on top of the sweat, she shivered. Cold on the outside, hot underneath, no temperature, hot and cold at the same time, no season, crazy.

Never mind Peavey-sayers anyway. Who cared what they said about her hair. It was her head it grew on, she could let it go horror-house style if she wanted, no clips or bands, long and locust-style, screaming frizz and audacity in their faces, today even louder than usual, in the dampness.

She walked into a cloud of her own breath, swallowed it, blew out another balloon and recycled it yet again, the same stale air.

Don't think about it. Jesse's would soon be plain as EAT.

Her eyes burned high and fixed, blue and set. Your father's eyes exactly, the blood-believers told her. James Blue.

The Daddy. Him. Longer-gone than *her*, less left of him to
go by or check on.

"Hey."

Emma turned.

A car. Close enough to reach out and touch. A boy was
driving. How did he sneak up on her that way? She quickly
turned away.

Not that he was anybody special.

"Emma. Want a ride?"

The window was up on her side but she could hear well
enough and should she go? It was a way out of her bad decision, a rescue more acceptable than the bus. She wanted to
and didn't, his name she remembered was John Robert, John
Robert Something, she couldn't think what. His hair was
shaved up around his ears, the skin there was dead white,
babies' feet white. His arms were leathery and dark and so
was his face, but that skin behind and over his ears was always white. John Robert was a bus kid. She'd never known
him not to ride. Why did he have the car?

And what in the world could she have been thinking
about that she hadn't heard him drive up.

He rolled down the passenger-seat window, going side by
side with her at her pace.

She kept her eyes on EAT and walked on.

Skin white as a frog's belly. She went back and forth, cold
and hot, yes and no, stirred up, angry, thrilled. Something in
her stomach turned.

"Emma? Hey . . ." He thought she hadn't heard.

John Robert What? She walked faster. No. She would not.
He had the family car was why he stopped, he wanted to
show it off. She finished the description: a bus kid *too*. No
way. She walked on, having made her decision, shaking her
wild Peavey hair back and straightening up a bit as she
went from her forward-leaning stance, to walk a little more
normally under his notice.

You look like a goose, Lucille told her, with your head and neck all craned out that way.

Yes Lucille, yes, all right. I'm ninety degrees to the road, Lucille.

Pictures went by. She had not moved; did not.

When Emma left, Lucille was sitting at the maple dinette table with a cup of coffee in front of her and she sat there yet, all this time later, thirty minutes at least, still sitting, the coffee long gone cold and stale, her hands flat on the table on either side of the cup, as they had been when Emma threw her last-minute 'BYE over her shoulder, slammed the door and was gone. *Clunch.* That trailer-door sound.

But coffee was not the matter, and Lucille Lasswell didn't drink or want any, but only sat with the cup for company, happy for a while, enjoying this very temporary spell of morning quietness to sit and stare at the wall and think . . . nice and easy like she liked. Nothing particularly on the wall to look at: a spot she didn't see.

Her kind of day. The daydreaming kind when you could sit, just sit, and not worry about needing to do something useful or productive, not on such a damp hot-and-cold day when everybody else was sitting still daydreaming too.

Pictures went by. Old connections. Memories and dreams . . .

All the *ofs* she had been.

Think.

Wife of, daughter, mother, grandmother . . . *of* this person and that. And how that small hook of a word had defined her. How it had been stuck at various times by various people in soft places over her flesh . . . like a heathen, decked out in ceremonial rings. By now the openings were permanent. The hooks might all come out, the people who put them there disappear, she'd still have the marks in her flesh to inspect and reminisce about . . . this one from the time when . . . war wounds to pore over and tell stories about.

Lucille knew Emma walked. Knew she skipped school sometimes too and where she went. But never said. Emma liked to think she did it all on her own and what was the harm? She took care of herself.

Besides, Emma was old.

Older than they were, Lucille sometimes thought. Older at sixteen than Granny even at eighty-two.

The radio was on, a battered old transistor in a torn black leather case she'd had for years. It had been Frank's before he left, he used to take it from room to room listening to the news and weather. Lucille hated it then, that tin-tinny sound going wherever he did, fading then coming back, no matter if she was trying to sleep or not; she hated it. But Frank was gone and he'd left the radio behind, and now Lucille enjoyed it. She turned it on every morning after Emma left, when the first call-in show came on. People called the station Lucille liked and asked questions. The first show was "Farm and Gardening"; others followed. An insecticide and fertilizer expert was on now, to answer questions about bugs and fungus and chemicals. Until nine.

Pictures came and went, the scene changed. A bright picture, as clear as the night it happened. The first time Lucille saw Emma.

"I hope you don't mind," Lolly's letter had said, "if the baby has our last name, with Blue in the middle instead of the end. Do you?"

Emma Blue Lasswell. Her daddy in her middle, her grandfather at the end, Emma frivolity: because Lolly liked the sound. Suddenly they had come back, it was summer and Lucille did not expect them and yet there they were, Lolly and Emma standing in the door, Emma holding

Lolly's hand, looking up expectantly at Lucille, with those clear set-high blue eyes shining, those eyes. "She has your chin, Mama," Lolly had written, "and Daddy's nose." She had never mentioned the eyes. Those James Blue eyes. Taking the world straight-on, at face value.

You never know. Girl, you just never never know.

They seemed impatient, as if something was Lucille's fault and she was supposed to correct her mistake. As if they'd been out there those six years since Lolly left, knocking and knocking, waiting for somebody to open up and let them in . . . when Lucille had sent Lolly money long ago to come home on but she never had. Yet there was that sense of blame, which Lucille stood in the door feeling.

In the next room, in the bed that had been hers until Granny and Emma started squabbling so, Granny Peavey turned over, coughed, made a snorting sound. Lucille's back drew up at the sound, a quick reflex. She'd be up soon.

"It's me," Lolly finally said. "Hi. It's me." That casual. Lolly never did understand anything.

As she sat at the dinette table, Lucille saw her now, this minute. After saying "It's me," she flipped a lock of that hair of hers back over one shoulder with a quick jerk of her head. A familiar gesture, one Lucille bet she still did.

Plain as day. As clear as if it was happening right now instead of ten going-on eleven years ago. Seeing it. Feeling it too. Remembering how scared she had been and yet relieved too; how both feelings had run through her at the same time, like cold and hot water coming down one spigot, icy and scalding at the same time, one neutralizing the other's sting, leaving her feeling neither. Only weak; watery in the knees. She held on to the door, they came in.

Lucille still had not spoken, could not, what was to say?

Emma came first, bounding into the trailer in her brash, incautious way, the same then as now, no holds barred ever, full speed ahead all the time. She had not changed and never would.

Then Lolly, clicking in high heels, dressed in bright blue, her hands in deep pockets. Lucille closed the door and watched her. She did not take her hands out of the pockets, she did not touch Lucille the whole time they were there.

There were four of them then. Four generations for a few hours, three women and a girl sleeping room by room in a too-small trailer, daughter of daughter, of daughter.

Except Lucille . . . who did not sleep at all, her heart was too full, expectation and dread had pumped it up too tight, full almost to bursting. Her eyes kept blinking, blinking, all night long, like small wound-up machines. Something was wrong, she couldn't think what, but something. Her senses were never off at such times; something bad was only going to get worse, if not one thing then for certain, another. Pray, put down the salt, don't tell dreams before breakfast, chant and pray, rub a rabbit's foot, make lucky signs, read horoscopes. Because you never know, you just never never know. What was it? What was going to happen? She could not imagine.

Pictures. Pictures.

It started with an O.
Odom . . . Oltrip . . . Olswan . . . no. O-no telling.
White as poster board behind his ears.
White as my behind.
"Hey, Emma, the bus's gone and it's past a quarter till. Come take a ride. You'll be late."
Last year he played right end on the B team, this year he didn't go out . . . he sang! Emma remembered it with surprise. That whenever the school chorus performed, John Robert O. wore a black robe with gold satin collar. It seemed strange. Somehow. It didn't fit.

She had to tell him something but nothing came. No flip
or glib response, no near-polite way to say no and yet still
let him feel good at least for asking, which should have been
easy enough, nothing so involved, just thank you but no
thank you John Robert O. Should be, but how . . . not a
word, her head was a rock. She had nothing to say to John
Robert O.

She kept walking as if she hadn't heard, as if he weren't
trailing along beside her like some idiot poking turtle. She
hated him. Him and his white ear skin and singing, those
hairy arms, his offer, this interruption . . . she remembered
something else: he once had a fight with a black boy.
At the end of it, John Robert had walked away red and
puffy and hurt-looking, his eyes ringed with a blue-purple
more resembling shame than bruises. The black boy however had sauntered away like nothing, like he could do it all
over again if he wanted. Not that he'd won, nobody won,
the black boy simply wasn't letting his hurt show. And anyway, in a sense he had won. Because not flat-out winning to
a white boy was a loss. Worse than, even. No wonder John
Robert didn't go out for football. Stupid. He was stupid.

"Last chance, Emma. You know how Leaks is about being
late."

Overton? No. Why wouldn't he just *go?*

Well all right.

She gave him an answer he could not mistake, shook her
head briefly then tilted her chin away from him into her
neck, giving John Robert for thanks the broad forbidding
tilt of her astonishingly wide and high forehead . . . in that
way refusing not only the ride but any easy show of gratitude as well, the same as she had the school-bus driver, saying in effect this offer is your affair and not mine, I never
asked, did not need, am feeling fine in this walking and no
victim, needing no sympathy and help therefore owing you

nothing in return, not even politeness: nothing asked, nothing earned, no gratuities, no victim, on her own.

Manners? Were only obligations. A limiting of options, a narrowing-down she could not afford.

Keep on. With the keeping on. Don't let down for such as this. She fixed on EAT. Nearly there.

Stories turned in her mind too. She had to go past them. Start after, and go from there. Keep her life boxed in. Stay inside this thick shell of self and option, safe from distractions, the past.

Stories about the Mama. Stories the Mama had told, in the night to her daughter, saying in her light fine whisper, "Listen . . ."

No.

John Robert got the message and took off, mumbling something unhappy and indistinct as he went. A thin spray of water lifted like surf from each rear tire, his car swerved on the damp pavement and he was gone, sucked quickly up into the dampness, vanished.

It made her feel dizzy: two ways at once. She wanted and did not want to refuse him, congratulated herself for feeling free to, yet was sorry to have done it. Might have been nice to get in out of the weather and ride, rest her feet and let her mind cool down some. Might have been pleasant. Looking at his white behind-the-ear skin. White as cooked perch.

EAT. She passed it. One quiet hurrah: halfway. Ahead was another sign, a new one. U-SPIRIT? Did it say U-SPIRIT? What in the world would U-SPIRIT sell?

And what in the world would she have found to say to John Robert O. anyway, for two and a half miles?

Never mind him, he was gone. Never mind that her throat felt clogged and her nose was running, it had been since the first, but now it was a regular faucet. Never mind. She pinched a bulb of wetness off and wiped her hand on her jeans. Should have brought tissue. In this weather every-

thing ran, sweat, trees, noses, everything; dripping and running like rain, everything but real rain itself.

Still looked like U-SPIRIT.

John Robert had said it was late and she was certain it
was. Had to be ten till at least, she'd never get there on
time. Late again, trouble again, Jamison Leaks' office again.
Jamison Leaks was the assistant principal, in charge of discipline, including unexcused tardiness which in his books
meant all tardiness, no such thing as excused lateness to
Jamison Leaks.

Emma! Leaks would say, I'm surprised.

He said that to girls. Boys he just paddled.

So?

Leaks couldn't touch her.

He was black, a feisty, sweet-smelling black man of
the old school who dressed spiffy and enunciated overcor-
rectly, the kind that slipped up and said Negro on occasion,
having been brought up when that was the more acceptable
term to use. Emma liked him. For holding on to his style.
For being that kind of black man at a percentage-integrated
high school, the preacher kind: he could have been a Mills
Brother, an Ink Spot, Nat King Cole. Emma couldn't help
admiring him, he was so outrageous, the out-and-out rascal
he was.

And John Robert was right, Jamison Leaks tolerated no
lateness. Better to be absent according to J. Leaks than late.
Absent you could get by with a "She felt bad" note. No such
thing however as an acceptable excuse for being late.

But what could he do? Emma had been late so many
times by now he had come to think she did it on purpose,
what more could he do?

So I'll be late again, so what. And he'll fuss again and lec-
ture and . . . what? Nothing. Feel dissatisfied that his pure
shame didn't touch her.

The air seemed to close in more. She was feeling really

hot now. A small seed of exhaustion sprouted, sending
shoots from her middle out to arms and legs. She perspired
heavily anytime and in such weather even more. Her shirt
was soaked, her hair jam-up in strings against her neck, like
a wet scarf.

Ought to cut it. Peavey hair. Ought to cut it.

For a breath of coolness, Emma lifted it against the back
of her head. Instantly, the tightness and anxiety lifted and
she felt better. She was hot, that was all, just uncomfortable.

Overstreet. It came to her. John Robert Overstreet. She
could hear the black boy taunting him. Holding up his bony
hands saying Hey O'street, come on O'street, git me.
O'street, he said, come git me O'street.

Her hair felt like animal fur, like a dog that's come back
inside after a rain. Shivering suddenly, she let it go. The cool
air on top of the sweat on her neck felt clammy; worse than
too-hot and covered. She shook it out.

Lucille nagged her about her hair. She didn't mean to but
couldn't help it.

See, she said, I have Peavey hair and I keep mine short.

It was hair, only hair: so what?

Lined up: her hair and hers and hers, Peavey hair, Blue
hair, whose-ever. Curl, no curl, frizz, a natural wave as
smooth and flowing as water.

You should have seen it.

No. She didn't want to hear.

Like no color you've ever seen before. . . .

The Mama, the Mama, she never went far. Stories, told,
retold, ignored, returned.

In the night. Told by and about the Mama.

Lucille heard Granny Peavey as she changed positions
once again, grunted, farted, coughed, settled back asleep
. . . if she was asleep. Either way, she'd deny it.

"Did not sleep a wink" was her morning song. Go in her room during the night, stomp, slam drawers, drop books, yell her name, she wouldn't rouse but snored away, rickety-rack, bones loose in her nose. Slept dead as a doornail except for all those sounds, rattling and hacking and spitting and farting, rumbling through her dreams like a thirteen-gear diesel.

Next day ask her how she slept.

Did not sleep a wink. Tossed and turned all night.

Never one wink, not one minute of any night, but was awake all the time according to her, day in and day out, night and day, tossing and turning.

"Lucille," she'd bark. "What time'd you turn off TV?"

"When it went off. One-thirty."

"I heard it." She always heard it. "Heard The Star-Spangled Banner, the Thought for Today, Lord's Prayer, the whole thing. Heard that fool rooster too, at five this morning. Heard Emma leave for school. . . ." Snoring all the while. Never admitting to one minute's peace or satisfaction or comfort, not an instant of letting go, awake or sleeping.

On the radio a woman called in to ask about her tomatoes. She had tried some in the spring, she said, and wanted to do it again now, in pots.

"The bloom comes on, you know, pretty as you please, and not just a few, a lot. Bunches of blooms, all up and down the vine, nice and yellow, pretty as you please, healthy-looking and everything . . ."

The woman went on and on; the gardening expert kept trying to rush her along with impatient mm-hmms but she was having none of it. She took her time.

". . . blooms right and left and I fertilized too with that 12-24-12 you recommended. I mean I did everything, red-wood stakes and ties and everything, got good sunshine, watered just right, sprayed for bugs. Still, would you believe it, those blooms every single one fell flat off before making one tomato. Zip zap, every one. Just like that. Like somebody came in one night and pinched them off. Now . . ."

Lucille cut away from the radio talk and went back to the old picture show replaying in her head. Lolly had followed the child in, click-clicking about the trailer, giving it the once-over good and proper, as if judging some kind of exhibit. "Well . . ." she kept saying. "Well." Lucille fell back into watching the story with ease and grace, like a retired night-club dancer who, hearing the beat of her tapping tune, ties back on the old black patents once again and gives it a whirl. . . .

The expert was recommending Bloom-set but Lucille was elsewhere . . . happy. Her arms were out in a graceful arc, a spotlight on her face, and she was gliding and time-stepping, heel-toe, toe-heel, shuffle off to Buffalo, slide-shuffle-hop, back in time to old loves and dreams and connections. Remembering. Hold a shell to one ear and listen. She believed: waves broke inside her ear.

"What's *this?*" the child had asked, picking up that old ashtray they'd had since who knew when, a clear-colored aqua-glass top hat, upside down with a groove in the brim for a cigarette.

How come? she asked, and Why? and What's this?

Emma ran from one thing to the next in the trailer, asking, asking questions.

Lolly watched.

Not U-SPIRIT. U-STRIPPIT. A new place where you took furniture to be stripped. Did it yourself. There were vats of a bubbling substance you put a chair into and left for a while; it came out peeled and raw. Born again. No past paint mistakes, no cover-up coats of varnish, no past at all, starting over. Emma had been there and watched. Seemed a

bad business. She kept wondering what would happen if
you accidentally stuck your hand in, what it would come out
looking like with its insides hanging out, like the chair, ex-
posed and unfleshed, raw to the world. She couldn't imagine
working in such a place, with violence so accessible.

She went everywhere. Not only to U-STRIPPIT but everywhere. Places she had not been invited. Brash, she just
showed up. To see what was what, at the heart of things. To
investigate for herself, and explore, an archaeologist search-
ing for signs. People looked at her funny, wondering why
she'd come when she must know they'd just as soon she'd
stayed away.

Never mind.

Adventurers stay on front lines, ahead of troops and gen-
erals, to scope out territory and information.

How come you can't ever sit still? Lucille asked, her eyes
narrowed to slits.

Maybe she would if anything ever seemed permanent
enough to stay for. So far, nothing had. A mama just up and
left in the middle of a thing, the trailer they lived in was
light on the land. If anything came along she could come to
think of as real, and a home, well then maybe. . . .

Signs of the town appeared. Lights in the haze, bright
colors blurred by dampness into soft halos. On the other side
of the highway she could see the Dairy Delite, not yet open.
The Eunola city limits sign was coming up too, not the original but a newer one, redrawn by city council eight years before, okayed in turn by the county commissioner's court and
then the state land commissioner's office. Emma knew the
exact spot where each was, the old line and the new, and
when it was drawn and by whom. She knew in fact more
about the town and its history than most people ever cared
to ask about. Having pored over old maps and plats and
documents and city directories, minutes of council meetings,
expeditionary journals going back to the town's first settlers,

she had traced the history of Eunola geographically, historically, politically.

Me, Emma, I am archaeologist to this town, here to testify what bones I have dug up, what skeletons were at work at which tables and pots, pursuing what activities, using which tools, sleeping where, making what kind of artifacts.

For Emma, the historical Eunola lay around the newer visible one like a shadow: its history, blurring its present, however far away the town got from its origins, whatever else it tried to be. The shadowy old self Emma knew and understood; the new one seemed less real, with less certainty what it was anymore. Now it was patched up; plastic and franchise and faddishness right next to remnants of the past: couldn't figure out what it was to be anymore, hanging on to some old things, bringing in new so fast that some better old things got torn down before you knew it. Zip . . . one was down, another put up in its place . . . that fast.

Some town. Not one thing or another anymore. Except here, where she walked. All that cotton and soybeans, as far as you could see, to the sky. Out there they hung on; elsewhere was a different story altogether, and even here. . . .

She'd heard of one entrepreneur who dug up acres of land, this rich alluvial soil, and sold it to make a parking lot. All those years it took to make the soil rich, all those floods and now . . .

Cars parked on it. Stupid.

But who was Emma Blue Lasswell, what did she know? Who asked her for testimony?

No matter. Emma did research on her own, at the library she loved, the downtown branch, where city documents were kept. She was an expert by now; she could tell you which streets had been laid out when, where cemeteries once had been, who did this and when . . . a delineator of real, measurable events . . . a charter of which choices had been made and by whom and with what results.

She passed U-STRIPPIT and the Dairy Delite.

You should have seen it. . . .

The story wouldn't go away. Something about seeing John Robert made her remember and hear it, this particular Mama story, which always began the same and once it started, no matter what Emma looked at or tried to think of to distract it, would have its say. It began to play behind her walking, like a musical accompaniment. The story about her hair.

Not Emma's hair . . . hers. The Mama's.

Had to be eight o'clock. John Robert said it was past a quarter till when he came by and that was a while back. The late bell rang at eight-twenty, no way to make it on time. The story came on. She neared a truck stop open all night and smelled its cooking before she got to it: bacon, coffee, eggs fried in grease. OLD-FASHIONED COOK-ING, one window announced. OPEN 24 HRS BEDS AND SHOWERS the other one said. She passed the city limits sign.

Should have eaten.

She didn't like breakfast food much, at least not this early, eggs or any of that, toast was all right except for the crunch it made in your head. Still, she was hungry from walking and the food smelled good. Should have eaten, something anyway.

Not like any you ever saw.

They all told it, her grandmother and great-grandmother, all her aunts and uncles, what kind of hair Lolly had had and how it had looked in sunlight, and always told it the same way in the same words at the same measured pace, making certain as they went that every point and detail sank in good and deep . . . year after year in the same language over and over, told and retold until she could have recited it with them word for word, so impeccably the same was it spoken. Like religious parables. Like Bible verses perfectly memorized, or one of Lucille's chants, the same however many times she might be induced to sing it. *You should have seen her hair!*

Main Street was a half mile ahead. Emma butted her head forward and tried to fix on it, the street ahead, where she was trying to get to. The school was on Court, one block past Main and three west to the right. Past the school was the railroad tracks and past them was downtown and the levee. Downtown was dead, a relic patched up to seem alive, a Frankenstein monster with electrified heart and mind. Just ahead of Emma was one of the shopping centers that killed it off.

She passed the truck stop, holding her breath, trying to get herself back exactly where she was, picking them up, laying them down one after another, trying to stay here where she was instead of off in old hungers and stories and dreams. Making it up, the present the present, as she went.

South. Toward Main.

Where she would turn west to go toward downtown and the levee, to school.

Downtown was dead.

The levee was hardly needed anymore; there had not been a flood in fifty years.

Downtown didn't know what to make of itself anymore, whether to go forward and sell, or turn itself into a museum piece.

East down Main however was a different story.

Turn left at Main and 84 and see.

Not dead in that direction, no relic of old times but new and moving and what it was altogether without question or regret.

Used to be, the land east of 84 past the cemeteries was planted in cotton or soybeans just as it was where Emma had walked; not now. Used to be the land in that direction belonged for the most part to one family and it planters, almost exclusively of cotton; not anymore, having been sold by one member of that one family, or most of it, sold not to farmers but whoever had hard cash and could immediately pay. *Now* was the spirit in that part of town, replacing the old reverence for family and past reputation. Who could? was the question, replacing Who has been or was and is. And whoever could, got it, whatever their business.

Some of the land was bought by an electric company to put a new power plant on, some was used as a site for a rug factory. There was a lumber company . . . the offices of a plastics concern . . . a giant discount store . . . town houses and apartments and small comma-shaped swimming pools and row houses in a tight bunch for those working by the hour in the new shops and businesses. Away from the road, hidden in trees, were some larger homes on half-acre plots. Real estate companies had bought that land, given it a fancy name and turned rich planting soil into backyards with pools and patios and self-lighting gas grills. Flowers grew like crazy there, in front of houses essentially in-a-row too, like the others only bigger, built in the so-called English Manor style, though what English Manor meant nobody who lived in one ever really knew. But the houses were fancy and big and that was enough; they had a certain elegant high slant to the roof. The address was prestigious and certain people were kept out. . . .

The ones who always had been. Whatever laws were made, who once was excluded still was. Same ones, no change.

Not so easy now to get away with . . . still, ways were found. To pick and choose, to say, *you* can live here but not you . . . for the most part, ways were found.

Turn left on Main, to the east, go a few blocks, you will see across a drainage ditch two cemeteries, side by side.

At the drainage ditch, just before the cemeteries, Main swerves to the right a little to cross the ditch, then ends. Court swerves toward Main there and picks up the east-moving traffic and takes it on out.

At the end of Main, take the curve, switch to Court and go on out. Pass the Protestant Cemetery, pass the Jewish, pass the new addition to the Protestant, a housing development, a strip shopping center, new homes and businesses. . . .

After a while Court turns to blacktop. Stay on it.

Some miles farther, the surface turns to gravel. Just there, at that change on the right, is an apartment complex and next to it a private school, hurricane fenced with barbed wire on top for extra measure.

Eunola Christian School: certain people kept out. Whatever the cost, certain people excluded. Whatever justification is called for, whatever use must be made of children, make it, in the name of the name. Public schools were wild now it was said, now that the you-know-whats were there. No discipline in the halls, no learning, everybody afraid of the kids. The kids. Send your (white) child to Eunola Christian. Avoid the kids.

The apartment complex next to the school was built soon after the school . . . for people who could afford to send their children to the school but could not manage to make house payments as well. Beau Manor it was called.

But the law and those excluded families had the last laugh there. When darker-skinned families insisted on moving into Beau Manor, even though their children could not attend the nearby school, the law upheld their right. And so the resident white families fled ratlike, and what once had been the place to move into now was the place to stay away from, according to some.

Had to move fast to keep up with those some. Had to keep shifting your feet or the ground would move right out from under you.

Now no child from Beau Manor attended school next door, or crossed the hurricane fencing in daylight hours. Vandalism however was a problem, in spite of floodlights and guards. Broken windows, small fires, shit in the halls.

At the gravel road the name of Court Street changes to Beall Road, for Lady Beall Cunningham, mother of the young man chiefly responsible for all the changes east of town. Lady Cunningham had been dead seventeen years.

Not long after that name change is a fork. Bear left there, go on another mile or so, pass another industry—the orchard of tung trees newly sapped, in rows—and you will eventually come upon a sudden, unexpected stand of bright green . . . on your left across the road, ligustrum and cherry laurel planted side by side to form a natural barrier to the house beyond and its lawn, that wide expanse of green as bright as plastic: winter grass, silky as rye, green in all seasons.

There.

The young man lives there.

Who'd done all the selling and speculation: him.

Carroll Cunningham.

The house had changed too. Used to be colonial style, with columns and wrought iron and the rest; used to look to the past for its inspiration, two-story, rising up over the flat countryside like something bent on dominating, meaning to show how grand it was in comparison . . . to prove what a better thing man was, to have planned and built such a thing. Used to but did not now, the house rambled and sprawled, one-story, running with the land instead of holding off against it, moving as the land did, flat and out and open to the light, using what was plentiful instead of shutting it out to create its own. Windows were all over, big ones wide open with no curtains, and there were domed

skylights in the roof. The house had an optimistic air, looking to the future now instead of backwards to see what it
should be and have to say about itself. The top floor had
been removed except for one section, the easternmost wing,
which served as an apartment for Preston Cunningham
and Judge, the man who looked after him. In the rest of it,
Preston's son Carroll lived.

It was his house now. Having been his mother's until she
died, having been his great-aunt Mattie Sue's before that
and the family patriarch Sexton Cunningham's to begin
with. Those influences were mostly gone now. It was Carroll's house, by Carroll's choice.

He sat on the edge of his bed waking up.

Time to get up, long past. He should be at his desk this
minute working. After eight . . . markets would open in
forty-five minutes, usually he was long up by now already
dressed and having breakfast. Somehow, however . . . it
was unlike him . . . he couldn't quite get on his feet and
moving.

He looked up. Across the room was a floor-to-ceiling window. For privacy's sake Carroll had had a drapery installed
but it was pulled open. He could see most of the backyard.

Two men moved across the window.

Carroll was naked and considered closing the drapes, but
the men were busy at their work and would not think to
turn around and notice, and so he sat with an elbow on each
knee and his hands clasped between, and watched. No telling how long they'd been up. With a farmer's routine dead-
set permanent in the clockwork of their minds, those two
were always up early, before dawn no matter what day it
was or season and no matter how they felt either. They simply pressed on, no matter anything.

Some merit to that, too. No sitting on the side of the bed

feeling lonely: get on up and do it. No questions. Picking them up and laying them down.

The day was gray. Looked wet out, maybe cold maybe hot, hard to tell, maybe neither . . . this time of year, no telling.

Judge pushed a wheelbarrow in front of him and Preston followed, carrying a folded aluminum chair under one arm, dogging Judge's footsteps so closely he seemed to be retracing them, as if fearful otherwise of losing his way. When Judge stopped and set the wheelbarrow on its elbows, Preston opened his chair and, placing it snug up next to the wheelbarrow, sat in it. He was oblique to Carroll: all Carroll could see of his father was a scant profile; his crossed blue-jeaned legs; shoulder and chest; one hand gripping the aluminum arm of the chair.

Above him, cool air switched on.

Carroll looked up at the vent. Air conditioning? This time of year, so soon? He didn't feel hot; he wondered if they wouldn't get cold under its flow. Still . . . must be humid out, must be awfully damp. The air-conditioning system was designed to turn on automatically when the temperature got to a certain point and the humidity came up to meet or even pass it. Still. Tomorrow they might need heat. Carroll felt the cool air drift in over his head then come to settle down about his bare shoulders and wrap around the stiff column of his long thin neck. He shivered.

He turned back for cover. Her form was still there, an indentation in the bed where she had lain.

Who? It took him several moments to remember. Visiting a friend from college, she had said, in town for Easter week. Then he recalled her exactly, and everything that happened the night before.

The white brick of the house was set off out front by a careful arrangement of well-orchestrated growth, lush in all seasons, planned by Carroll and kept lovingly by the handy-

man, Judge, who'd been on the place since Carroll's childhood. Carroll enjoyed plants . . . any sign of life to perk him
up, if he didn't have to invest in too costly a reply . . . but
for Judge, the yard was a deep source of pride. Indoor
growth he didn't fool with . . . foolish, he maintained, to
bring dirt inside a house when people were all the time trying to keep it swept out . . . but he worked the yard with
care, his own special brand of slow, precise gardening.

In spring, gardenias and camellias and azaleas bloomed
alongside the front wall and down the front yard, and roses,
nandina, plumbago, verbena were planted in between, in
well-coordinated clusters of color and style, on a lawn built
up to roll, landscaped by a local nursery to drain, so that
rainwater ran off, instead of staying lakelike in the flatness
to rot new seeds and roots and the bases of stalks trying to
naturalize and grow.

From the road you could not see all this. Could not see
how right now the rain tree was in bloom, with grape-heavy
clusters of pale flakelike gold and pink flowers tugging at
every branch, pulling it low. A pyracantha by the house's
left corner had already filled out . . . with Christmas-red
berries as thick as a hive . . . and an acacia was spectac-
ularly yellow. Nandinas blushed pale red, a clump of spe-
cial-order lilies were in their fourth bloom, a three-colored
bush called Yesterday, Today and Tomorrow had white
flowers next to blue next to near-purple, as the blooms aged
and grew dark. Beside it, tiny white tea roses had been convinced by Judge's expertise to make one final appearance
before turning into dry hard sticks for the winter.

None of this: you could see nothing of this color from the
road. Unless you got out and went through the ligustrum
and laurel, to make a special point of getting inside to see.

Actually Carroll wasn't as keen on flowers as Judge, who
did the planting and much of the choosing too: it was Judge
who phoned orders to the nursery, not Carroll. Carroll liked

tropical plants best, green nonblooming things, philoden-
dron, aspidistra, ivy, elephant ears, palm, all kind of fern.
The backyard was planted with these, more to Carroll's
taste.

Far to the rear of the house beyond the yard was a pond
Carroll had had dug and stocked with bass and perch . . .
for Preston to fish in, to help fill up his days.

Or so Carroll thought. But it was a waste, hardly if ever
used. Preston was a farmer, accustomed to getting up and
on with a day, he didn't like to fish. Sitting all day waiting
for a cork to bob was simply not his idea of anything to do.
Judge went occasionally, so did the maid. But the pond was
three years old now and had not been fished nearly enough.
Probably the fish were on top of one another by now.

Judge reached into the wheelbarrow and drew out a
twenty-five-pound sewn paper bag. Several dozen small
hairy bulbs were beside it.

He had tilled the earth and dug the holes the day before.
He took the sack to where the holes were.

Judge had protested when Carroll asked him to do this
planting: it might be too early, he said; late October to early
November was soon enough. This time of year, he said, you
never can tell, summer might come back and burn up the
flowering. And if winter went on too long, the cold would
bite off the first blooms. Might get it from either end.

But Carroll insisted. He wanted to make some move toward a change, even if a sign had not been given to assure
him it was coming. Planting was a trust he somehow
needed.

A light cotton blanket thrown over his shoulders for
warmth, Carroll stood and went to the bathroom, his back
slightly hunched and drawn in.

Too late for air conditioning, too soon for heat . . . if both
were turned off, the stillness would be stifling. A bad time.
No way to know. No way to prepare for it or figure how it

will go. Might be either way. Or might hold like this for a
while, close and sticky and damp, for no telling how long.

He thought of the girl again and winced.

Good Lord. He just remembered.

He'd called her Snow White.

Getting better now: she could see the end of it, in her
mind if not really. With less than a third to go it was better
all around. Her pace picked up. With things to entertain
her, the time went faster and she didn't mind it so . . . now
that she could see colors, sights, people, cars, stores. . . .

If only she'd eaten.

Now it would be hours. Horrible school food at that, watery soup or soggy limp spinach, probably salmon croquettes, those mashed together leftovers from the week
before, not a sign of fish in them except those round
knucklelike little spine bones . . . but wait. No, on second
thought it wouldn't be salmon croquettes, Monday wasn't
fish, Friday was. Catholics didn't have to anymore and everybody knew it; still, the school went on same as always,
doing what they'd done forever, every Friday of the world
fix fish. Sometimes salmon croquettes, sometimes fish sticks,
sometimes a thing they called cod flake fillet, bits of fish
which if you caught it you gave to the cat or threw out. Fish
garbage, packed together with junk and filler in a patty as
round as a compass-drawn circle. Today might be canned
ravioli, those gummy crimped pure-starch squares drowned
in a stand-alone orange sauce. Or boiled wieners and sauer-
kraut, what a smell, made the whole school stink. Maybe
liver, thick slabs of grit-grainy fried mudlike stuff, onion-
camouflaged to look like steak: take a bite expecting steak
and oh, well. The texture, and what a taste. No fiber to tear
at like steak, all organ, something's *insides* for Christ's sake
. . . viscera. Afterwards, that grit in your teeth and the

smell: take a bite and it fills your head; belch and it bellows out nose, ears, eyes, mouth.

Oh liver, liver, deliver me from liver Yours Truly Emma Blue.

Her blue eyes winked, her arms swung hard, back and forth.

Only the ice cream's any good.

Cornsticks?

Right, cornsticks.

Red jello with whipped cream?

Fake. Pure plastic. Not a sign of milk, cancer in every bite, all additives and chemicals . . . shortening I've heard, whipped up to look like cream.

You never know. Girl, you just never know.

Then again, if you didn't think about it but held it in your mouth until it melted and let it mix with the red jello it wasn't bad. Can't think about everything all the time.

She came to a service station and turned in. In the ladies' room, she pulled down a wad of toilet paper cut in stiff squares, blew her nose three times, threw the paper away, yanked down another stack for the road, hard on the nose as it was. Stiff as notebook paper. An attendant filling up a car with gas watched the girl walk back to the highway's shoulder and head off toward town again, leaning in that direction as if dead set on getting there. Like she was being pulled.

Emma never looked back. She saw him watching her but never gave him a sign.

Briarheather Shopping Center was ahead. ALL-WEATHER MALL, it called itself, with flagstone walks and waterfalls. A worldwide flag display. Baby-sitting arena. Game machines. Balloons. Clowns. Bake sales. Movies, tacos, ice cream, pizza, Tak-a-Foto, special seasonal exhibits.

No wonder downtown died.

This was where people went to be entertained. To have fun.

She'd heard so many stories so often and they were so old to her by now that as soon as she lifted up her hair this one came, like a song you keep hearing over and over in your mind and can't get rid of, in the exact phrasing and intonations the singer on the record gives it, never changing from one hearing to the next:

You should have seen it, it went. *You should have seen her hair.*

And: *Isn't it a shame Emma didn't get it? But has Peavey hair instead?*

Thick and *wavy, naturally curly same as yours.* But not frizzy. *No, not ever frizzy: smooth and flowing. Like water.*

Like water.

And the color?

Oh the color. *Brown like mud with an overlay of red and gold on top, like rust and sunlight, like the sun was inside it instead of shining on it. Mud-rust it was. Mud-rust. Picking up light. Like the gold suit she wore. Picking it up.*

Such hair and such a mama, year after year they told Emma the same story, same, same over and over again, in the same language, *you should have seen her hair.*

Baloney. She had seen it . . . didn't remember it like they did, but had seen it all right.

Please. Emma plain. Just Emma. Peavey if that's so, anything but hers, anything but daughter of. If long-gone was what Lolly wanted let her stay where she wanted, far away in time and space, all right. Just let Emma be: Emma. Making choices, deciding, choosing to ride or walk or go or not, whatever she felt like, one by one.

Step by step.

Briarheather was not yet open. The huge parking lot was empty. Yellow lines zigzagged across it in pairs, waiting to be filled up.

Just keep on, pick 'em up, lay 'em down, Granny knows. On with the keeping on.

She bowed her neck and put one foot in front of the other, hoping it was enough.

Lolly had not stayed long and Lucille had found out soon enough what the bad thing ahead would be . . . the next morning in fact. She wondered if Lolly knew that someone had watched her go. Or if it mattered.

Lucille fit her hands one inside the other around her coffee cup, making a tender wall, as if in its defense . . . smooth, pale hands, long and graceful fingers, like her face without wrinkles, lost from time and schedules.

Her hair was fresh-trimmed and neat; it made soft curls about her face like a gilt frame around a painting, setting off her deep hooded eyes and frail egglike cheekbones. Her eyes were blue, like Emma's, but not so certain. A trembling was inside them, as she remembered. . . .

She looked up at the window. It happened again. As if brand new.

She had lain on the living-room couch, not sleeping. Granny was in her room, the one that had been hers and Frank's, and Lolly and Emma were in Lolly's old room.

Early, not yet dawn, Lucille lay awake, her eyes dry and wide open, the door to Lolly's bedroom opened.

Lucille did not lift up or let on she was awake but lay very still as if asleep, somehow, she didn't know why, waiting to see what would happen without disturbing anything, or imposing.

Lolly had on her bright blue dress again but was not clicking anymore. She tiptoed toward the front door. The only sound she made was the swish of her dress, sliding back and forth against her stockings.

The front door opened. The arm of the couch was between Lucille and the door, and Lucille craned her head around to look through that slice of open space between the arm and back, to see. Lolly opened the door, only a little, and went out: left foot, hip, body, right hip, foot, gone. Facing the trailer, she eased the door shut.

Clunch!

Should have known. She'd lived there. Should have known a trailer door wouldn't ease shut but always made that terrible sound, like the door to a meat locker, everything inside shut up for good, no air, no escape, clunch, that trap.

Lucille got up and went to the window. Too late to do anything. Through a slit in the curtains she watched her daughter go, for good it now seemed. It was the first time she'd seen her car, a new and fancy one, big, an Oldsmobile Lucille thought, a maroon color below with white vinyl top and a stripe down the side. Two-door; sporty. How could Lolly afford such a car? She said she worked at a restaurant making change, turning paper to silver, coming up with little, as always, foolishly believing in clank and glitter instead of a soft fold's quiet worth. She started the car and backed it up.

Lucille watched.

LOLLY.

The license plate said LOLLY, red on white, in raised letters. LOLLY.

She turned the car around to head it toward the highway and when the rear plate went by, it announced her too. LOLLY coming and going, a tag to single her out: her name, announced like the flashing parade signal she once had made, that twirling baton in the sky and the gold stab of her sequined, shiny suit, reflecting against the sun, all coming together to say Hey, it's me, look out I'm coming, me the Lolly, the famous one. Me. It's me.

"Hi," she said. "It's me. Hi."

LOLLY.

One last secret glimpse of her too: as the car passed
alongside the trailer, her profile. Her hands were light on
the steering wheel, her fingers gracefully curved, as casually
in control as if around a baton, her frailty only an act, part
of the illusion she created, this very businesslike, plain work-
manlike young woman. As she went by, she made a small
gesture, one of those private things a person does when no
one is looking . . . she shook back her hair in a final loosening kind of way as if getting free of something, as if saying
well, that is over with, I am free and clear once again, to go
on. She was gone.

She pushed her chin out and high, threw back her shoulders, pressed down her foot, turned north and disappeared.

Free. Spewing gravel, she moved on, her attention set
ahead far outside the windshield and beyond the street
ahead, beyond what was visible and hard and real; higher
up than others', focused on what she never shared, that
sheer entrancing dazzle, the brightest possibility, chance.

No talent for sticking. No way to set herself simply to get
through, not that one, no way she could simply swallow her
fate and say oh well. Not her. Had to shine. Had to be
queen bee. One way or another she was going to get what
she had always figured was rightfully hers, some kind of notice, some kind of way to be set apart from ordinariness,
acclaimed in some way. And she would give up whatever
she had to to get it.

Even . . .

Lucille drew in her breath. After all these years she still
could not think of it without feeling such disbelief it made
her breath stop and a chill run down her middle, like she
was being sliced open there.

Give up even: her own child.

Yet and yet . . . Lucille would not judge. Lolly was her
daughter, by whom Lucille had not done so much better;

she had stayed and Lolly had fled, still and all who was to say?

Oh girl, if it's not one thing it's another for sure and you just better not say, not ever, because you never never know.

Lucille looked back down at her cup. The coffee was cold. A shadow of cream floated on its surface. Quickly, as if afraid to look, she covered it up with her hands.

And if it had been as special as they said, why couldn't she remember it? Or her face either?

Nothing was left. No pictures Emma could depend on. Lolly was gone, crumbled back to dust like flowers in a memory book kept past their time. She had only the photographs left behind and the stories people told. Neither of which Emma gave much credence.

Her own sense of Lolly could not be held down to paper or a picture: Emma saw her in movement. How she turned her head, lifted a hand to her face, tossed back her hair. A certain slipperiness, a lightness; floating above the ground, never touching down where a daughter might come to depend on her. A memory of pulling at her, wanting to hold her down, to bring her face child-level to look at. As if Lolly were a helium-filled balloon Emma had been given to hold the string of for a while.

Fat chance.

She was always going to fly. From the beginning it was set how the story would go, finished before it started, so slippery she was with her head up and her mind on flightier things by far than the squarish earthbound daughter she'd given birth to, this Capricorn goat-child butting her way through, asking for more than a baton twirler could give: herself, now, on the ground where she—Emma—was, asking asking, where are you, where are you now?

The Mama. Like a fairy princess told about but never truly believed in, not in fact and time.

The face was all gone, but certain things did remain. Besides the slipperiness. Some other leftover traces as well.

Like the memory of fear, every day at the baby-sitter's. Lolly dropped Emma off there in the morning and every day Emma sat waiting and every day believed today she will not come, today I will be left, no one to catch me when I fall, today is the day she will fly, here today gone tomorrow, head in the clouds, zip: good-bye Mama and all that, good-bye to stories in the night, good-bye. Emma remembered.

It took so long to get past Briarheather! The parking lot went on and on, forever it seemed like, nothing to say for itself, as if it had the whole world to take up and just might. Coming up next was something as bad, a car lot called Used Car City, acres of cars and service areas and showrooms and repair garages. Downtown suited Emma better where things were close up together and more defined. Ugly was better than this, uncontrolled and audacious, going on and on as far as you gave it room to.

And one other thing, her prized possession, kept safe like a jewel in a velvet-lined box.

Emma told no one; in fact, she refused to say anything about that time to any of them, much as they wanted her to. Nothing of those five and a half years with the Mama. Or what she kept of her now, in her head, and how it turned and kept her going, just angry enough to set her fine line of bitterness taut and keep the not-stopping in gear.

The sign announcing Used Car City was a huge silver pole. On top of which was a car, a real car, junked, and inside it, cardboard figures representing a family. There was a mother, a father, a small boy and smaller girl, a dog leaning over the father's shoulder. The father drove. The mother wore a red hat, a beret kind of tam on the side of her head, rakishly set. The children were smiling broad smiles at whatever they saw through the windshield.

Emma went past it. Past car after car and color after color, lined up like so many toys to pick from, stamped out one after the other, forever it seemed like.

His office was in the house, toward the back in the space that once had been a bedroom and hall. Carroll had had the wall torn down and the carpets ripped up, had bare oak floors sanded and refinished, a floor-to-ceiling window installed, the gray silk draperies removed.

He came in, dressed, carrying a thermos and cup and several newspapers.

It had been Lady's bedroom but Lady's things were all gone now . . . either stored or sent back to her family, some given away, some auctioned . . . until little of Lady Cunningham was left, only that car in the garage and the road named for her and the look in Preston's eyes, still missing her, hardly anything else. Carroll's choice: a person had to go forward, had to move on and away or risk being drawn in.

His desk was a large table, a huge slab of Italian marble set on chrome sawhorse-type legs. The marble had been special-ordered from New Orleans, a beautiful black slab, cool and white-grained and as big as a door. Behind it was Carroll's reclining chair, of black leather and chrome. Across the table was another chair, a smaller version of Carroll's. There was a filing cabinet, a wastebasket, one bookshelf, nothing more. The walls were stark white.

The house bounced light and sound about like rubber balls, the walls were flat white, the ceilings low. There was space and light, gaps, plants. The furniture was of leather, velour, canvas and chrome. Floors were bare and well kept, hand-waxed to a dull, elegant glow.

No more rugs and plush and gilt. No gloomy and conspir-

atorial family portraits. No dark dangerous corners to get
lost in. No Lady.

Carroll sat down and checked his watch. Eight-twenty.
Not so bad. Still time.

As he poured a cup of coffee, he looked out the window
beside him: the two men were still in sight; in fact he could
see them better now. Preston watched Judge intently. As if
his very life depended on the success of their endeavor.

There had to be a time when change was possible. When
the drift of things could be made to go in a different direction, simply by choosing differently, simply that. If you refused to yield to the current, if you opted to swim against it
and were strong enough to reach a new shore, well then . . .
wouldn't that shift the flow?

It would; it had to. After all, history was no more than
that, what people did. He had it now. He knew. If he could
just keep it in line and not feel depressed, if he could just
hold it together. . . .

She did look like Snow White. Embarrassing that he
should say so, but she did. White skin, black hair, red lips.
And red shoes. It was the red shoes that intrigued him. How
shiny they were, and how red, her lips and shoes, and the
white and black in between. Something like that always
caught him up. He had seen her across the room, someone
new, a gay young woman with an aura of merriness about
her, and red lips and shoes . . . and for that one instant had
loved her. From that distance. His heart had leapt inside his
chest and all of him went toward her and he loved her. That
quickly.

Now she was gone and with her, his feeling. No use to
pursue it; nothing there beyond one night.

Judge was preparing the earth for the bulbs. He would
not set one in the ground until the ground was entirely

ready. He tore open the large sack, shaping its top corners into a spout.

Looking back away from them, Carroll opened a newspaper and began to read.

Had to be eight-twenty at least.

Right now, crossing Highway 1, she had to be late.

Late, Jamison Leaks, I am late once again. Once again I am Unexcused Tardiness: Emma Lasswell.

A smell; she closed her eyes. And, oh Lord, she would never make four hours until lunchtime.

First John Robert and his white ear skin.

Then the truck stop.

And the stories.

Now this.

The Gold'n'Crust Bakery. It was across the highway from her, turning out loaf after loaf of the soft hole-y white kind of bread Emma detested. Plastic, she called it, especially when Granny was within hearing range, though not to Granny directly. Usually to Lucille, the in-between. The tin plate they bounced shots off of, to get to one another.

Granny liked Gold'n'Crust and Emma liked whole wheat, and that was nothing, they could afford to buy both. Except that they were so alike, the two of them, that they couldn't let it go at that but had to poke at one another constantly, knowing full well the poking would do no good, that neither one was ever going to give the other the satisfaction of thinking the poke had even registered much less hurt, still doing it, time again, poke poke, never getting ahead of it enough, or past it to say, well who cares: doing it. In this case, whole wheat against Gold'n'Crust was not really the point of argument, just something handy.

No room for opinion either, only right and wrong and certainly, each believed, truth was on her side. *Her* side, my side. Granny Peavey and Emma could sit for a solid morning arguing over something unprovable like that, like white bread as opposed to brown or who gave the best news commentary on TV or whether or not some umpire had called a ball or strike correctly, long after the game was over and the score history. That childlike it-is, it-is-not, yes-I-am, no-you're-not kind of battle nobody ever wins.

Except in this case each thought she had. Each went away triumphant, thinking truth had out and it was on her side again.

I won! I won!

But the smell from the bakery, plastic or not, was warm and inviting and Granny would never know: Emma breathed it in in gulps, though it only filled her stomach with more wanting. She should have eaten, the smell was making it worse, her head ached not so much from hunger as from thinking about food. She was nearly past the bakery yet the smell was strong as ever. Congealed into the thick damp air, it stayed, held there, around her face like the dampness itself.

Warm bread. She could taste it. So soft and hot, butter melts into it.

Preserves on top.

Strawberry preserves. A mound of strawberry spooned on top, soft starchiness and butter and grainy sweet red . . .

That voice.

Emma heard it still, could hear it this minute winding in and out of the bread smell, like a smell itself, like that odor of smoke that stays long past the time of the fire. This long after she was past it, after she had tried to forget, after she had made up her mind to set it aside and pay it no mind . . . still, here it came, stirring her up once again, making her more aware of her emptiness than anything.

"*Emma,*" Lolly said in the night, as the child Emma lay on

her pillow, eyes wide open, goose-bumped and anxious, waiting. Tales from the Mama, told in the night.

"*Emma. You should have seen me.*"

At the window with the curtain pulled back, long after the LOLLY rear tag had vanished, Lucille still stood until, sensing other eyes, she turned.

Lord, the child. Those high blue, James Blue eyes.

Emma stood in the bedroom door, once again looking at Lucille as if Lucille was at fault. Those eyes. . . . Lucille drew back.

Without a word the child came straight to the window.

Lucille moved aside, not knowing what to say or try to do or how to explain what she did not herself understand. But Emma Blue Lasswell didn't seem to be after explanations: she only came on, direct and unflinching, ready it seemed for whatever was ahead. Unsurprised as well at having to face it. As if she'd always known.

"Emma . . ." Lucille held out her arm to keep her from seeing. She didn't want her to know, not yet. If she didn't look or see the LOLLY car gone maybe . . . maybe what? It didn't matter, she would put it off, face it later, she wasn't ready to deal with it, not now, wait.

But Emma jerked the curtains wide apart. Such a small thing, her back and shoulders so square for a child, so old and stumpy already, seeing the new car gone, she stood looking for a long time, her arms straight out, her nose barely cresting the window's sill . . . making sure, letting it sink in it seemed until she was positive. When that was done, she threw back her head and let out a strange mourning wail, a low and guttural sound more like a man or animal than child. Lucille went to her but before she could get a hand on her, the girl was gone . . . running as hard as she could in the other direction, straight into a wall. Following,

Lucille went there but by the time she got close, Emma had switched around again and run to the bedroom wall then back to the window again. Lucille was soon out of breath and gave it up. From wall to wall the child went, banging her body, as blind as a headless chicken trying to find head and nest and sight again . . . with no destination in sight, no light to see by and no clear notion what good the running might do, only doing what came to her, twisting and flapping and turning, butting against one wall, bouncing off, running to another.

And what could Lucille have done? Scream? Run after her? Chase a car? Scream and yell and make a fool of herself over somebody that determined to leave?

No. She could not. Let her go. Watch from a crack in the curtains as one of the hooks gently slipped itself out.

Granny Peavey had been wakened by the noise by then and came into the living room. Lucille told her what was what, but if either woman ever got a hand on Emma and tried to stop her, Emma only squirmed out of their grasp—she was so strong!—biting their hands and, gathering herself long and stiff, her arms tight against her sides, rolling loglike across the floor away from their help. This incoherent running was the form her grief took: banging itself against walls and chairs, running at as high a speed as it could . . . like a Peavey, with no respect for rules or manners, without a glance in the direction of what anybody else might be thinking or feeling, with no sense of timeliness, only going on and on as long as it was in her to, without giving the least nod or gesture toward a natural rhythm of how long a thing could continue without turning stale or boring. Simply going on and on, no break or rest, in that way of hers, the way she still did, even now, with her head set ahead of her body in that gooselike leaning stance, even now, after all this time, she had never changed.

This . . . *fit* was the only way Lucille knew to describe it

. . . lasted almost two hours, with hardly a letup, until Emma's face was wet and red and her hair stood up around her fat baby face like wire. Until she could go no farther but finally despite herself simply ran down, in a heap against the couch, sobbing, choking, mad it was over, that was all, simply furious she could not go any farther. When she did stop, she went to sleep there on the floor, whimpering still, in her dreams, like a fresh-weaned puppy, and it was over. Lucille tried to lift her to put her to bed, but could not. She was in such a clutch of unhappiness, so rolled up in that baby-sodden lump of misery that she seemed nailed to the floor, altogether dead weight, impossible to carry. So she slept there. And when she woke, did not move. But stayed on the floor all morning long, staring, solemn and distant, doodling her bottom lip with her thumb. As if plotting. Making a plan. Figuring it out. When she got up she got up. It was over, for good. She never said word one to any of them about Lolly or her leaving or what it had been like in Tennessee before they came or anything. Not a word.

And was wild yet, as furious as ever, tormented as ever, only not showing it, insistent on staying how she was, on the raw leading edge of her own resentment, leaning forward, keeping it tight inside. She had not changed, Lucille thought, or let up on her feelings one jot, not in all this time, in which eleven years Lolly had not been seen one time and was heard from twice a year only, at Christmas and in January on Emma's birthday. Cards she sent, with money orders enclosed, a generous amount to be sure, but still . . . sometimes Lucille thought nothing at all would be better. No return address was ever on the envelope; she asked for nothing and expected no demands in return. Like Frank. Lucille thought the two of them must have read the same book. Or heard the same song: ask for nothing, be asked the same, free and clear, free and clear.

Lucille shifted her weight and looked down once again at her hand on the cup.

Still smooth. Speckled with age now, but taut yet and quite white, with a graceful look about the fingers . . . nice hands. She was proud of them.

It was right Emma was that way. It kept her from sitting still and turning in on herself the way Lucille had. *Had.* She still meant to change. Still had time? Yes. Still would. Lucille put her left hand over the right one on the cup, to hold it steady. Sometimes she felt so carried away, sitting in the same place so many years while others went away and went, and she was the only one to stay and do nothing but nothing, in a trailer she had hated since the day they moved in yet there she still was . . . how many? . . . nearly thirty-five years later. Sometimes she felt like something caught up in a current she did not have the strength to swim against, it went so fast.

But she could not swim, she had not been taught to, she was afraid to put her face down in water. Rescue had to come some other way, from the shore, from . . . but who was there anymore? With hook and rope and life preserver?

The expert was describing grass diseases, brown patch and fungus and St. Augustine Decline, or SAD, as it was called. The old man who called kept butting in, his voice a gentle, creaking whirr, trying to say he didn't think it was brown patch his yard had but something different, the grass was not dead in circles like the man was describing but in a widening, irregular shape.

Judge sprinkled two measures of bone meal into each hole then tamped a bit of dirt over it to seal the nutrient from the plants' tender roots. A good and careful man, as diligent in caring for irises as for Preston, Judge worked slowly, tediously, precisely. He used to drive Lady near-crazy, Carroll remembered, doing things so deliberately and so thoroughly slow.

Absorbed, Carroll sat facing the window, his chair pushed back. He tapped a pencil on the marble table, hitting it first on its eraser end then sliding his fingers down to the point . . . a dull sound, a sharp one, back and forth. Preston gripped the arms of his aluminum chair as if it were about to get away, his eyes were steady on Judge's hands, watching every move. As if it were that important.

Should not have come to this, never had to, would not again.

He couldn't remember when the girl left or why. She must have driven to his house, to have left this morning on her own.

One spark of love then nothing. He remembered her body, there was a funny shape to her chest, pigeon-breasted, he thought it was called.

His pencil tapped more slowly.

She was laughing when he saw her, they were at a party he wished he had not come to the minute he walked in the door. He didn't like parties much anyway . . . the same people saying the same things time after time . . . but sometimes it was worse; sometimes he felt particularly alienated; then he was altogether set aside; inside himself. Then the conversation of his friends turned into meaningless chatter and his friends themselves became mere stick figures lined up, one after the other like snapshots, nothing between, no soft edges, no understanding. Then he was alone. Then gloom and cynicism got him. Then he could not get back into his life. His inherited discontent, this impatience, intolerance, this inability to reach out and across.

He was by the bar, sulking, when she caught his eye and brought him up out of himself. For an instant. One flash of life.

Only that long. Now he couldn't care less if he ever saw

her again and she was lucky to be gone. No use to pour salt
on her gay spirit, watch it melt like a snail.

Judge moved down to another spot. Dipping into the bone
meal sack, he turned to look back; his mouth was moving.
Talking to Preston. Preston rarely responded but Judge
talked on anyway, telling Preston no doubt step by step what
he was doing and how it had been to do the very same thing
all the years he'd been there, what the weather had been
then, compared to now, how much more agile his fingers had
been then, less arthritic and bent, more sure. Preston's gaze
never wavered. He was completely bald. His hard square jaw
had melted and become uncertain wattles.

Carroll looked like *her* he was told. Same bones, same
coloring, same aloof tilt of the head, same measuring light
gray-green eyes. Same temperament too, brooding and apart
. . . perverse even, the way they changed moods so quickly
so that you never knew where they stood on any one subject
or which way they might be likely to go next.

Carroll didn't *drink* however, the way Lady had, and that
was his saving grace.

And yet not alike. Carroll held on to small differences. He
could not be too much like either of his parents, he would
not be sucked into old family patterns or give in simply to
regendering them the way Preston had, losing his nerve in
the end, turning finally into his own father. Preston had sat
still for it; he had waited too long and one day he simply became Sam Cunningham, his own father all over again, and
never had to.

Not if he'd taken a stand against it. Sexton Cunningham
had died standing up; his great-grandson Carroll meant to
imitate him, not the others . . . meant to get the momentum
back in that direction, and change the pattern of its flow.
Imitate Sexton, imitate Mattie Sue.

Choice was the difference, the option for change.

When Judge moved even farther away, Preston picked up

his chair by its seat and walked toward him in that sitting position, the chair cradling his back, across the yard.

Judge, sitting back on his heels, turned to Preston and held out his hand to show him something. A pecan perhaps; they were falling. The two of them looked content, making these exchanges in their own small world, sharing some measure of delight, whatever was left to them, taking it. Leaving everybody else out.

Might not be so bad a life.

Better, perhaps, than his. Sitting behind this wall of glass and light, alone and apart.

Abruptly, Carroll sat forward and ran the damp fingertips of one hand across his eyes to wipe away the cloud of reverie that had come across his mind. It wasn't like him. Even when he'd felt that way at a party he ordinarily did not give in afterwards to remorse or regret. But sometimes there was so little satisfaction it felt like nothing would ever be over and done with, or solved, but would just go on and on instead, like this, without culmination or point. Carroll didn't want to be manipulative or isolated, he wanted to live his life full-out and share it. If he was to attain his goal, he needed to spark a new Cunningham generation, find a wife, have children. So far, he had neither. But what could he do; only what he could, no more. Women were a constant; he had no idea how many he'd been to bed with by now, yet and yet . . . Lord how it did go on, how long it took to come to anything.

And the bare truth was he felt most easy, most himself, when he was alone. He had no group; his life seemed suited to solitude. Disconnection seemed a nourishment not a drag. He liked bright, quick-witted women yet every time ruined his chances with them by putting their brightness on the line, testing it, finding some way to discover it wanting.

Perverse. Character was perverse, personality was perverse, nothing went in a straight predictable line but all jogged willy-nilly . . . zip . . . as it would.

This damp, heavy, no-season day. It suited his temper.

Tossing his pencil aside, Carroll picked up a pen, decisively. It wasn't like him to go slogging off in his mind that way. He didn't like indulging in easy sentimentality or slacking off.

Must be the weather. Such a gray day . . . easy to sit and stare, do nothing.

Frowning, he scratched out one suggestion he had written down the week before, circled another and put a question mark after it.

Which way to go next . . . buy, sell, hedge . . .

He glanced at his watch. Eight forty-five. He was due to call Mattie Sue at nine. He reached for his coffee cup without looking, came to it before he expected, touched the lip of the cup and set it off balance. The cup stuttered then went, before he could stop it. Coffee ran over papers, contracts, letters, in a widening puddle over and across his desk.

Flushed and furious, Carroll stood and threw his handkerchief down onto his desk. It turned quickly brown. He went to the kitchen for paper towels.

All her stories were the same. About herself. And what she had been and how she had glittered, marching in front of the high school band in her gold-sequined suit, bouncing light, twirling her silver baton. How she had made magic, turning a solid simple stick into a shining circle of light.

Not a majorette, you understand, so far in front of majorettes they could barely see me, in their skirts and big hats and fat legs, trying to catch up. They never even got close. Not to me, with no hat, no skirt, my hair loose and free, way out front. Me, she said to Emma, me. I was the star, the one they came to see. And it was . . . everything.

To be out front that way. Was everything.

Nighttime stories Emma took with her to sleep, to dream on. Stories told by a mother to her child in the night, the child asking for more, more, for light . . . clues to know herself by. She could still hear them now, exactly in her pure silver singsong, like a child's. Lolly's voice was still clear. And the stories. And what had been missing from the stories. Something. Same thing every time.

Herself.

Emma. The daughter. Waiting to hear some mention, some notion, some glance in her direction, of love. Never once, not even close. Lolly was alone always, first and last, whoever was with her did not matter, she was inside herself alone and apart.

Without Emma the story would have gone differently. Would have had a different ending. Would have . . .

Wait, don't, not that.

Who didn't ask need not feel responsible. Not when none is required, let it go. No guilt.

I was Lolly Ray Lasswell, do you understand? The star of star twirlers, marching, and turning my baton like fire.

Yes.

They had not lived in Eunola when Lolly told her stories, or in country anything like it but were in higher, firmer ground, on rockier surfaces where there were high peaks to look up to and lifts and rises in the land to move against and mark time by. No flat rich deep dark swampiness then, no air to take more than it gave, but a light swiftness every morning, a provision of energy instead. There the stories could fly. There was different. A lift in the air.

Emma remembered it well. The voice. The feeling of ease. The ridges and peaks to look up, the wind light and bracing, and the voice of the Mama, telling stories. The Mama in motion, poised, ready to go.

A fly on a sugar cube: think about reaching for it and it's gone.

Gone. Before. Like a smell, like smoke. Sounds, that voice. These Emma still had and would not share. Chips of gold in her stony memory, she would not let them go.

She was coming to houses. Traffic picked up.

Think elsewhere: of Jamison Leaks and what excuse to give.

It was required. Even if he knew you were lying, Jamison Leaks expected you to give an excuse and furthermore to act like you believed it while you were telling it. Emma grinned again, thinking of him. Most likely he had her name in his hand, this minute. Late again: Emma Lasswell.

Another contest; she did enjoy them. Peaveys after all were like wood: you had to sand them some to get their best qualities to show.

At the intersection she had a choice, either to turn right and go down Main or stay on the highway for one more block over to Court, the street the school was on. She turned.

A grassy esplanade went down the center of Main Street, separating its west- and town-bound traffic from its outgoing flow. Crossing the north lane, Emma turned down the esplanade, rubbing her bare toes as she went to cool and clean them on the grass.

Oak trees went ahead of her and behind, on either side of Main close to the curbs, their limbs branching out low then reaching across heavy and gnarled to make a kind of tunnel over the street. She looked up. Not yet. Every so often she checked, to see if the limbs from both sides of Main had joined. Not yet but close; only a pale seam of sky kept them apart.

Beyond the oaks, the houses on Main were squat and heavy, some two-storied, of white clapboard mostly, with large, sitting-type front porches. Most were outfitted with

double-seated porch swings in which old men and women
sat mornings waiting for the mail. Not lavish houses particularly, but comfortable. Merchants had built here when the
town was first settled; this was the seed of its past, its mid-
dlemost heart, solid and enduring and close in.

In time, Eunola's life had moved elsewhere, but Emma
liked it better here . . . where you could feel comfortable
and safe and at ease, with room to spare and who you were
announced firmly all around. Inside a heritage quiet and
solid and secure, not fancy or rich particularly, but solid and
safe, with ghosts and comforting stories all around and tes-
timonies at hand: house, furniture, street number, things to
look at and pick up and feel. Things to be reassured by.

Know who you are and tell about it. Pass it on, make it
come true all over again. Was it so much? It stirred her
heart to imagine.

A trailer was light on the land and spoke of nothing:
made to be used up and junked.

Skeletons were in these houses, and secret passages, myth
in porch boards and the sweep of a roof. Here you could
have a quiet heart and know.

She could see no one. She seemed to be the only person
alive on the street. Inside the tunnel of trees, she was alone,
except, wait, one sound. A swush-swush: someone sweeping
concrete.

A car passed. After a time, another.

Pick them up and lay them down. You never know, you
just never never . . . She heard the sound of her own feet
and breath.

Had to be past eight-thirty, maybe even a quarter till.
Might as well be absent as late, got in less trouble actually
absent, might as well not go. Absent, all you had to have tomorrow was a note saying *She felt bad.* Might as well keep
on, why go to school now.

She crossed the railroad tracks. There the esplanade

ended, and Emma—happier now—moved over to the sidewalk on the south side of Main, crossed Hawthorne and
went on west.

'Bye, J. Leaks. No late Emma Lasswell. No Emma Lasswell anything today. Not until tomorrow. When she will
have been absent.

By the time he got back most of the coffee had already
been soaked up into the papers stacked in careful piles on
his desk. Carroll crumpled up a wad of paper toweling,
sponged up what was left, wiped the table, threw the paper
away.

Quarter till. No preparations made, no reading. As soon as
he got this done and was a little calmer, he would go ahead
and call Mattie Sue, even early. That would help. Something. To help him get past it.

Past Hawthorne on her right across Main was the county
courthouse. Behind it was the new jail, stark and angular
compared to the older red building.

Immediately to her left, just beside her walking, was the
only house left on that block . . . or, for that matter, on
Main at all west of the railroad tracks, the others having
been torn down long ago or set on truckbeds and moved
away. The whole block was empty lots, weeds and For Sale
signs, in the middle of which was this one strange house.

Pink. And nothing like those sturdy ones east of the tracks
but delicate . . . a rare confection, left over from a more
luxurious time, gone shabby now and out of date, sitting
there waiting to be moved out too. Three stories high and
slim as a chimney, it seemed too tall to hold up against a
strong wind . . . a town house, built in New Orleans city-
style, to take its space where space was available in cities,
up, not out.

Emma slowed down.

Trembling now in the face of time and changes, the house was so eaten up by ivy and weeds and honeysuckle, grown tree to tree and bush to bush like a blanket, that the most you could see from the street was bits and pieces . . . the edge of a shutter, the rainbow glare of glass, a whip of curtain, trace or two of age-paled pink. The oldest woman Emma knew about lived inside it. Older even than Granny Peavey. Ninety-four she had heard.

Another daughter, her life set aside for ebbing, old Mattie Sue Cunningham, Carroll Cunningham's great-aunt, Mattie Sue, daughter of the first Cunningham, Sexton, sister of Sam, aunt of Preston. Old woman, old maid Mattie Sue. Still holding on.

And still bright, Emma had heard. Living mostly alone in the pink house, still able to care for herself with Carroll's help, refusing, in fact, so the story went, to move out. Saying no to all offers. And Carroll for some reason let her have her way in this, ignoring talk of what a scandal it was for an old woman to live alone in such a house. Carroll kept to himself whatever thoughts he had about Mattie Sue.

It had been an exclusive block to live on at one time . . . had meant something to have that lower Main address. Emma knew the names of other families who'd lived there too. Had been fancy but was no longer. When the old woman went, no doubt the pink house would too.

Emma peeked through the bushes.

Looked cold inside. Wrapped up and covered over that way . . . looked eerie and cold. There was a curving peagravel drive that went in an arc from Main up to the front stoop and back out again. The steps were cracked, and the stoop had pulled away from the house by nearly an inch, leaving an irregular lightninglike crack between it and the front door.

Drawing closer, she looked up. Above her, the house

seemed to sway, its roof leaning toward her and away . . .
toward her and away.

It looked inviting.

Lucille stood and took her cup to the sink.

So much had gone by, so little was left to go on . . . she
and Frank had bought the dinette suite on time, tearing out
coupons month by month to pay for it, they had been so
proud to pay the last one, now look: scratched and scarred,
no Frank and yet . . .

Yet she still sat at it, dreaming her life away.

Frank had left, and Lolly. Only Lucille stayed, shaped by
a wind she could not predict the vagaries of, ever . . .
which way it would blow from next or how hard.

You just never know.

She turned on the water, hard. It ran down into the cup in
a gush and bubbled over the top, foam and bubbles. She let
it. Run and run.

Somehow she would make it stop, this progression, this
same direction and flow, these *ofs* she had been and was,
how one by one they slipped in and out, never asking per-
mission or letting her know. Somehow.

And then . . . ?

"*Shit.*"

Oh Lord, Granny. She'd be up soon.

Lucille turned off the water.

Was it the magnolia tree moving or the house? Emma
couldn't tell. Neither, most likely, with the air so still.
Pushing a limb aside, she tiptoed into the pea gravel.

Old woman, old daughter, old maid. Lived too long was
the problem. Lived past anybody's need or expectation.

Except her own. Which wasn't finished yet. This old and yet. She wasn't through. Had to hold on a little longer, just until. Until the circle finished itself out.

She still kept up, by reading the magazines Carroll brought. Watched television too. News at night.

"Accident," she'd read someplace. Some new kind of woman said being a woman was an "accident of birth."

Accident's ass.

Written in the stars as far as Mattie Sue Cunningham was concerned, destiny she called it, unavoidable and inevitable, not prey to puny earthbound slip-ups or collisions . . . or co-incidence, as "accident" implied, but set from the beginning. From before. How the story had to go. Never any question.

Her sheets were white and so was the bedspread, she lay flat on her back staring at the ceiling, her black eyes fixed on a brown watermark she liked to look at. Sometimes it be-came a swan with a fat neck if she looked long enough.

Daughterhood was no accident but what she was, played out now to its end, what she was meant to be. Firstborn too, but that was puny, comparatively speaking; it counted for nothing except if you were a son, then oh, well then firstborn was different. Then the flowers were all yours. But be a daughter and that's all you are, first or last or in the middle: daughter forever.

She slept in the servants' quarters behind the kitchen and used only that room and its accompanying bath, the kitchen and the sun porch. The rest of the house went silent and un-visited.

She did not hate men. Not one by one, if you consid-ered a *particular* man. Only sons and their bounty, from birth, and the infernal unfairness of that. From the first min-ute of her brother's life, hers had changed. As soon as the son came the thing had turned in a different direction and she had been set aside, smart or not, hard-working or not, capable or persevering or diligent or willing, all of which

Sam was not, was never, which didn't matter, he was the son
and that was that; she could still see her father's face when
he got word he had a son and set out for town to spread the
news.

The only thing left was to choose how to live it out . . .
with how much grace and health and passion and integrity.
Only thing left was to hold on to whatever you had and believe the rest would eventually come around. And it had. It
had.

Mattie Sue got up slowly, piece by piece, starting with
fingers and working up. Lying flat, she flexed her knuckles
and made fists, let them go then made fists again. She raised
her elbows up and put them down, like a bird testing wings,
and turned her ankles side to side. It had, it had; she had
got some satisfaction after all. Not enough, but some, more
than anybody'd given her hope for.

Without changing the position of her back or shoulders
she gently swung her legs to the right and over the side of
the bed until her feet were on the floor, her back still flat on
the bed. She lay that way awhile. Even twisted, it was easier
to raise the back up when your feet were solid placed.

Have to baby a back. It creaks the most, threatens to give
way. The back you have to be carefulest about.

Just living this long proved something. She'd seen Cun-
ninghams born and buried . . . some younger than she by
far . . . had watched some leave and heard how others got
sick or lost their senses. All the time she stayed on. In the
pink house Preston had dumped her in the minute he married Lady, like a sack of used-up clothes set out for the Sal-
vation Army's weekly pickup.

No use to give in and moan about should-haves however.
No use whining. You have to take it as it comes and not look
for too much and at the same time expect it all, everything
you ever wanted. You have to keep that balance and believe

you'll finish, you have to. Close up and far away, look for nothing and at the same time everything.

Her mind blazed, it was as keen as ever. Ridiculous to live in such a worn-out sack of a body when your mind was so bright and quick. Infuriating and undignified, absurd and a shame.

She pushed up to her elbows and rested. Only for a minute. Too hard on the neck to stay in that position long.

Ninety-four years old and she had waited long enough: the flower basket had finally swung back in her direction, roses at last on her gray shaky head. She was eighty-something when it happened, after all those years of neglect, finally it had come.

Dumped. "No way for a house to have two mistresses," Preston had said when he married Lady. "This is Lady's house now." Not that it was Lady's fault, Lady didn't even know. And so they shoveled her out of the family place and set her aside in a downtown pink house to live out her life a daughter forever, aunt forever, old maid. With no pay for the work she'd done, no wages for all those years' pure hard work, just set aside—like that—without a second thought.

Until Carroll. Until Lady was dead and Preston half-gone in his mind, when Carroll came by to see if she was still alive and if so, how.

She sat fully up and slid her feet into backless slippers and pressed her hands down on the mattress to force her back straight. Oh, the back. She waited for it.

No bitterness however: it had never been fair but she knew better than to use herself up hating and blaming and fighting what never paid off, even—*even*—if you won. You had to play it out was all, and see. You had to keep to a farther-off point and hold your vision there and train it to go both ways, far-off and yet deep-close inside too. So deep nobody else could know or see. Close up and far away, at the same time. You couldn't let day-to-day get to you. Had to reach beyond that, without ever losing track of where you were.

There. She turned her head as far as it would go to the right, to the left . . . loosening up. And finally, she stood, hands on her lower back, and went to the bathroom.

The risk was, with all that looking in and out, close up and far away, whether you'd live long enough to see your patient waiting pay off. So far she had.

Emma knew all the stories about Mattie Sue; everybody knew those ghost tales. Family going back and coming to such a seeming dead end, down to one man, Carroll.

The pink brick of the house was chalky and soft, like tinted marshmallows, held together by melting. The whole thing looked ready to crumble. There was a round window between the second and third floors with an X in the middle and four wedge-shaped panes. One was broken out. A piece of cardboard had been taped in its place.

Emma walked through the pea gravel. Tiny rocks crawled between her feet and sandals. She stopped, shook one foot and then the other, then went on.

In front the windows were all curtained and dark. She headed for the backyard.

At the side of the house, an enormous pyracantha, the biggest she'd ever seen, blocked her way. It had crawled up the house to the roof and reached out sideways as well, so that it took up all the space between that wall of the house and the bushes marking the lot's western bounds. Pyracanthas had thorns . . . poison in them, she had heard, enough to make you sick. Pushing through the ligustrum, Emma went out of the Cunningham property into the vacant lot next door until she was safely past the pyracantha, then came back through.

She stood near the corner of the house. She could see the backyard.

Mattie Sue struggled. Stockings were a pain, but stockings were a measuring point, a fixed rung to go by. She still got dressed every morning before taking one bite to eat . . . even though she never went anywhere . . . still managed it. Down to stockings and real shoes. Not slippers; shoes you could tell were shoes.

Wasn't easy, but she did it.

Skirts and blouses she'd had to give up on, and the lace-up kind of shoes she preferred: too many buttons and strings, too many holes for stiff fingers to contend with. But she held on to stockings, with rolled garters at the top.

One thing at least to keep to.

Stay in your nightgown all day and pretty soon you don't know what time it is, day or night or what, and then how can you tell what's what, if you're awake or asleep or alive or dead or dreaming it, after a while? Got to train time and habits. Like a pet in a box. Got to keep it to a schedule, keep it tame and docile, manage it as much as you can: keep it under your thumb. Otherwise, well, forget otherwise.

Stockings up, she zipped her dress, a shapeless one-piece affair she wasn't thrilled to be wearing but it was the best she could manage and anyway she wore a sweater on top. She slipped her arms in and went to the kitchen.

Put water on to boil; a measure of instant coffee in a sterling-silver pot.

She lifted a long rope of pearls over her head, looped them once around her neck, twice, let the rest drop, past her breasts. She used to wear chokers until the fastener got impossible. She liked to hide her neck . . . cover up that sag, that loose and feathery skin there. She still had her pride. After all Carroll still came. And her doctor occasionally.

Which wasn't the whole thing anyway. She had her pride even if *nobody* came. People who thought when you got old you weren't vain anymore didn't know anything. Lose that and you give up.

She ran a comb through her hair and smoothed her skirt. The television set was on the counter next to the sink; her pillow-backed wicker rocking chair was in front of it. She turned the television on but left the sound off. News was still playing. She didn't like news in the morning.

She fixed her breakfast.

No way to get this old and not have lost much and she had: her teeth, much of her bulk, all resilience and most color. Her blood ran slow and made her cold all the time; sweaters were a necessity in every season, the house seemed always cold. Wrapped up and shaded over like it was, it never warmed up altogether, even when the streets outside were boiling hot according to TV and Carroll.

A window was open over the kitchen sink . . . nothing to see but a thatched, impenetrable tangle, limbs and twigs and vines.

Her face had once been called too manly for a girl, too strong to be pretty, her features too large and imposing. Her profile was stern: solid nose, high cheekbones, square jaw, board-straight forehead with heavy brow protruding. No wonder she never got a man it was said: no wonder. But those strong features aged well and only in the past ten years had it begun to catch up with her. Now it was all softening, more it seemed each day, and pale, almost white, without edges. As if somebody had shattered all the bones then let it stay, too loose, not strict anymore. Pasty, except for the eyes: solid black; centerless; sharp as ever. No need for glasses. A milkiness had blurred the edges; the white was creeping into the black part, but still . . . when they moved about, fixing on coffee, spoon, water kettle, her eyes looked like black grapes in a bowl of milk.

Her request to Carroll had been simple.

Ten acres, she said, and the roof over my head.

She was in her early eighties then and Carroll was just starting to take over the Cunningham affairs. Lady was dead and Carroll had come to ask Mattie Sue to move in with him and his father.

But Mattie Sue wanted no part of it. No deal; just her back pay: wages she was due from the time she had worked out there, when her brother Sam proved so useless after Sexton died and it was up to her to keep the place afloat. All those years keeping books, making decisions . . . to be shoveled out when the time came, like some welfare hag, put on a dole, set aside to get old and die. Good-bye Mattie Sue, thank you very much you've been wonderful. She wanted what was owed her. A day's wages for a day's work, she spelled it out plain to Carroll, ten acres and the roof over her head was a fair price to ask, and one more thing as well: it had to be free and clear, no strings. Did he understand?

Carroll nodded, grinning, sparkling, his eyes crinkled, overjoyed she thought . . . *thought* . . . by the very notion of her asking. Oh well yes. And where had he been the rest of her life?

No strings. Mine to do with as I please, crazy as it may sound and I have no idea what that will be, I only know I want that freedom and have earned it. To have something in my hand before I go, to pass on as I choose.

Not to a son. Not this time.

Free and clear. Unconditionally . . . Lord . . . *mine*.

Yes, he had said without flinching, yes, fine, which ten acres did you have in mind? She didn't care, any ten. Never had seen them to this day, didn't care to. Just to have them was all, in her possession to give away.

Her teeth were beside the telephone on a table. When Carroll called she'd put them in but not before; the breakfast she ate was soft enough to gum.

Now she had it but still had not found the appropriate heir, to finish her life out and give it the meaning she required. Not yet. Still waiting. As of now, it would all go to a Methodist orphanage. Which was close. But not perfect. The texture wasn't exactly right. The orphanage didn't know, so if the right thing came along and she changed her will they wouldn't have lost anything.

She carried some things to the sun porch.

Halfway across the back of the house was a room made of glass. It stuck out from the brick part of the house, which otherwise was a pure rectangle, and looked newer than the rest.

Something moved. A flutter of gray and black in the glass room. Emma drew back, flattened herself next to the pyracantha, waited.

The backyard was more wrecked than the front.

Covered with sticks and fallen limbs and dead brown unidentifiable things, it had no real grass in it at all, only weeds and crab grass and Johnson . . . sticking out between a mulch of leaves fallen and fallen over the years, run together now, never raked. There were thatches of ivy and junk trees all around . . . like hackberries, the kind that multiply like fire and eat out the lives of prettier, better trees. A mess. A solid run of waste and neglect.

But you could still see where a flower garden once was: along the left side of the yard was a weaving scallop of stepping stones going all the way to the back fence. Monkey grass went with the weave; monkey grass could survive anything. Some other things had lasted as well: nandina, the boxwood, the shrimp plant and ivy. Ivy was thick; it had not run outside its boundaries but over the years had doubled up on top of itself instead, growing higher and higher, layer on top of layer, staying where it was supposed to.

At the very back of the yard where the stepping stones led was a huge ash tree, bigger than anything else in the yard, bigger even than the oaks east down Main. Emma wondered she hadn't noticed it from the street. A shaggy thing, the ash came up slow and regal from the ground and held itself high. Its lower and middle branches however curved in toward the yard in a wide, protective arc . . . like something watching over it, some benevolent papa making sure no harm comes to it. Only, the limbs had grown too heavy over the years and the tree's very life was threatened by the weight of its own unchecked growth. The tree forked early; those two main limbs pulled hard in either direction, farther and farther with new growth every spring. One day no doubt it would simply split down its middle and die, from the heaviness that tugged at it, from the growth that, untended, would not slow down. It looked magnificent and proud, yet hopeless. Like a kingly creature being sucked into a common mud puddle.

Should have done better by it. Something so old and grand.

Emma peeked around the corner once more at the glass room.

Nothing. Nobody. Must have gone. She went around the corner, keeping her back against the house and her eyes hard on the glass, in case. She went sideways, step by careful step.

The *solarium*, Lady had called it.

Fancy. Like Lady. Fancy word from a fancy lady: it was Lady who had ordered it added on and Lady who most enjoyed it, until she stopped coming to visit. Mattie Sue hadn't much cared one way or the other at the time, but she did like it now, it was a pleasant place to sit. Even though the glass was so grimed and webby that little or no light came through it anymore . . . still, it was pleasant there, and gave some sense of being outdoors. Not that Mattie Sue looked out: nothing to see out there but that junky once-was backyard. She sat catty-cornered to the glass, where she could see it from the edge of her eyes but not dead-on. The sunlight that came through on the brightest day was as gray as her own gray head.

She couldn't handle the whole silver service and brought it out one piece at a time . . . tray . . . sugar bowl . . . creamer . . . coffee. She placed the silver pot down on the tray and started to sit, remembered she had forgotten a cup, went to get it, remembered her sweet roll, got it. Came back and, with a sigh, sat down.

Too old, too old, running out.

She reached for the coffee. Her hands were short and stubby and strong, her fingers still able to flex, if stiffly, and grasp, though hobbled when it came to finer, more delicate pursuits. She held the pot in both hands, one to direct, one to steady, and poured her cup two thirds full . . . not too. Can't stop on a dime anymore. Got to leave plenty room for mistakes.

The table was wrought iron with a glass top: also Lady's choice. Four matching chairs were pulled up to it but Mattie Sue sat in a different chair, one she'd brought from the dining room, a tall mahogany chair with a tapestry kind of upholstery on the back and seat. The wrought-iron ones hit her wrong, at the shoulder blade with those hard round backs. This one was straight and held her back up but had some comfort to it too.

She dumped two sugars in her coffee and a fat glob of real cream.

People used to come by asking did she need help, a gardener? plumber? new roof? siding? leveling?

Let it rot, was her standard answer. Firm but not loud: Mattie Sue never raised her voice.

Let the roof cave in and the pipes clank to dust, let the
pea gravel choke out the monkey grass and Johnson take
over the St. Augustine I couldn't care less. Let it fall down
on my ears.

Then came real estate hounds.

Would she be interested . . .

No she would not. . . .

Not when she had only just got it, not when she had not
found what to do with it yet that would leave her mark
behind properly. Having a piece of what she had done and
known and been and stood for to pass on was the whole
point and money was shit compared to that: nobody understood. Footprints were what she wanted. Something to look
back at, that proved she'd walked there. Until Carroll came,
there was not a sign of her. As if she'd been shuffling in sand
all her life, with somebody jam-up behind, wiping out whatever tracks she made, leaving no trace of what she'd been
and done, only that soft swift leveling shaped by the wind.
Until Carroll. Until him. A son too, yet and yet . . . enough
of Lady in him; he understood.

She stuck a knife into the wrapper of the sweet roll and
opened it.

Let it rot! she said to tree surgeons and termite inspectors
and carpenters, her black-as-raisin eyes crackling in her
white white face. Let it rot. Said the queen of rot, standing
majestic and firm in her shambling doorway, her chin high
and steady.

Cajun eyes, some said. So black. Must be some cajun back
in her family.

She pulled out a sweet roll.

The glass was almost impossible to see through, but
Emma could make out a table, some chairs . . . and her.
Had to be. Sitting at the table. Herself. Her head went up

and down. Her back was sideways to Emma, at a safe enough angle that Emma could move toward her, probably without the old woman knowing.

Anyway what can she do? Like Jamison Leaks? What?

She went on a few more steps, keeping her eyes on the gray bobbing head.

The trees dripped with moisture, and vines had grown from one to the next, catching limb to limb, jumping across one tree to join with the next, leftover, dying honeysuckle and still-blooming morning glories and some other vine with a thick, woody stem. A yard wrapped up, set aside from time and changes. Like a mummy? Almost.

Like one of Lucille's blouses, in a NOT-A-TOY sack.

She edged along the house toward the glass. Why was she sweating so, when the air felt so cool? She felt for sticks, stretching her toes ahead to test the ground. A drop of sweat ran from her forehead into one eye, blurring her vision; she shook her head, it went away. She snuffled. And wouldn't her nose keep on running at a time like this, wouldn't her bowels feel like they needed moving when she hadn't eaten a thing, wouldn't all that just.

But her hunger had passed. And there was a kind of trill in her chest which rang louder than the stories and voices she heard on 84. Like a wire pulled so tight it hummed.

She leaned forward a bit and, closing off one nostril, blew out the other one down and out onto the ground, keeping an eye all the time on the old woman's head.

Of necessity. She'd never done it before. But all things come to pass to those who wait long enough and look hard enough.

"Shhhit *FIRE!*"

Lucille's quiet time was over. Granny had announced herself.

The talk show was winding it up, they were on flowering bushes and how to make sure they bloomed, oleanders and such, and if they did bloom this year, what to do afterwards, year after year. This particular call-in show went off at nine but another one came on afterwards, on the same station, and then another. Until noon.

Actually nine wasn't exactly right: news was at nine; the call-in at five after. But before the news, the topic would be announced and Lucille waited to see what it would be, to see if she'd rather listen to the talk show or turn on TV for a game. ESP was a popular call-in topic, also assassinations and psychic phenomena; conspiracies, child abuse, capital punishment, local murders, astronauts and the moon; UFOs, welfare reform, the President, welfare chiselers, taxes, fortunetellers—whether they were phony or not—the occult, government scandals, mistresses, common-law arrangements, premarital sex, oil and gas, sex change operations, carcinogens; miracle cures, pyramids, killer bees, life after death, reincarnation, rejuvenation drugs; face lifts, what to do with old people, retardates and criminals, the high salaries athletes get, cholesterol, violence on TV, such as that.

Granny sneezed and honked her nose. All her noises.

The psychic and ESP kind of shows were best. Conspiracy theories and politics were too scary, they set her teeth on edge. Too hopeless, too few options, too little control: her mind couldn't hold all the implications. No possible solutions or even resolutions. Nothing to do or say.

The bed creaked. Granny rubbed her feet back and forth against one another. Every morning. Scratched her feet, rubbing sole against dry sole, scrrch, scrrch, sandpaper to sandpaper.

The gardening expert was saying how much he enjoyed being on; the host was thanking him.

Lucille took the radio and put it on a small end table beside a comfortable chair and sat down. The prayer was next.

"God-in-heaven."

There.

"Oh Jesus. Oh *crap*."

Every morning, Granny's diagnosis of the day . . . of life itself, the morning, Lucille, whatever came within the scope of her vituperation and its arms were mighty and long: shit, it was shit, all pure shit.

Lucille slipped her glasses on and leaned over on the arm of her chair to look at herself in the mirror. They were new, with a lighter weight powder-blue frame that didn't rest so heavy on her nose. Before, she'd always had the same kind, with a plain frame and glass lenses. These were plastic: the opticals man assured her she'd be happier with them and said the powder-blue frame was, in his words, "most becoming." But she didn't know. Blue looked funny. She fluffed her hair up, from beneath her ears. It was true they felt better. But she didn't think she'd ever get used to how she looked in them.

Shuffling footsteps: Granny. She was up.

Lucille picked up a small sink rug she'd been hooking and found the spot where she'd left off working the week before.

Instant coffee was terrible and Mattie Sue didn't like sweet rolls either, at least not this cheap brand, baked at a local bakery . . . made out of paper it tasted like if you ate it by itself: The Gold'n'Crust Hunnybun it was called. She'd read the list of ingredients. No honey in it, if honey was what "hunny" promised. A cinnamon roll actually, the pastry was rolled in two perfect pinwheels and laced with cinnamon and covered with a thick white icing so sweet it left a film on your teeth. . . .

If you had any. Or wore the ones you had.

But the cheap rolls worked better. Carroll had brought her some from a fancy bakery and they wouldn't dunk right.

Mattie Sue tore off a piece and held it headfirst in her cup, swirling it decisively until it was well soaked and dripping. Now. She leaned over the cup and, bringing the rag of wet drippy bun to her mouth, sucked it, let it go, sucked it again, let it go. A warm sweet paste dribbled down her throat. She sucked again, keeping up the on-and-off rhythm, making it flow, and murmured as it came, a low satisfied hum to guide the flavor down.

Good, it was good, mornings were fine, every day seemed to start with promise, old as she was, far off as it seemed, close up as her last day very well had to be. But never mind. Sitting in the sun porch there . . . in the *solarium* if you will . . . sucking sweet coffee toothless through a rag of cheap bun, Mattie Sue Cunningham felt perfectly fine. Felt . . . she couldn't say why, the way her life had gone, the way no light came through the filthy windows behind her, the way her house and yard were, so wrecked and wasted . . . felt despite all that and anything and everything else the well-known stories about her might prove or point out, at the moment that sweet warmth ran down her throat and she murmured how good it was, touched by a certain *grace*.

A stick. Emma didn't see. It popped.

Mattie Sue turned her head chin-to-shoulder in a listening pose, her better ear aimed toward the outside . . . something? Somebody?

She sat so still she might have been part of the furniture, waiting to see if anything-next occurred. But no, there was nothing. Only the drawing and creaking of the stairs and floor, the clanking of old and rusty pipes, the scratching of vines and bushes against the screens, an occasional mouse, roach, bird at the window, squirrel on the roof.

She tore off another piece of the sweet roll.

Something.

As soon as the stick snapped.

Emma didn't see anything. It was a quick blur, not of vision but sound. By the time she could say something moved it was over and done with, the thing was still again and there was nothing to hear: that fast. No chance to decide or choose, no second opportunity to turn quicker. A brushy sound from under the house behind her feet; like something soft rubbing against a solider object. A swish, a cry, a scampering panicky rush, the quality of speed, crackling in the air. Something popping, the run, the: escape. It went from directly behind her in the same direction she was going, to beneath the sun porch, taking the same route she would, never coming out from under the house however to make a catty-cornered shortcut, going down the pink brick part to its end, making a right-angle turn to the left, coming to stop at the far corner of the glass room, behind a supporting pier at its corner.

Emma looked up. The old woman's head was cocked, her ear set for listening. She flattened herself harder against the house, until her wet palms made suction cups and stuck.

The thing was beneath Mattie Sue, almost directly under her feet. Something that lived there. Like the ash tree, in protection. Something warning whoever trespassed: *their* territory. Their turf.

Probably nothing.

Cat or rat, maybe a raccoon. Likely nothing to get excited about . . . yet her archaeologist's mind was on edge: quickened for signs. Whatever it was, the thing under the house had yielded no clear definitions as yet. It could be anything.

The old woman's head turned back once again to its bobbing and nodding. Emma waited a second then squatted to look.

From under the house in the dark, two bright yellow eyes met hers. As she thought. Only a cat.

Leaning against a silver gas meter beside her, Emma rested her head. Its insides hummed and ran, its small clocks wound on and on, tiny black arrows turning around and around.

She looked at her feet: dried mud circled every nail and went up and down between each toe. She curled them up. Underneath, an outline of toes was on the insole of her sandal.

Only a cat. Leaning forward, Emma blew out her other nostril.

It wasn't real hooking but a special needle you only had to poke through the backing: automatic and magic, color came through. All you had to do was change threads from time to time, and keep poking.

She wondered what a big fancy car like that cost, with a stripe down the side, and how Lolly paid for it and if she still had one.

Didn't look as good as real hooking, Granny said and it didn't, but well it worked, and at least she had drawn the pattern herself: a gold eagle on a wine-colored background. Not original actually; copied from a magazine. Still, she had done the drawing instead of buying a pattern and Emma said it was pretty. Emma said Lucille was talented that way, said she ought to try her hand at painting. Or sketching.

She had not been much of a mother to Lolly but she did

remember spending hours copying cartoon pictures from the
paper . . . amazed at her own hands, that they could turn
out funny mice and cats and people, exactly the same as in
the paper. Of course Granny was talented in that way too.
She could crochet like a demon. Or used to. Before she declared it useless and full of shit. Lolly on the other hand
couldn't draw water and Emma wasn't willing to try.

A psychic. Good.

". . . bends keys with the power of his mind, from behind
locked doors . . ."

Oh good.

The gas meter felt nice. Cool. Emma pressed her ear into
it.

Now what.

There came a time when you did one thing or the other,
either went through with a thing or gave it up. A time when
you left off being afraid or hesitant or whatever and just up
and did whatever it was, or gave it up and didn't.

Off the pot, Granny said.

Squatting beside the gas meter, Emma considered her al-
ternatives.

One was, to leave now and still have been farther than
ever before and probably not miss out on anything anyway;
after all what more could there be, so why press it.

Do it or not. Go up to the glass room and look in or don't,
it doesn't matter which, but one. Ride or walk, go with the
consequences, don't whine. With the keeping on. Walk or
sit, stand or run, something: choose.

Time. She stood up abruptly and, as if she'd always
known she would, walked directly to the glass room, just
up and did it. . . .

Don't look back, don't measure, just go on.

The cat didn't stir. Emma put her hands up around her eyes to shade them and, through the thick accumulation of grease and grime, peered boldly into Mattie Sue Cunningham's sun porch.

Up and down. She was dunking toast it looked like into a cup, holding it there for a while then bringing it to her mouth. Emma could see her perfectly. Her hair was short and combed, her clothes freshly ironed. She wore a kind of housedress with a sweater over it and pearls. A cloth napkin —also fresh and ironed—was tucked inside the pearls to protect her clothes.

A silver service set was on the table, coffeepot, sugar bowl, creamer. Mattie Sue's cup looked like china, ivory-colored with a single gold stripe around the lip. Beside it was a cellophane-wrapped, half-eaten sweet roll. Emma recognized the red and yellow label immediately: it was from Gold'n'Crust, a Hunnybun or Sweet-Thang it looked like.

Suddenly everything changed. Mattie Sue pushed back her chair and in as big a hurry as the cat made a terrible scrape and fuss to heave up out of her chair and go across the room away from Emma. She turned, fumbled with something, put her hand in her mouth then turned back around to face the east windows, the exact windows Emma was looking into, her face pressed against the glass, her blue eyes glittered and shining, even through the grime.

She put the phone to her ear . . . who . . . was somebody . . . ?

On tiptoe, she moved over a fraction to find a cleaner spot but kept her face flat on the glass. Her breath made a fog she kept having to move out of.

A perfectly white face, no color, no eyebrows, no pink. No blood it seemed, so pale. But her eyes were black and keen and beady, and sharp as darts. Mattie Sue was talking on a telephone. And her eyes were directly on Emma.

"Yes?"

Her voice was deep and harsh, almost mannish but not so strong anymore. Barely more than a whisper. Carroll relaxed. Something in his stomach uncoiled at the sound of her. She had not gone yet. She had survived another night and could help him again. One more time.

"Good morning." It sounded more cheerful than he felt. "Are you all right?"

She didn't answer.

"Mattie Sue?"

Two blue eyes peered into her glass room. Hands around the eyes. Fog on the glass where her breath came. Bright blue eyes, lit-up and high, such a fixed look, like marbles. Eyes with energy behind. Fire and life.

Mattie Sue squinted and moved toward the girl, raised a hand and stopped. She did not want to frighten her away, didn't want her to leave, knew how crazy and old she must look to anybody on the street. She stood trying to decide what to do, with one hand up beckoning and the other holding the telephone which carried Carroll's wondering voice.

"Mattie Sue?"

"Wait . . . don't go . . ." But it was only a whisper. No one could have heard it even close, much less through a window.

The girl frowned, as if she heard, then turned abruptly

and ran. Fell. Got up, made the corner of the house and was gone. Gone.

"Mattie Sue. *Are you all right?*"

She tripped once over the gas meter, fell, scraped her hand, stubbed her toe really hard, got up and went on. As she rounded the corner, here came the cat out from under the house, zip right in front of her, she almost tripped over it and was so frightened she fell flat and open into the pyracantha bush. The cat went on, back under the house and down the other way. As if it had done it on purpose: run out from under the house just long enough to scare her then gone on about its business, as soon as it was sure she was hurt and scared and leaving. Emma saw it only briefly but registered its looks precisely: the ugliest cat she'd ever seen. Mottled, brown and black and a kind of rust-orange, no telling how old, ugly and beat-up looking. Huge.

It was like flinging yourself into a tree of needles.

She yelled, feeling pain cold and hot prick every inch of uncovered skin and then some, coming through her shirt in places too. Shit! She was furious, madder than hurt, at herself for being so stupid, at the cat for causing it.

She pried herself loose and, without stopping to see how badly she'd been cut, went on. Out into the other lot, back through Mattie Sue's, through the pea gravel, the bushes, onto the sidewalk once again, feeling like something let go. Like somebody released from some terrible place.

Yet she did not stop but kept running, on down that block of Main past the empty weeded lots and across the next street. When she was safely on the other side, she did pause to look back. Over the top of the house and all the other trees, she could see the old ash, bent and huge, lonely.

Something she was afraid of. Something to run from. That look, her, the cat . . . she wasn't sure what but something.

Down Main and on down it she kept checking, looking back over her shoulder again and again, every few steps, to make sure nobody and nothing was following her, not Mattie Sue or the cat or . . . whatever. She couldn't think what else. Whatever.

Sweat ran off in buckets, she still needed to move her bowels and now the other came down on her too and her nose was still going like a faucet but she never stopped; kept on, one foot after another, not really afraid after a while but not willing to slow down either or think about it.

Just go *on*.

Mattie Sue returned to Carroll.

"Yes . . . I'm all right, dear. Just distracted for a second. As all right as an old old lady can be, that is."

Who was she? Whose eyes were those? Something went down in Mattie Sue's chest, a loop of fear and joy, that the girl had been the one and was gone, that if whoever she was waiting for came by and she missed the chance, would she be allowed a second? Or was it going now? That slight dip in her chest, a loosening . . .

She reached over and turned up the sound on the television, low, so it wouldn't interrupt their conversation but loud enough to hear. The program was "Spin for Luck," an especially ridiculous show she particularly liked. Irony was such a joy; stupidity pleased her. Just how absurd people could be.

She pulled her stomach in and tightened it up, holding together what she had left, one time more.

"Listen," Carroll was saying, "Judge is planting caladiums out here. You think it's too early?"

He knew his voice was high and shrill . . . panicky. Mattie Sue would help; she always did.

Now he could go on, stop feeling bad about Snow White and the spilled coffee, now he could work. As long as she lived, he could depend on being pulled up, on his circle of self including at least one other person if no other. He had no idea how he'd manage when she died.

More women he supposed.

She passed a giant store: SHOELESS? PAY-LESS it was called, a grocery store-type business where no one came to wait on you or help you find a fit, you just walked around between row after row of shoes trying on whatever you liked until you found a style and size that fit your needs and feet. HELP YOURSELF, signs on the wall urged. The shoes were arranged by size, on shelves that started at the floor and came up to eye level. At the door there were four check-out stands. The clerk there took your shoe box from you and kept it, threw your new shoes in a plastic sack with a string around the top, drew the string up tight, took your money, gave you your receipt and that was that. Nobody knew anything about shoes there. Just cash registers and figuring tax and operating bank charge-card machines: ring it up, add it on, draw up the string, let the customer beware his own bad choice and fit.

Used to be a movie theater there.

She used to twirl at that corner. Remember?

Twirl? Twirl! Used to bend her back so far her head came between her legs. Used to do the splits at that corner where the Delta Theater was. Used to go down in a pure splits right in front of it, under the traffic light, with those batons all the time going . . . used to . . .

Used to be three movie theaters downtown.

Now were none. Only drive-ins out from town and multicinemas in the malls, like the rabbit-hutch houses in that direction, lined up to take your pick from.

Emma rubbed her arms. Needle-point pricks were all up and down them, tiny points of blood. Didn't hurt so much as they made her feel hot and sweatier. She crossed another street, against the light.

My turf: downtown, a relic, leftover, dead. Cat has his and I mine, archaeologist's territory, where the past leaves behind signs to know the present by.

Junk jewelry stores and pawnshops, easy credit, fire-sale bargains. Insurance offices, government agencies, empty windows. Empty windows. Empty. Vacant buildings. Department stores once the town's finest still had LAST CHANCE! GOING OUT OF BUSINESS painted on the windows, the paint flaking faster than anybody was showing interest in reopening the stores. Inside were ghostly cases and tables, littered with tags and dust and remnants of last then lost opportunity.

Buildings torn down, replaced by nothing. Destroyed for the sake of it it seemed. Empty spaces waiting. One successful business was a block-long bargain shop-and-save store, lay-aways their specialty.

Emma rubbed the tops of her arms, where the scratches were, against her jeans.

One drugstore had not changed. A Rexall, it still had the old-fashioned orange and blue sign: like Mattie Sue, the owner was old and had lived past his time. Soon as he died his son would see to it the store was moved or changed or sold. What once was a fancy furniture store was now a government agency set up to help working women with small children, another former movie theater was a pool hall. But Deacon Penn's office-machine shop remained and was still the only decent place in town to get typewriters and adding machines repaired. Deacon refused to give in too, like the druggist and Mattie Sue.

Emma neared the end of Main. Ahead was the levee the street ran into and in front of the levee the old war memorial, that ship-shaped tile monstrosity that in Lolly's time announced the name of every white Eunolite who died in World War II. It was different too.

. . . used to lean on that memorial and watch for her, ever see him? Standing there, just standing, every Friday of football season, waiting for the parade.

Not the parade: her. Which he used to watch from the time she turned down onto Main all the way down it all those blocks until she got to the end of it, where he was, just standing there leaning against the same name every Friday. . . .

James Blue. The Daddy. Blue in the middle. He used to.

Carroll picked up his phone, checked his book, dialed.

Better now, better, Snow White forgotten, things getting smoothed out in front of him. Mattie Sue helped. He didn't care how she lived, in which house in what kind of shape or who she might decide to pass what on to. Anything she asked for he would do what he could to get. Her eyes, crackling with spirit and life, her very life: there was the fire his family had missed out on. There was Sexton Cunningham's true inheritor. He would feed on her spirit and draw from her example. As long as he could. As long as he had.

Inside his ear, the phone buzzed; clicked.

He had decided to sell. His energies were gathered in that direction for a while, he was ready.

Mattie Sue watched as three wives got on giant red wheels which their husbands spun around. Where they landed told them what to do but by the time the wives got there they were dizzy from the spinning and wandered around for a time trying to get straight in their heads, in order then to do what the instructions said . . . go through a maze, run hit a mallet on a bell, pick up a pie and hit a husband in the face with it. Whoever finished first won. Whoever did it fastest for the day won even more. And who did it fastest for the week, well the amount of screaming and hollering that went on over dining room suites and boats and cheap cars was almost unbelievable.

Mattie Sue sat in her wicker chair and rocked, fixed on the foolishness.

The faintest kind of weakening in her chest . . . like a tight string let go of at one end.

Maybe the orphans were in luck.

No names were on the memorial now, not one. Having come to some power, black people had protested the exclusion of *their* dead soldiers on the memorial all these years and had come to city council to air their grievances and make their wishes known: take down the white names, they demanded, and put up the black. Separate, equal, equal time for each.

Next week, came another tribe to council chambers: white daughters of ancestors of other, longer-ago wars, to make a different threat. Their civic project the year before had been to restore the memorial's dedicatory message, which over the years had lost many of its letters. TO THOSE WHO SERVED, the memorial now read, IN ME-MORIAM, whole and complete for the first time in twenty years. The daughters would not stand for outright rebellion, they said as if they owned the town. The minute one white name gave way to one black one their new blue letters were coming down, period.

City council scratched and pondered but came to no decision except to take down the white names, and so the memorial was blank white, no names, the message intact still but underneath it, nothing.

Even the black people gave up: why fight downtown battles when downtown was dead.

Emma came to the end of Main where Jesse's Cafe was, the Jesse's of the yellow beat-up EAT sign. EAT was on the window too. JESSE'S was on the top in a rainbow arc and beneath it, straight across, EAT.

Emma turned left at Jesse's and walked parallel to the levee for one block down River Road.

Two people saw her. Sitting in Jesse's, they happened to look up as she passed, happened to be pausing, between lifting the cup off the table and drinking from it, between taking out the rag and wiping the table off . . . happened at that minute to be gazing out the window thinking . . . not much, dreaming, wondering how the weather was going to be the rest of the day, just sitting looking up and out the window, when . . .

One was her great-uncle Bo Peavey, Lucille's oldest brother who was in there sitting with the cafe's owner Jesse Brough having a morning cup of coffee. The other was a pale fat waitress with pink-orange hair who'd once had a close friendship with Emma's grandfather Frank Lasswell, who in fact to her mind had not been with as good a man since. Neither was particularly glad to see Emma. As a matter of fact, by the time Emma turned the corner and left their sight and headed down River Road to Duncan's Dunkins to buy a sack of still-warm doughnuts, they were already regretting having looked up in that spare moment and out the window at the exact time she chose to be walking by it. Now their day would go differently. Just from seeing her. Bad enough already, so wet and close and lousy, bad enough without her going by too, with her head jutted out a mile, steady leaning forward like that, head out front like a turkey. Bad enough. Without having your whole day colored with remembering as well, thinking back and thinking back . . . remembering things dead and gone, times dead and gone, things and times the girl didn't even know about.

Emma did that to people. If she caught you by surprise in particular, it happened, she made you think back . . . not about her but her mother. And what a time that had been when Lolly Ray Lasswell was twirling that stick on their streets. How different a time it had been. How much more on top of things Bo Peavey had been then, how many pounds less the waitress had weighed, how poorly things had turned out.

"GodDAM, Jesse," Bo said, loud enough that the waitress and two other patrons turned around to look. "It's *hot* in here." He wiped his bald red head with his handkerchief, trying to think about only that, how hot he was and what work he had to do in his dump truck, thereby keeping himself in the here-and-now in Jesse's.

At the end of that block of River Road, Emma turned left, swinging her doughnut sack, and went down Court, bouncing: she felt good now, happy and hungry and expectant, even with the pyracantha burns. Would be a good day after all, no matter weather, old woman, cat, thorns or what, who cared, it was going to be *fine*.

After another half block, she turned down a curved and broken sidewalk with grass running through its cracks like a stream of water.

Home.

The building at the sidewalk's end was ugly to be sure, even Emma knew that, but no wonder, nobody took care of it anymore and so what anyway, this kind of ugly was better than new plastic fantastic lovely.

But today didn't help, dampness only made it more woebegone than ever as its rough and porous surface absorbed the air's moisture instead of bouncing it off and its windows —in sunlight so sparkling—took on the day's predominating hue. Damp and dour, gray and rueful: who'd want to go in it?

Me. My place. My excavation site. Chip away with my hammer and pick-ax gathering clues.

The Sexton Cunningham Memorial Library: Eunola's first public library, Est. 1882. First then. Last now to get new books and magazines. Nobody came there anymore.

Halfway down, square in the middle, the sidewalk was broken up altogether. Earth from underneath had erupted and made a small mountain there of concrete and dirt. Emma skirted it automatically without looking. The building was not level but had over the years on that wet deepdown ground shifted back, away from the street so that, tilted back that way, with the top floor leaning back, it seemed to be settled momentarily on its haunches, in preparation maybe for attack. Nothing beautiful about it people said, an eyesore, their fingers probably itching to tear it down too. And not only that but poorly situated too, in the wrong place all these years.

Half a block from the water: hadn't old Sexton ever heard of a flood?

Before the river's rerouting, floods had periodically come into the library and ruined the books, time and again so that by now they were so water-damaged pages wouldn't turn without being unstuck. New books went to the branches instead, while the Cunningham became another downtown relic . . . like the old Rexall, the druggist holding on to his sign. Only old things were there: classics, histories, expeditionary journals, city maps and plats and ledgers, philoso-

phy, some art . . . all kept by one librarian, Emma's friend
Alice. The building itself was tended to by a janitor who
came twice a week to dust and clean the floors; the lawn,
what was left of it, by a sometimes gardener.

Emma came straight on up the stairs, feeling good, heat
and sweat and edginess having flopped over and become an-
ticipation. Good now; the day would be fine; Alice was
ahead, Alice's sweet openness, a day in the library.

Sexton had been proudest of the library's doors, as well he
should have been, and still would be if he could see them:
they were beautiful, the old building's finest attribute.
Watched over at each corner by small, tailed gargoyles
etched into the concrete, the doors were only half wood, the
bottom section being a warm golden oak enhanced by carv-
ings of curls and curves and daisies, of fleurs-de-lis and
curlicues, all hand-done by a Memphis artist Sexton had
commissioned for the job. All this hand-carving was inside
the panels that made up the lower part of the doors and
over the top, outlining the corners there. The rest was
made up of two matching oval panes of heavy leaded glass.

Real glass. Not the imitation stuff you get now but real
leaded glass, beveled at the edges.

After a while city council got tired of the same flood-song
being sung in their ears—and having to produce revenue to
replace ruined books and shelves—and had two branches
built, out from town. By then the river had been rerouted
and a lake run in beyond the levee so the danger of flooding
was pretty much subverted but it was too late then, the Sexton Cunningham Memorial Library was a dead issue; attention was going elsewhere by then, no matter what, flood or
no flood.

The janitor lovingly kept up the doors. He came every
Friday with soft rags and ammonia and lemon oil, to polish
the wood and keep the glass sparkling because in return
they gave such positive testimony to his efforts.

Familiar with its weight, Emma put a shoulder to one of the doors, turned its ornate brass knob and pushed hard. The door opened abruptly, only a crack, got stuck again, then with her second push became noisily unjarred. A blast of cold air shot out of the library as if aimed, hit Emma's face, ran over her damp sweat-soaked body in a wave, sent a shaft of ice-cold deep down her neck and spine. A chill ran up and down her arms; the pyracantha burns prickled.

At the front desk, Alice, startled by such an energetic entrance, looked up and at the sight of her friend started to smile . . . until she realized what day and time it was . . . Monday, 9:00, Emma should be in school . . . and at that, changed her mind.

Alice made Emma feel a way no one else did: of all things, shy. Not that she meant to, just the opposite, Alice's intent was to have no effect at all, to be altogether collected within herself, drifting weightless and apart, never maneuvering, manipulating or imposing. But that was what Emma couldn't straight-off cope with. She wasn't used to it. A fight she could handle, but this . . . just Alice, standing there wide-open accepting . . . made Emma have to find new ways of approach. Shyness wouldn't do however; and so Emma turned her discomfort into a swagger. A defiant cockiness which, against this threat, she wore well.

She held up the doughnut sack.

"Hi!"

All sparkle and bravado.

And yet deep inside, she shivered.

Alice wore a sweater against the air conditioner's chill. Central air and heat had been a tax-write-off gift from Carroll Cunningham two years before, useless when what they needed was books and repairs and readers but what did Carroll Cunningham know, he never came in there, just furthering his name and his income was all. Now their few

patrons froze in summers and in winters boiled, the old
building just didn't seem to want to handle the machinery
properly and settle on an in-between temperature, it was always too one thing or another.

Emma waited for Alice's full moon face to change.

Alice, small and delicate with so sure a sense of herself,
safe and private Alice no string pulling at her making her
walk slant-forward, even her name felt light as you said it:
Alice. Sat high in your mouth and flew swiftly out, without
barrier or need for heat. Only Alice, natural as light itself, so
still and quiet and serene, needing, it seemed, no testimony,
or charms to rub for luck.

Leaning against the cold leaded glass feeling the glass like
ice against her wet back, Emma held up the doughnut sack
and with her head cocked, she hoped winningly, waited for
her friend's stern expression to change.

"You can't bend keys, it's a trick. I read how to do it in
Science Digest."

"Oh, yes? How do I do it in *Science Digest?*"

"Well, I didn't understand the whole thing but there's a
kind of stuff you use, see, that looks like metal but isn't.
Sounds like metal when you hit it against a table, feels like
metal when you touch it but isn't metal, but some kind of
frozen stuff that after a while starts to thaw and lose its
hardness. Bends. All you have to do is sit in the next room
and pretend to do it with your mind and it's in there bending by itself."

The psychic laughed.

"*Science Digest* ought to go find such a substance and
have it patented. Or maybe they should rename their story
and call it what it is, pure fiction. Pure unadulterated make-
believe."

Lucille changed threads. A lighter shade of gold for the talon.

She had to get out, that was the first thing . . . which she'd known for years but so far had not been able to do, for one reason or another, no reason, every reason, you name it, the trap had been set. For one thing, Emma. Who refused to move into a subdivision house. Wanted an old one she said. With wood floors and a fireplace.

Old meant bad plumbing and wiring, no dishwasher, room air-conditioning units if any, meant repairs and leaks and work. Lucille couldn't see it. If she was going to move, she wanted every modern convenience money could buy, drapes and wall-to-wall, the works.

But. That was only in the second place actually because in the first Lucille could not seem to get herself to up and go look around, much as she combed the classifieds, reading about three- and four-bedroom houses with built-in ovens and dishwashers and concrete patios and gas grills and sliding glass doors . . . magic houses in magic places, with names like Briar Hollow and Winding Willow and Lazy Lane Estates . . . houses waiting, OPEN FOR INSPECTION the paper said.

Wasn't money either, she had plenty. The savings Frank left her plus the monthly checks he'd sent over the years, a generous amount she spent so little of there was certainly enough for a down payment, maybe even enough to buy one outright.

Still when you'd been in one place so long it was hard to just up and do it, it was. Granny said she hated houses with no bare floors to feel under your feet except in the bathroom and at least she and Emma agreed on that; they didn't agree on much else.

You could choose your own color scheme, Lucille heard. Avocado seemed to be a popular carpet color, also harvest gold, which she thought she'd probably like best and get the least tired of. Kitchen appliances came in those colors too, although she wasn't sure if it would look good to have everything matching that way. Maybe, she'd have to see.

Which was the problem, actually.

It was hard to do anything if you couldn't first imagine what it might be like. Without seeing it in your mind beforehand, with at least some idea how it would go, how could you? How answer questions? Bedrooms . . . ? colors . . . ? patio or not, fence or not . . . ? no, she couldn't, not yet. Not so far.

She hung on to *so far*. There was time still, it had not run out yet and she was working on it. One day she would just up and announce it: they were moving to Leaning Oaks. Or Shadowcrest. Whatever. Soon. When she could imagine such boldness, soon.

One talon was complete . . . that was the problem with this easy kind of hooking, it went too fast. Lucille moved the needle across the rug to the next.

"Sis-TUH!"

Oh Lord how she hated that name and how well Granny knew it. The whole family had called her baby sister all her life and Granny only did it now to remind her once again that to her Lucille was still that baby, that know-nothing youngest daughter, never smart enough to do anything but run errands, never taught anything useful like the rest, only sent here and there with messages or quarters tied in her skirt, everybody's, the whole family's go-for, the youngest of eight.

One reason it had been hard for her: to learn every single thing so late, even how to think straight, made it that much worse.

But as far as Granny's thinking went, Lucille Lasswell might as well be Lucille Peavey four years old, sleeping with her sisters. Would always be that too to Granny, no matter how old she got. Liver-splotched and gray, she would still be the baby daughter, empty-headed and addle-brained, to Granny.

Lucille listened to her show, hooking her rug. She would not wait on the old woman hand and foot, it took every bit of strength she had not to get up, but she had made up her mind.

"We have a long distance call waiting. . . . Hello? . . ."

"I brought doughnuts."

Emma changed the tilt of her head, from right shoulder to left.

"They're still warm even . . . fresh from Duncan's."

Alice disapproved of Emma skipping school and Emma knew it but made no apologies and gave no explanation . . . waltzing around the disapproval instead, doing special little dance steps she knew Alice could not resist, seducing her good humor, knowing it would come around in time. After all it was too late to go to school now, the bell had rung and she'd be really late now and Mr. Leaks hated lateness more than absence, a lot more, as a matter of fact hated lateness more even than gum-chewing or long hair on boys, more than . . . she had her. Alice was smiling, disarmed. Emma addressed the cold air's patron saint.

"Carroll Cunningham, it's *freezing* in here."

Alice tossed her a sweater from the lost-and-found. Emma took it with her to the bathroom where she sponged off her scratched arms.

The library had just opened for the day; no one else was in it. When Emma returned, Alice had brought out her thermos and two cups. Pulling on the sweater, Emma sat down beside her behind the desk, and began to eat.

Warm now. Warm in the cool places, cool where she had been sweaty. All right now. Safe. In a warm circle surrounded by books, encompassed by Alice's sweet accept-

ance. No need for swaggering or a closed-off mind, no John
Robert, no bread smell, no Lolly. No cat, no thorns. She
sipped the warm, lemony tea. She would stay all day, reading, browsing, helping Alice.

Granny Peavey called Alice Chow a chink. No defamation
or insult intended; no dislike or malice in her mind when
she said it, only clearly and simply stating what as she saw it
was what, firmly in the here and now without regard for
consequence or effect. To Granny, things had a pure and
ruthless simplicity, so did people, places, furniture, whatever: were either this or that, period, no soft edges or
qualifications; one name, that was it, last chance. One thing
or another. And once you knew the name, all you had to do
was say it for everybody else to know what you meant. It
was that simple, you didn't dawdle or mess around but
called shots as you saw them, everything clear and distinct.
A Chow was a chink, just as a Yee or Lou or Chum was, always had been and would be and that was that, what more
was left to say. Nothing according to Granny, nothing.

Other Peaveys, younger than Granny, had become in-
clined, by force of circumstance and the law, to speak otherwise and name other names. Not that they didn't always
agree with her on what was what, or see the same as she,
not that they had any less intransigent a fix on what was
what in the world. But they did talk in a different way.
Called new shots. Said new names.

"Don't say chink, don't say nigger, not supposed to say
wop, don't say Jew," Granny's great-grandchildren, Bo's
grandchildren, told them both.

"What's wrong with *Jew?*" Bo pleaded.

They weren't sure. But something. Just weren't supposed
to say it.

When younger people spoke of Alice at all, however, they
mostly still did tell you what she was but in a different way.
"Charlie Chow's girl," they said. Or Alice *Chow,* with par-

ticular emphasis. Only not saying it straight-out the way
Granny did, in the process convincing themselves they were
smarter than she; nicer too . . . than she or Bo either one.

Either way, one name or another, they all did what Emma
did not, recognized Alice as one thing and that only, before
sex, inclination, religion or occupation; the stamp of her heritage taking first and only place in their minds. First and
last and always she was a Chow, Chinese Charlie's daughter, to Granny a chink. And for Alice herself, that factor had
been—like the breathy stories in Emma's memory—the over-
riding one in her life, the cogwheel everything else turned
on. But Emma, with her clear raw way of looking at the
world, missed all that. Alice was her friend; it was enough.
In this, as Peavey as Granny, seeing nothing beyond what
she made up her mind to. Past was past; Emma moved on,
whenever she could.

The floor creaked under her step. The wide, warped
boards were of high-polished dark wood, beautifully
grained, like wind-shaped sand. Every room smelled musty
and dank from the old floods. You could still make out water
lines along the walls, and ceilings were decorated with
formless brown water stains. Doors stood permanently ajar,
too transfigured by time and water and neglect to properly
fit a frame anymore. The room Emma was in had a fireplace
with a marble hearth, inside of which stood empty andirons,
rigid protectors with bulldog heads. Beside the hearth was a
useless set of antique fire irons, of gleaming brass, lately
polished. The janitor took pride in his work, especially here
in the old branch where rewards were immediate and satisfying: new ones all looked the same all the time, nothing to
polish, all carpets and formica and plastic, no pride to take.

Emma shelved some books, took one down, opened it and
went toward a table; still reading, sat . . . turning water-
rippled pages without annoyance, running a finger through
two stuck together, her attitude here the same as on the

highway, all the intensity once set on making the journey now focused here, zeroed close in on the book. She still wore the sweater from the lost-and-found; sitting so still under air conditioning, she needed it.

Alice came in and, seeing Emma so engrossed, left. Returning to her place at the front desk, she resumed the work that took up most of her time and attention, the repairing of books. Tenderly she laid back a cover and rubbed the end-paper flat and picked up a pot of glue. Was nice having Emma there. She should be in school. Still . . . the library felt better now and Alice felt more comfortable having her there, especially on such a gray depressing day.

Alice believed in education. It was the only way she had helped herself come up from her behind-the-store life to something better. Now she had some respect for herself; some prestige. And the work she did was not tied to this place either, but went with her; she could be a librarian anywhere in the country, her credentials gave her that freedom.

The book glued, Alice put it into a special vise to hold it until it was dry, then looked up at the front doors. Nothing new. Such a heavy dreary day . . . around the edges of the oval panes, even more so, distorted the way it was, magnified even. In a year, Emma would graduate. She should already be sending off for college catalogues, making inquiries. Alice had decided to make it her business to help. To give Emma what advice she could, and help her map out the rest of her life to her best advantage.

Shivering, she drew her sweater up closer. The air-conditioning flow seemed never to stop, but to go on pouring cold air out on her head in a solid rolling never-ending stream.

Mornings, whatever the weather, Granny wore the same thing, a blue and white seersucker robe tied loosely at the

waist. Her nightgown was longer; it hung below the hem
of the robe, dipping up in front and back, hanging long and
raveled on the sides. But who cared how she looked, mornings or any other time for that matter. Not her. She pulled
her fine yellow-white hair up into a hard twisty knot and
pinned it on top of her head with two silver bobby pins.
Ugly old thing. In the mirror: old and ugly, ugly and old.
Her feet were freezing, she slipped them into a pair of black
pumps worn out in just the right places for the shape of her
feet, with their corns and bunions. Ugly didn't matter anymore; neither did old. Only holding on to what you had
mattered, keeping things shaking just right, so you never
settled back too far or got too comfortable . . . do that and
what happened? She knew. Sleep too long and you don't
wake up, this age. Sleep too long and you can't tell the
difference between it and. Sleep's about it anyway, little
difference between it and the other, close your eyes and
you're out, what's the difference. None. Not to the one
doing it. She farted; sighed. Lucille hated farts. Never said
so but did. Funny how people liked to talk about diseases
and sores, cancers and such, but hated farts. Talking about
or doing, especially hearing.

"Sis-TUH!"

Lucille hated being called that. So what, served her right.
For . . . whatever. Didn't matter what, something. Served
everybody right, everybody who was younger and would
live longer . . . would, devil take them, still be here poking
around when she was long gone to the worms.

"Yes?"

Always said something like that too, Lucille did. Hated to
call her Mama, didn't like Granny either, always said something like Yes? or What is it? to avoid having to say either
one. Shit, how she hated it all. How she'd like to chew them
all up like so much tough old meat and swallow them gristle
and all . . . family, children. Didn't mean shit. Showed how

little you actually got. What a pitiful amount. And no satisfaction at all. Down to this: a fat whopping nothing.

"Fix me a cup." Her voice as gravelly as a choked cat's.

Hunched over, she went from her bedroom to Lucille's
kitchen, calling one room hers and the other Lucille's, because her room was always a stinking mess and Lucille kept
her kitchen so stinking clean: you could eat off her floor.
Stupid. Useless. A waste. Wiping and wiping, sweeping up,
same, same, stupid.

Sitting, she farted again and let it spread, without lifting
her cheeks. Let it make all the sound it would against the
hard maple seat.

All the damage she could. In as little time as she had.

At two-thirty, Emma checked out her book, told Alice
good-bye and plunged out the front door, taking the steps in
one leap . . . only to discover in the outside air she was still
wearing the lost-and-found sweater, which she took off and
carried back up the steps and threw inside the front door,
onto Alice's desk, saying "Hey!" to warn her. Then shot
back out, broad-jumping the crack in the sidewalk, going on
again, her head set in a new direction but set nonetheless,
fixed on where she meant to go, which she always knew
ahead of time. Like Lolly, she always had a goal to fix on.
But was less intense now, from sitting so still and reading so
long, still wrapped up in that time; the wheel burning lower,
circling lazier around.

Alice, come to the door to watch her, smiled. Something
positive should be in store for such good, simple energy.
Something to reward the head-heavy drive and rolling flow.
Something toward which Emma might finally head and, getting there, find solid, palpable, real. A profession. College.
Work. Her energies could grab hold of those and use themselves up profitably. Something that would not fade as soon

as she got to it but would occupy her time and mind in a
satisfying way.

At the school, Emma went around to the back next to the
cafeteria door and bounded up the steps of the school bus,
elbowing her way through the crowd collected in its aisle.
Finding a seat next to a window, she settled in and began to
read the book she'd brought from the library, about the
flood of 1927, which had wiped Eunola out for a time.

Feeling fine. Taking a ride home.

She'd been wrong about one thing. The day. It had light-
ened some after all, instead of staying the same. Crickets
and birds were out, announcing the break, and the pale
drifting clouds covering up all the blue had parted somewhat—only in small cracks here and there—to allow the
faintest hint of sky to come through.

Maybe a dry norther was on its way; maybe that crack of
sky was the first sign of it; maybe the dampness was getting
ready to break. Maybe . . .

Not much relief, but some, some.

Lucille began dinner to the sounds of her mother's favorite
soap opera, watching the clock, anxious for Emma to get
home. Emma made her feel instantly better.

The pale fat pink-haired waitress packed up her umbrella,
said her good-byes and left, still haunted by the remembering that girl had called up.

With a weekly news magazine before him, Carroll ate a
light snack in his office, having skipped lunch. Now that the

markets were closed for the day, he allowed himself to un-
wind some. Soon he'd freshen up and leave, head for town
and Mattie Sue's. He hoped selling was the right thing to
have done.

Alice Chow removed the repaired book from the vise.

Mattie Sue had on the same soap opera as Granny but
wasn't really watching. Wondering instead, who had been at
the window and if she would come back.

Bo Peavey worked on. Sweat poured down his bald head
and into his eyes. Hot now, hot, it was plain pure-D *hot;* he
couldn't think of anything else.

The kids around Emma giggled, screamed and fought,
and the book in her hand went up and down with the
bouncing of the bus, but Emma didn't look up or glance out
the window at the weather again, she'd noticed it and that
was enough. She fixed her eyes on each line of words as she
came to the left margin, so the jostling wouldn't make her
lose her place or jar her concentration.

Women and children had left town during the flood, to
wait for the water to recede. White planters and their black
help had camped out on the levees, and kept lanterns burning there, to find one another by . . .

She rubbed her arm as she read. The hairs stood up wherever she rubbed, from the brisk sensation the pyracantha
burns provoked, and that made her look up from time to
time, to think back over her day and its adventure, going
into Mattie Sue Cunningham's backyard and seeing her

there, in the glass room eating breakfast. And the cat . . . that ugly old cat, why did it bother her so? She'd go back one of these days. When the time was right. Go right up to the pink house and knock on the front door. Or maybe stay at the window when the old woman discovered her and find out what she was trying to say, making that come-and-go gesture.

Maybe by then the cat would have died.

One other thing she couldn't ignore: the smell of the bus. Like she knew, worse in the afternoon than the morning.

Country. She hated it.

II

THE FIGHT

No light from outside came into her room. There was a window, but it opened out onto the back fence of the trailer park, so that in winter Emma couldn't tell when she wakened whether it was early morning yet or still deep into night. She felt for her clock without opening her eyes, in case she had time to go back to sleep, and brought it into her bed under the covers.

She'd slept in her clothes. Her jeans were open, unzipped, uncomfortable; she must have fallen asleep reading. Somebody must have come into her room while she was sleeping to turn out her light.

She pulled a blanket up to her neck and held the clock against her chest. Did something happen during the night? She had a leftover feeling of something. Like something bad had happened since she went to bed. She put off finding out what time it was; early or late, she didn't want to know. Something lay heavy on her mind. Like a mask snapped down over her eyes, something oppressive. . . .

But wait: it was a holiday. No need to look at the clock, it was Friday, Christmas Eve's eve, the first day of her Christmas vacation.

Uttering a small sigh of joy, Emma put the clock back on her bedside table and settled deeper down in her bed.

Granny.

She'd had a dream, that was what stayed with her and covered her up in fear. The dream was about Granny; Granny was in it. Lord. And scary. Granny had said something terrible.

Her eyes popped open and Emma lay on her back trying to reconstruct it. She couldn't quite catch hold of what it was.

It was morning, no doubt about it now, her room was softly lit, the sun had been up quite a while. She checked the clock. Nine-thirty.

What had she said? Something meaningful, directly to Emma. Emma standing over Granny; Granny talking.

She put her hands behind her head on the pillow.

Not Granny in the flesh-and-blood: Emma could not recall seeing her. But Granny's voice, Granny's spirit, what Granny was, beyond bones and flesh, the force Granny represented and was. Granny all right. Without doubt. Not her face but Granny herself.

Emma had been standing over her and. . . .

She was dead and she was talking. She was dead and she was talking. I was scared but couldn't leave, she was talking to me, I was standing over her and couldn't leave, the force of her words held me. Standing over Granny I knew she was there but could not see her in front of me in the casket but did see her too: she shook a pointing finger and stared into my eyes and spoke. I couldn't see her mouth but she spoke. She said . . .

"Don't shake the tree. I'm still in it."

Don't shake the tree. I'm still in it.

Granny was dead and she was talking. Lying there dead;

still, she issued warnings and threats and bulletins saying how alive she still was, and defiant as ever, making trouble as usual for the rest.

But so what.

It didn't seem too fantastical a notion: Granny would. Whoever's life she had touched would never be the same afterwards; whichever Peavey's life she touched at any rate, others Granny fussed about too but not with the same vigor: Peaveys were who she felt called upon to grate against, Peaveys who she felt were her God-given charge. To irritate and rouse up. To keep from getting too lax or lazy.

Emma sat up. No use trying to go back to sleep now, time was numbers and she was into the day, herself inside herself; might as well get on with it now, no use trying to go back. Granny again. Granny had got her going too, just like she did the others. And who was in the tree now? Getting shook out of her warm treetop bough before she was ready.

Emma zipped up her jeans and, barefoot, padded out of her room toward the bathroom.

But Lucille was not in her bed and the bathroom door was shut . . . in there already, no doubt, and would not be out soon . . . grieving again, most likely . . . when Emma had to go, and bad. And the other bathroom was past Granny, whose door was closed too.

Don't shake the tree. I'm still in it. Her voice as harsh as rust itself.

Which way?

Without question.

Emma moved ahead. Toward the one who never slept a wink anyway, so why should she care?

She eased the door open.

Lucille sat up tall and alert, listening, hugging a sheet of paper close, in case anybody came in. If they did, she'd hide it quick, before they saw. She heard Granny's door open and close. The trailer got quiet again. Lucille relaxed and brought the piece of paper close to her face and began to unfold it. She'd forgotten to bring her glasses.

Still in the tree: not dead yet.

The old woman slept on her side with her knees drawn up and her hands crossed over one another at the wrist. Like she was tied up. Her hands were loosely curled, her thin white hair lay across the pillow like a swatch of gauze, her mouth was open, her teeth were out, she was snoring. "Did not sleep a wink," she would say later on. "Never shut my eyes once. Not for a second. Heard the whole thing." Her lips fluttered as air went in and out; she made the snoring sound when the air blew out. Her eyes were tight shut, so deep-sunk beneath that great white brown-spotted forehead you barely could find them. Tiny beaded things: when they were open, fierce and unyielding.

A Peavey forehead. Which she said Emma got from her. According to Granny everybody got something from somebody; nobody had anything on her own or for free.

She wore a white cotton nightgown. Her daughter Zhena, who had to buy them, always fussed. "Can't get cotton anymore," she explained. "Nylon and polyester's the thing now. Won't that do?" No. It wouldn't. Don't shake the tree, I'm still in it. Order from Sears, Granny told Zhena; Sears'll carry cotton. Which Zhena—fear-obedient like all Granny's children—went home and did, carping all the while.

Like Peaveys needed to.

Satisfaction never came and couldn't. Then they'd be let too loose and couldn't keep up.

You had to sand Peaveys some to get their best qualities to show. And Granny had flint paper for fingertips.

Emma tiptoed to the bathroom, shut the door and sat. She

relieved her bladder as quietly as she could, holding back a
little so it didn't come out in a gush and wake Granny.

She looked so tiny in bed asleep. Like a baby in an infant
sleep-sack.

When she was finished, Emma held the toilet handle for a
minute, looking toward the bedroom, wondering if the
sound would waken her.

Better not chance it. Better to let her find it unflushed and
fuss about that instead. Better than shaking the tree; she
was still asleep in it.

Lucille, hearing the door once again, listened for signs. No
yelling; it was Emma. Emma would leave her alone for a
while. She sat with her feet on the bathtub. She'd had the
letter only a week, but Granny said she must have read the
words off it by now, she'd gone over it so many times.

Well. One time more wouldn't hurt.

Emma pulled out a cast-iron skillet and a pot, some eggs
and bacon, coffee and grits. The grits box tilted over as she
reached for it and grits poured out onto the floor. Emma
pushed at the white corn-powder with her toe so that the
grits sprayed out finer, and couldn't be so easily seen.

"Like a mad woman scattering shit," Granny always said
of her efforts.

"You should clean up as you go," advised Lucille, always
the arbitrator.

Like a mad woman scattering shit.

Emma took down a container of frozen orange juice.

She pictured Granny, high in a frozen, leafless tree, and
the rest of them at the bottom trying to shake her out. The
old woman wore her white cotton nightgown; her hair was

loose and flying; her small prunelike face screwed up in rage.

"Don't shake it! I'm still in it!" Granny yelled down at them. And hard as they shook, they never budged her by an inch: she would not fall.

Emma squeezed out the frozen cylinder of orange juice; missed the pitcher; scraped the juice off the counter back into the pitcher; poured water over it; ran more water into a pot for the grits.

Granny: they never got over or past her, she held on too tight to her limb. They could sit—Peaveys—telling stories about her from now on. Like the one how she "up and flat left" as they told it, sold her place to Carroll Cunningham without asking anybody's advice and moved into Lucille's. She had done all that seventeen years before yet they still told it . . . you might at any time hear that "She just up and flat left" suddenly interjected into a quiet conversation between them. And once it was spoken the story then came. The rest of them would cluster in like pigeons to a popcorn hull and each would peck out his or her expected contribution and the story would come on and would not stop until it was finished.

Without saying boo to a soul she just did it . . . after all we did for her too . . . she just up and sold her place to Carroll Cunningham and moved out. Like . . . snap . . . that.

Like . . . a snap of the fingers . . . that.

Up and flat left was their once upon a time: when grandchildren and great-grandchildren heard that phrase they ran from the room and found some game to play or some TV show to watch, some activity that took long enough that it would occupy them until it was done.

Which was the only choice you had: either to participate in the telling or at least sit and listen; or to walk out on it. One thing was certain, you couldn't stop it, their stories were like the locusts' tree concerts: if it was their time to

sing you might as well hush and wait it out. Only somebody
like Lucille would bother to yell "Shut up" out a window to
them, and look at the good it did.

Emma liked the stories though, as long as they were not
about Lolly. She had heard the "up and flat left" one so
many times she could sit down right now where she was and
without coaching recite it word for word; taking parts, mim-
icking voices, imitating their Peavey-hurt, indignant tone in
the same back-and-forth, in-out language they used, and you
would believe as she did it you were right there too, hearing
it the way Zhena and Esker and Johnnie Ruth and Bo told it.

Face facts, Bo. That was Zhena, Face-facts Zhena as
Emma called her. Zhena said "Face facts" every other
breath.

She read the instructions on the back of the grits box to
see how much she should pour in, to match the amount of
water already on the fire set to boil.

"Emma, you'd do a lot better if you read the instructions
first." That was Lucille, plus every schoolteacher she'd ever
had.

Read the instruction, *then* take the test.

Emma was glad for their stories; it was the best thing
Peaveys had; as close to the kind of legacy you got in those
squat houses on Main Street as anything she might come up
with. Nothing you could reach out and touch with your
hand, like a house or furniture was; still and all, something:
their one claim to grace and permanence. And say this for
Peaveys, they never let a good story die. The "Up and flat
left" tale was seventeen years old now . . . how Esker went
out to her house to take out her trash and found Granny
gone; how he came to Zhena's house and the others came
too, and flew into a panic thinking she'd been dragged off
and killed; how nobody thought she'd ever go to Lucille's
house, she hadn't seen Lucille in fifteen years and after all
Lucille didn't even have a proper house but a trailer to live
in, a trailer house when they all had yards and brick houses

and such; what had happened when Lucille finally called
them and told them what had taken place, how Granny was
sitting right beside her there and had, it looked like, decided
to come there to stay, to live there she supposed; what they
had all thought then, how they had hmmphed and hmmed
and hawed thinking of that, sitting there wondering every
one of them one thing (though this part they didn't mention
in their story) which was, how much she had got for the
place and where the money was and if they'd get their
hands on it or persuade Carroll Cunningham to tell them
where it was since most likely Granny would not . . . yet it
was still told as if it just happened yesterday. So what,
Peavey reasoning went: no need to let a good story die just
because it was old; if it was a good one and the telling was
still fun, tell it again. New stories never seemed as good anyway and besides what had happened was never the point;
events weren't the thing as far as Peaveys were concerned,
but how you told about them. How the story was shaped
and shared and passed on, who took which part every time
and got mad in the same places all over again, as if it were
brand new and happening while they told it; who claimed
to have known first where Granny had gone; who was the
most hurt, the worst wounded, the most put-upon. These
were fixed and stable; they never changed. Zhena always
said "Face facts, Bo" at some point toward the last of the
story, reminding him he had *not* known Granny went to
Lucille's to live as he claimed because none of them had had
the least suspicion, defying him to challenge her on that
which he did not; no one much challenged Zhena. Next to
Granny she was the toughest one.

The mail. Emma suddenly remembered. First-up in the
trailer got certain privileges, like going out to bring in the
mail. She hoped Lucille had not beat her to it.

Clunch. She ran out to the aluminum mailbox, one of many, in a row in the gravel beside 84.

And so they stressed how a story was told and clung to that *how*, and shaped their tales carefully and kept them the same word for word year after year (*You should have seen her hair . . . She just up and flat left . . . Face facts, Bo: none of us knew*) so that if Bo, say, was telling and left out something, his wife or sister could step right in, like . . . snap . . . that, and fill in his blank, not to help Bo out especially, but to keep the story honest and the same, so they would have it year after year to depend on and pass on. Like somebody else, some other family, might preserve stocks or bonds or a special inherited piece of jewelry.

Clunch. She came back in, put part of the mail in her back pocket, threw the rest on the counter next to the stove.

Lucille flinched, every time the door slammed.

Granny shifted in her bed and turned over onto her back. The snores got louder.

When the up-and-flat-left story was over and Granny was living in the trailer with Lucille and nobody still, to this day, knew how much she'd gotten for the place much less seen a penny of it, after all that there generally was a period of quiet. Homage to the tale, thinking how they'd felt that day when after all the panic and to-do they found out the simple truth: that Granny had gone to Lucille's to live, when Lu-

cille didn't live in a proper house but a trailer, when Lucille
hadn't helped take care of her all these years but had been
more married to Frank than daughter to her own mother.
Now Frank was gone and Granny ups and goes there to live,
when after all . . . after all . . .

From what they began to say then, anybody listening to
them would have thought they were all jealous of Lucille,
that each of them wished Granny had come to live at their
house instead of Lucille's, the way they all began to holler
and shout, saying what an outrage it was, not only that
Granny had up and flat left without telling anybody or asking the opinion of a soul, not only that as if that weren't
enough but then to make matters worse, had gone of all
places to Lucille's house to live. When Lucille didn't even
live in a house proper but for God's sake a mobile home. A
trailer house and she goes there. Hmmphing and howling
and fuming they took up that juicy tidbit and began to peck
at it, squabbling like always but as usual not listening particularly to one another or stating counter-arguments; doing
what Granny and Emma did: yes-I-am, no-you're-not.

Like turkeys in the rain: they lift their heads to greet it,
mouths open gobbling, until they drown. In their tracks.
Head up, mouth open, they went on and on with their testimony, stating their case, as much to the heavens as to any
one person. As blood-believers, thinking who you were determined what you were, they knew of no place else to look
for a listener.

And if anybody else not a Peavey had been there that
day, and heard what was being said word for word, and
tried to make it come to a logical conclusion, what it seemed
like was that every single person in that room was deeply
hurt, not only because Granny had gone off without telling
them, but that she had made that cut even deeper by going
where she did, to Lucille's mobile home instead of one of

their houses. When they'd have been glad to have her. More
than glad in fact: proud.

But if Granny had made a different decision that day and
gone to anybody else's house instead, *any* of their houses to
live in, they'd have all been exactly where they were now,
doing the exact same thing, and the one whose house she
went to would be screaming loudest of all about her going
where she had . . . just as loud and long as he or she was
right now about her *not* going there . . . and nothing would
have been different at all. The only difference would have
been that one of them would have been saying that well,
after all somebody else did have more room and fewer
mouths to feed, it looked like Granny could have gone there
instead and *after all,* they'd done the most for her over the
years and it did look like they deserved a rest now that they
didn't have to go out that rutted road anymore and *after all,*
somebody else was younger or older, had fewer children,
more space, better beds, more beds, a bigger stove, a smaller
family, a front porch for her to sit on, yard enough to plant
her flowers on, so on and so forth now and forever, on and on,
whatever came to them. The point being, why couldn't
Granny have gone someplace else? After all . . . after all
. . . there would have been an endless run of after alls, just
as there were now, explaining why what had happened—
whatever it was, whichever way it went—shouldn't have.
Should have, shouldn't have, but didn't, didn't, never did,
always it went the wrong way and they yelled and complained, getting what they needed to keep them going, that
grit and fire and abrasiveness. And more than likely, the
thing would sooner or later have come down to somebody
saying that well, after all Lucille hadn't really done her share
over the years and after all, Frank had moved out and Lolly
was gone, so why couldn't Granny have gone there, Lucille
had plenty of room now. By means of Peavey logic, it would
have gotten to that, eventually; inevitably; without ques-

tion; would have. But now that she *had* gone to Lucille's, it had to go in the other direction, they had to scream about that instead. If it didn't go one way, it went the other, but one thing was certain: it went. Living on the edge, Peaveys never could let themselves be satisfied with what was, not enough to let down their guard; they always had to fuss and fume about the way things went, no matter in which direction, *which* never being the point but *how*. Every time they seemed to be losing their balance and in danger of falling, something happened like this to save them, and they could grit their teeth and start to fuss and fume and fight again, and eventually would pull themselves back up and together again, by scraping themselves up against it, sandpapering their skin down so they could tell it was still there, alive and hurting.

Which way it went was not crucial: only that it did. On with the keeping on.

Don't shake the tree. I'm still in it.

Five years later Emma came and Lolly left her and they were there in the trailer together, three generations, one skipped. Lolly was gone. Granny had a high forehead and so did Lucille and Emma but Lolly did not: Frank's, Granny declared. Lolly was never a Peavey, the old woman insisted. Emma was but Lolly had never been.

And from then on it was going to happen. Once they both got there. Like locusts, like a Peavey tale, the point had to come where Emma and Granny no longer could tolerate each other's sameness.

"Just smell one another," Lucille often told them. "All you two have to do is get close enough to smell one another and I don't know what. Like dogs: no telling what's liable to break loose."

You never know girl. Except sometimes.

An accident waiting to happen, Lucille might say.

WHAM. Emma slammed the cast-iron skillet down on a burner and turned it on. The drip coffeepot had grounds in it from the night before, which Emma dumped into the sink without bothering to turn the disposal on. Her bare feet picked up some of the spilled grits and spread white powder all around.

She liked to cook but couldn't keep up. Always the stuff got ahead of her and she made a mess Lucille would later have to clean up.

If you started in the middle and kept your eyes on the goal you couldn't help it. The details got fuzzy. You lost track of the in-between.

Like a mad woman scattering.

Emma wished Granny would get out of her mind. First Granny and now her. Now that Christmas card. From her. In her back pocket with the gift she had enclosed.

Usually it came earlier; she had thought perhaps this was the year it might not come at all. But no, here it was, no such luck and why. Why remember and remember year after year long after the thing is over and done with, why not let it go instead of coming back twice a year on-the-nose regular, like the knife of a carnival expert right on target: zap, to the heart . . . REMEMBER ME: The Mama. Your Mama and not just *the;* I send money and greetings to prove it. To remind you that you are to me and in the world still and all, after all this time and no-show, my daughter. The daughter of . . . remember, my sweet Emma Blue, re-member . . . Love, Lolly.

Shit.

Laying a strip of bacon in the skillet, Emma accidentally

touched its handle which, cast-iron too, was as hot as the bottom.

Shit.

She stuck it in her mouth; it hurt, would blister.

Always going to. Fuel to the fire.

No word from Lucille. Usually as soon as anybody was up she bustled on in full of help and doom. Crying again most likely.

The envelope was square and not quite white . . . that cream color fancier by a mile than pure white, and thick classy paper too, not just Hallmark from the drugstore but something expensive, engraved the way those things are done by such people, people such as her, such as.

The ink was blue, the envelope addressed in the tight, cramped, almost schoolgirl hand Emma recognized immediately: Miss Emma Blue Lasswell, in care of . . .

The card showed a homey scene: a laurel- and holly-trimmed horse and carriage pulled up to a large, columned white house, snow on the ground, tracks behind the carriage, wreaths and Christmas swags and fancies on the front door and in every window pane a candle, with a yellow-orange haloish glow. Everything fuzzy. A water-color reproduction, with indistinct ends and edges. Two white horses pull the carriage . . . between their ears, jaunty red-feather plumes. At the reins, a top-hatted driver, eyes properly forward . . . behind him, on the carriage seat, a stack of wrapped, beribboned boxes. Stepping from the carriage, a girl. A beautiful and blurry young dream girl, seen through a rain-wet glass.

A happy occasion, children no doubt singing carols in the big white house, a merry storybook Christmas, silver star perfect on the tree: pie-in-the-sky brass-ring perfect.

Catch it!

Listen, she had said in the night, *listen.* . . .

To me. About me. Star on the top branch. Silver dream

angel outshining the rest. Higher than. A chip of the sun shining in the back of her mind, burning her up. *Me!*

Not a chance of it not happening, not today. Not when the girl was so stirred up and the old woman was so talented at spotting such weaknesses, not a prayer, it had to: the water was simmering too wildly, the fire was up too high. No way to avoid it; it had to come to a boil.

She stuck her finger in a cup of cold milk to ease the red blistering pain. Shit, she hated to burn herself. A burn hurt worse than anything. She swirled it around in the milk and watched the circles.

Like something in a dream, the girl on the card was smoky and sweet, dressed Victorian style in a blue tight-fitting long coat with a full skirt. There was a bonnet on her head, rakishly tilted like Used Car City's smiling mama. Her hair was pushed up beneath it, except for soft wisps about her face, only brush strokes, just so. *Mud color, with an overlay of rust and gold. Like the sun was shining in it instead of on top. Like no color you ever saw before, mud-rust and flowing, like water.* Calculated curls, escaping just so. One foot reached from her skirts, a tiny black thing pointed toward the ground, poised, hesitant it seemed, feeling to see how far away the ground actually was. A tiny foot, it would doubtless make a light step, barely disturb the new snow. One hand was on the carriage rail, the other was lost in a fur muff with tassels.

A picturesque scene to send to a daughter, that perfect young lady. Perfect Christmas night visitor with gifts to bestow.

But who was in the house? And why wasn't someone at the front door to greet her and make her seem less lonely . . . so tentatively perched there, one foot reaching, to test the snow.

Emma took her finger out and sucked it. No good. It felt no better. She dumped spoon after spoonful of coffee into the well of the pot, only to realize when she reached for it that she had not filled up the kettle or boiled any water. The bacon sizzled and curled too fast, the fire was up too high. She turned it off and leaned heavy on her hands on the stove.

The trailer was dead night-quiet. No one stirred. Granny's snore was too low to hear through the door. It might have been 3 A.M. instead of past ten. It seduced her, the quiet, the opportunity. . . .

Checking to make sure everything was off . . . except the grits, which could cook awhile . . . Emma left her breakfast preparations and stole back off to her bedroom.

Just for a little while. A quick look.

She closed the door behind her.

In the bathroom, Lucille heard it all, the kitchen noises and Emma tiptoeing back to her room, the door shut. She sat on the toilet seat with her feet up on the tub, reading. She'd had the letter only a week, but the stationery was already worn at the folds, she had reopened and closed it so often.

Her long bare feet flexed back and forth on the cold enamel and one by one she bent her toes down then straightened them, starting with the little toe and moving up, one foot and then the other, then both at the same time, a small toe-parade.

Dead. As Zhena said, face that fact.

Face facts, Lucille, she had said: your husband is dead.

Dead, let it drop. Dead. Let it sink to the bottom of her soul like a lead fishing weight, let it stay. The word. The fact. The absence of him in the world for the rest of it. Dead. She would never absorb it entirely, but let the information at least, the fact of it, the truth of that one word, drop down into her and stay, like an old something made of metal you swallow but never pass: dead. Face facts.

She couldn't quit reading the letter. She kept it in her pocket to feel of, and took it out in off-times during a day to check one more time. Yes. Still there. Still dead. With one of the *ofs* erased, she was *wife of* no more. Of what man? None, a dead man, if wife of a dead man then wife of no longer: that hook had been snapped open and removed, her flesh was free of it now and from now on until however it stopped.

She crossed one foot on top of the other as if in consolation, as if the pain was there, as if one foot might check the bare loneliness of the other.

And yet the opening was still there, where the hook had been. It would scar but never leave, it was as much a part of her as knees and shoulder: wife still, wife always. *Of* no one, yet and endlessly, to her soul, wife. What she was. And was.

"Dear Mrs. Lasswell . . ."

Lord but would she never get past it. It caught at her heart every time, and she must have been through it two dozen times by now.

Inside the card, the imprinted message was simple and to the point: SEASON'S GREETINGS, that was all, in an old-fashioned type. Underneath was a surprise. LOLLY LASS-WELL TURNAGE, it said, engraved, her new last name, which she'd never revealed before. It was crossed out. Beneath the X was her signature. *Love* it said in that same tight blue hand, *Lolly*.

Couldn't stand not, could she, had to leak information out, drop crumbs behind her for people to get hungry by. Couldn't do like Frank, leave altogether with nothing behind: had to always be showing somebody.

A blue paper had fluttered from the card. Emma bent to

pick it up and discovered there were two: money orders, fifty dollars apiece, bought at a convenience drive-in grocery store, anonymous enough. Usually fifty was all Emma got, this time there were two. As if she'd thought better and at the last minute doubled the amount. Both, along with the card, were in Emma's back pocket. She was not too proud to accept the money. Principles broke down elsewhere. This she would take.

The Mama. Ermine muff, wasp waist, blue rakish bonnet and snow. Silver tinsel, grit in the eye. Standing on a chair, Emma reached up to a shelf and got down a large leatherbound book. It was time to forget instead of making things go backward, time to go on from it. She sat on her bed, fluffed up two pillows behind her and opened the book. It fell apart naturally, to a certain page.

She filled it up entirely . . . from top to bottom and side to side without margins or white space, nothing but her, but her, flashing her sign, telling her name. She stood on grass that had white lines drawn across it and behind her in the distance was a giant fuzzy H. A goalpost. Incidental backdrops, her stage, a football field. Her. The one. All shining. Coming and going, LOLLY.

She stood on one foot with the other leg drawn up so that the boot toe of that foot, the left, rested hard by her right knee. In profile, the hiked-up left leg was on the far side of her, while the right standing one was nearest the camera. The right knee was bent slightly, making a gentle very natural arc ankle to thigh, from high-top tight zippered boot to the elastic of her suit at the top of her thigh. So easy. It all looked so easy. Altogether unforced and right. The left knee made a perfect right angle up over the other one.

Me . . . I was the star, she said and she was, you could see it, she did not lie. Starshine and flash were there, perfection itself, all glory and wonder and true flash and style, born not made. In the blood, running like Peaviness, like high foreheads and the need for grit.

They were nearly the same age: Emma would be seventeen in January, Lolly was that age when the picture was made, her senior year.

Such thin childlike legs Lolly had, bony at the knees like a little girl's. Her body too . . . it seemed not finished somehow, still stuck in adolescence, the thinness around her midsection above the waist, those ribs, cheeks like pads. Like a child.

Not like Emma, whose body had matured altogether too soon, when other girls were still at doll babies. In the fourth grade: there she was in full bloom, as tall as she'd ever grow, with breasts and hair and soon afterwards bleeding too. Well it wasn't something you could control but still . . . in Emma's case it seemed everything either came like a pie in her face too soon or too late or not at all.

But look at Lolly. Graced with such luck. How could a brass ring slip from such sure, agile fingers?

She wore her famous gold-sequined suit. It was sleeveless and legless and barely covered her butt . . . in fact a glance of skin peeked from beneath the elastic at her thigh, the tiniest suggestion of what was underneath, enough however, just the right amount, just enough. Lucille still had the suit, wrapped up in tissue in a drawer. Couldn't see it was gold in the picture of course, the picture was black and white; what you could see was what it did: a blurred white starshape was at her hip where the sun had caught up the light of one sequin and flashed it pack. Trading licks light for light.

She stood on her name. Beneath her standing foot was one word, LOLLY. *Me, I mean, I was it, Emma, It!*

The book was open against Emma's propped-up legs. She had kicked off the covers when she got up and they lay where they'd fallen, on the floor at the foot of her bed. Around the room were piles of her life, dirty clothes, magazines, papers she had worked on, cookie wrappers, towels she'd wound around herself then dropped. Beside the bed was a stack of library books.

Like a madwoman scattering shit, Granny said . . . slob, she called her. Takes one to know one, Emma snapped back.

Spitting and spiteful, one against the other.

So taut and yet so fluid; the Mama had not lied, she was everything she hinted at, the chipped-off fragment of pure glory she told about. Everything came together there, as in the night-stories, all the energy one body was allowed, brought together for this one concentrated and very radiant moment, nothing held back, an explosion contained, fireworks in a loose ribbon, endless promise in the most casual glance.

Oh . . . hi. It's me. Fake wonder and surprise, spoken with such commitment and integrity, who could bear to disbelieve?

Her back was bent impossibly: her spine curved back on itself in an astonishing upside-down horseshoe shape that tolerated no rigidity or denial but gave altogether, so that her shoulders came back in toward her butt. Her arms were out, the right one reaching toward the top of the page, the left pointing at the line-marked grass beneath her. In each hand was a baton; they lay against the length of her arms from index finger to past her elbows. Her head was back, her hair nearly dragged the ground, her face was toward the camera, she was smiling. Nothing held back. It seemed.

A flash of promise. Give them what they ask for but never all. Never. Let them wonder, need more, wonder where it came from and if it will be there again.

Emma turned the book sideways.

That was the only way to see what was beneath the flash and glory: there, in her eyes. Which did not flash or sparkle but were dead serious . . . businesslike and calculating, they gave her away, proved how it was possible for her to leave a daughter behind without looking back except twice-

a-year cards and money orders, no return address, nothing
promised or asked for beyond that. The eyes revealed just
how far she would go. . . .

Two feet off the ground, abstracted, never responding to
a daughter, always off in some cloud or other, fixed on
things flightier and more important by far than a small
squarish daughter who seemed to have inherited none of the
good stuff, none, but was Peavey at its worst and Blue and
Lasswell too: all the bad genes, foisted off on one girl. Ordinary.

With her finger inside to mark her place, Emma took the
yearbook and set it up on her dresser next to the mirror, and
propped it open with a jar of hand cream. Standing on the
bed to be high enough to see, she did it too.

Bent her back. Let her hair fall. Looked sideways to the
mirror. Hiked the other leg up. Fell. Hit the bed. No way.
Except she did look thinner sideways and her hair was prettier falling down loose, but her back was like a shelf, flat and
stiff and unyielding. Instead of bending back on itself, it refused: this far, it said, but no farther and threatened to pop
if she pushed. Her foolish head looked unnatural hanging
down that way, her neck was too stiff, her knees refused to
give at all, and oh Lord, the look on her face. How in the
world could a person just stand there and *smile* . . . and
smile . . . and smile.

Emma rolled off the bed, took the yearbook off the dresser
and threw it against the far wall.

She put on her shoes and went back to the kitchen.

WHAM! Lucille jumped, feeling something hit against
the wall next to her. Now what. What in the world was that
girl up to.

"I am sorry to have to write you this bad news, but the
day before yesterday your husband Frank Lasswell was
killed on the job. It was an accident. We were laying some

pipe when a chain carrying one section suddenly snapped. That piece of pipe fell free on one end and swung around and hit Frank Lasswell on the back of the head. We thought maybe he would only be stunned, but then the pipe came back from the other direction and before we could do anything about it, and with him so dazed, it hit him again. That time he fell, and was dead. We couldn't actually tell which blow killed him, but we didn't try to find out. Seemed useless. The man was dead. The pipe had killed him one time or another. Nobody, I assure you, was to blame.

"Mrs. Lasswell, this is not an easy letter to write to someone you've never met, but I was Frank Lasswell's foreman, and as such it has fallen upon me to do it. Also, I hope you approve of what we did about the burial. Frank's will said he should be buried inexpensively, in the cemetery closest to his death and we did that. He was a private man, as I'm sure I don't have to tell you, and he didn't say much about his past. We only got your address from checking at the company insurance office. (Who I'm sure you'll be hearing from soon, if you don't please let me know.)

"Mrs. Lasswell, there is one thing more. What should we do with his things and do you want any of them? There's not much, but we have put it all aside in case you might want some of it to remember him by. Also, there's his pick-up truck which one of the men here would like to buy if it's agreeable to you. He has offered one thousand dollars which I would say is a fair price to pay for a two-year-old GMC in good condition. But of course it's up to you.

"Please advise me on these matters.

"My deepest regrets to you and your family, one daughter I believe, name of Lolly Ray Lasswell.

"Sincerely,

Lucille went to the sink and splashed her face with cold water. A lonely thing, to grieve a death alone, cold and bone-chilling lonely. No one to tell. No one to swap stories with, about what funny things Frank had done on this occasion or that, how maybe he had looked when, this or that . . . no one to tell . . . her family never had liked him and Frank's own people were bound to be long-gone from remembering him by now, he had left them so early, when he was only fifteen; nobody left to say Frank Lasswell to and see some brightening about the eyes, Lolly was the only one. And look at her.

Lucille turned her face from side to side in the mirror, inspecting her skin, the folds under her jaw, her pale vanishing eyebrows and paler brow. Somehow on her, sorrow never showed. She always looked the same whatever happened. She dried her face and put the letter back in her pocket.

She thought of her own: the two letters she had sent out. After all these years never putting word to paper, she had written two. One to that foreman, the other to her daughter, whose last name or address she didn't even know. She had addressed it after the license plate, simply LOLLY Ray Lasswell, care of general delivery in the town her cards were postmarked. Maybe she'd get it, maybe not; Lucille didn't know which she wished for more.

She raised her eyebrows and turned to a three-quarters profile, her best look. Holding her head up at a nice angle, she smoothed down her hair.

It felt like pieces of her, cut up and sent in envelopes out into the world, to be handled by strangers.

But at least she'd done it. At least she had taken a notion out to its end: that was something. She was anxious to get to the mail first every day, to see if either one had replied. But Emma had gotten up first today. Probably the mailman had already been by. She opened the bathroom door.

"Good morning."

At the stove, Emma turned. "Eve's Eve special, coming up," she said.

Emma seemed bright. As she cracked an egg into a pale

yellow bowl, a slip of white slopped over the edge. She
didn't seem to notice. At one glance Lucille took in the
spilled orange juice and grits, the coffee in the sink, empty
containers all around.

Granny would say: like a madwoman scattering shit.

"Need some help?"

"Unless you want to set the table."

Lucille went for plates; Emma stayed busy at the stove.

Lucille had never thought of herself as waiting, she had
not taken that string out to its end to see what was there.
But now it was fact, now she knew: all this time she had
kept the idea of him ahead of her to go toward, light at the
end of the tunnel, something hard and real, her last chance
for . . . she owned up to it . . . rescue. There, Frank was
who she had thought was on the stream bank with boat and
paddle, the one she had thought would save her from swift
currents and rising tides. She had turned his monthly checks
into scraps of a promise. She had pieced them together herself and made them into a vow with no help from Frank,
who never promised idly. Or went back on his word.

She set silverware in three places, folded napkins under
the fork, thinking it might help to have things look nice, it
might give them all a lift.

Not coming back. Of all the comings and goings this
worst one finally had an end, was over. She had never expected it to be so completely blank. Frank was dead, never
coming back, there was nothing left over to go on, nothing,
she was free. Weightless and free and released, like it or not.

Reaching for salt and pepper, Lucille spied the cream-
colored envelope face-up addressed in blue ink to Emma.
No wonder she was so frantic and noisy. With her back to
the girl, she turned it over. No return address either place.
Where was the card? Had Lolly mentioned Lucille's letter?
Good chance she would never get it.

"Emma. Has the mail come?"

"Nothing but a bill and a card from Bo and Francine and . . ."

And?

"Shall I wake Granny?"

Emma turned and for the first time looked at Lucille. And a card from Lolly. She hadn't said it. Her blue eyes were such a high color they seemed about to pop out of her head and fly away. Those terrible blue eyes, like marbles. Like his. Her daddy's eyes. The girl was in a panic, that was clear, it happened every Christmas and birthday when she got those cards.

"Oh no," Emma said. "Let's put it off a few minutes. Wait till the biscuits are in."

There was real affection between them. Each recognized the other's pain and in a sense shared it, eye to eye and across all barriers. Yet they did not speak of it ever or spell out what they understood.

"Listen, Emma, if we're going to have a tree you better get after it. Tomorrow's Christmas Eve you know."

"Didn't I say this was the Eve Eve's special? Going today. There's a tree lot up the highway not far. I can walk unless somebody's coming out. Is anybody? I need to go to town anyway. Do my shopping."

She poured the eggs in the iron skillet and picked up the biscuit pan.

Set now: on its way and always going to happen.

"Zhena I think."

"Good."

She slammed the oven door.

"Okay, call Granny."

Lucille settled her shoulders back and went to do it.

They had a car. It stayed in one place day and night, on the far side of the trailer next to the clothesline and never was driven or fooled with by anyone except Esker Peavey.

It wouldn't run, Emma said. Nobody knew for sure if it would or would not, nobody else but her drove, maybe it did, maybe it didn't, one way or the other, Emma refused to drive or ride in it so it might as well not run like she said and they might as well never have been given it for all the use it was.

Granny hated it too, unless it served her purposes not to. Then she might suddenly love it, you never could tell.

She barked at Lucille for waking her up, said there was no need, since she hadn't slept a wink all night anyway. Lucille came out rolling her eyes and Emma grinned.

Esker gave it to them.

That was wonder enough to take your breath away if you knew Esker Peavey because Esker never gave away as much as the time of day without asking for sales tax, and yet he did: he flatly gave them that car.

Years back. When Emma was little. In case they needed it, he said, for an emergency. Especially, he said, now that *that girl* was going to be living there. Which was how most of the Peaveys referred to Emma for years, as *that girl.*

So they did have a car. Esker was retired but he still dabbled in cheap real estate and used cars as a sideline and he had given them what had to be called a car since it was nothing else but, though Emma said it didn't deserve the name of one.

She refused to ride in it.

"Not that I'm too good to," she explained to Lucille. "There just isn't anyplace I ever need to get to that I wouldn't rather walk to than ride in such a poor excuse for a car." No distance was too far, no day too rainy, no wind too cold that she wouldn't prefer either to be out in it walking or waiting for a bus or hitching a ride. She'd as soon not go at all, in fact, as to ride in it.

"No wonder Esker gave it to us," she told Lucille. "Shows what he thinks of us, what they all do, thinking it's good enough for us but not for them. Who get a new one every year. Nossir. But for us: we're too low even to refuse it."

She just wished she'd been old enough when it was offered. She'd have let them know quick enough what was what.

It was ten years old when they got it with no knowing how many miles; the odometer was permanently stuck at 78,002.8. A Nash, from the year all Nashes looked like tubes with the roof blown up to a hump, its color was as much a mystery as its mileage. From any distance it seemed to be something between the shell of a brown egg color and a mixed-up low-key kind of yellowish-brown. Sort of. With some green thrown in.

Puke, Emma said. Color of puke.

Ochre, Esker declared. The owner had told him and he'd looked it up and sure enough: ochre.

Poor Nash. Just ugly: like a bad cross between mutts, just plain mutt-ugly.

Emma dumped the eggs on a platter. Lucille took it to the table. With the same spoon she used for the eggs, Emma scraped out grits.

Granny rubbed her feet together, sole to sandpapery sole.

Not even any chrome to interrupt the patchy puke-ochre either. Not one decoration, not one ornament: Esker stripped all he could get away with off any car before selling it and, since this one was only going to his mother and sister for emergency use, and since after all he was *giving* the thing away scot-free, why he might as well strip it all off. (Lord, he said to his son Wymer as he pried off a line of silver from the right front door . . . what they need with *chrome?*) Every last inch of it was gone. Not a hubcap or stripe was left, no hood ornament, no decoration or fancifulness, down to skeleton practically, and then some. Some bones, even, left off. Esker took off the front grille and replaced it with window screening, and around the headlights where there should have been a rim of chrome and over the top where there once was a tiny awning of it, now there was nothing, only the glass lamp, stark and bald as a lashless, lidless eye.

Well but to be fair to Esker, the car wasn't exactly beautiful in its first, beginning best. For some reason, Nash made its cars that particular year all turned-down-looking . . . and it a year of fins and tails too. Every line of the car was rounded, its main over-all direction front to back and top to bottom, its main course in life, it seemed, downward. Everywhere there was a tiny swoop made upward, something else went back to the street again, all rounded over and nose-dive beat-down streetward again, head and tail tucked, back rounded up, like something too ashamed to raise up and face the world or lift its eyes and take it head-on.

That was the outside. The inside, because you rode closer to it, was even worse. Esker had taken out the radio and had removed the chrome-decorated door to the glove compartment. What was left of the upholstery was gray and scratchy but had that been intact, gray and scratchy would have been a better accommodation to your back and behind than what was there, with rubber foam leaking out and places for your butt to roll into, to make your back feel permanently twisted out of line, and bumps and lumps and gouges to make you shift your weight constantly trying to get comfortable. The paint on the steering wheel was worn off except at the bottom and there was none at all on the gear-shift knob. Esker had broken off what was left of the horn rim, to salvage the chrome, leaving only two small jagged points which you had to search for to find and had to know just exactly how to operate in order not to cut your finger when you needed to honk it.

Nothing worked right on the inside except that horn when you knew how and the heater sometimes and the speedometer, though it made noises like chains dragging and seemed off, Wymer said, on the slow side. But as Esker said, what counted was it ran and it could get them where they needed to go in case of emergency, and it did. It did go. *Run*, however, was a flat exaggeration.

Wymer brought it to the trailer. He was supposed to teach Lucille or Granny or both to drive. Granny refused, but, surprisingly, Lucille was a willing and competent pupil . . . as long as Granny stayed out of her way. With any kind of better car, Wymer said, she'd have been a fine driver. Her only trouble was carrying through what she started: she'd pull out on a street and as soon as she got there begin to doubt the wisdom of it and put on brakes and look wildly around to see what or who was coming . . . with Wymer yelling all the time *Go on, go on, you got it go on!* his hands over his ears to muffle the crash.

But Lucille did learn the basics and, in a pinch, she could drive. Only, once Wymer was gone, she brought the car keys inside and hung them on a hook Frank had put up by the front door and never lifted them off again. There was a grocery store within walking distance, and a small shopping center besides. Plus as soon as Granny moved in, all the other Peaveys started coming out to the trailer all the time making sure they had everything they needed, asking did anybody need a ride into town for anything or anything brought out the next time they came, so they really had no need for a car, and once Emma got old enough to have a say-so, the thing was less attended to than ever.

Only Esker bothered to notice it anymore. Every time he

came out, he took the keys down and cranked it, fooled with
the engine, kept the points and plugs up, and the battery.
Emma learned to drive in it, on gravel roads that wound in
and around the trailer camp, but got her license in Francine
Peavey's car instead, arguing that the Nash had no inspection sticker and besides had a stick shift which she had not
learned to master. So it sat there, rusting, on the far side of
the trailer. Just sat there, as much a fixture as the clothesline
and television antenna.

*Had to. If not the car, then something else. Anything.
They would have found it. But something.*

Granny sat at the breakfast table and let the plate of
scrambled eggs, grits, bacon and biscuits be set before her.
She said nothing, not a word, and did not cough or fart like
usual, but only waited for butter, jelly and her cup of coffee
to come, then began to eat. She had still not looked at
Emma or Lucille.

The other two chairs scraped and they sat.

Ate.

Waited.

For? Her. Always. They were always playing her game,
waiting for her response. She found a way to disapprove of
everything somewhere along the line and they waited each
time for her flat unswerving *no*. No way not to, for either of
them. She had them. They ate.

Finally Emma cleared her throat.

"Anybody want to walk down 84 to the tree lot with me?"

Not thinking anybody did; knowing in fact nobody
wanted to; just starting the ball to roll, making talk, a way
to break the silence.

Coming to a boil. Had to.

"I don't believe so, Emma." Lucille's voice was trembling.
What was the old woman up to? "You go on after breakfast

if you don't want to wait for Zhena. I'll clean up the kitchen."

Granny's fork clattered against her plate where she dropped it. She spoke without looking up.

"No use in it. No tree this year. No."

There was no reason to argue that; she was just stirring up dust. They could have just gone on about their business and ignored her and after breakfast Emma, as if Granny had never said a thing about a tree, could have walked out the door and down 84 and gotten one and what could she have done . . . nothing. But no, they couldn't stand it, the thing was going to happen, the wire was pulled too tight by time and circumstance and there was no way in the world Emma could keep from doing exactly what Granny wanted her to do: spit back.

She didn't get far.

"What right . . ."

Granny butted in and raised her voice, nodding toward Emma without looking up from her plate.

"Was one thing when she believed in Santa Claus, that was one thing, no use now to bring a tree inside, hang trash on it. Go downtown if you want to see trees. They're there. On every corner. No use in it here, not going to."

She went back to her eggs and grits.

That was how she did it: by reaching past their logical responses down into where they lived, gut tender. She squeezed them where they could not stand it.

Plus never stayed the same on any issue but went where it suited her to, here this time, there the next, perverse, adamant about staying perverse, keeping her power intact, by making them wonder which way she might go next.

Keep it flying. Got to keep feeding the shit into the fan and watch it fly. Watch them dodge and duck, see how they scramble, like roaches when the overhead light's turned on. Got to keep it shaking. On with the keeping on. Make it move, not sit still too long.

She scooped up a mound of grits, piled eggs on top, then peach preserves and spooned it into her mouth.

Sit still long enough and you don't get up. Got to keep the shaking alive.

Lucille watched her. She knew Granny so well and what she was up to. Granny didn't care one way or the other about a Christmas tree, she was just up to no good, gouging Emma where she hurt worst, especially today when she'd gotten Lolly's card. Which Granny couldn't have known about. But probably sensed something . . . that Emma was already on the edge of panic, before Granny ever said a word. The problem was, Emma did care. That was what Granny had over her: that Emma cared about having a tree, cared about getting the card, cared enough to jump in tooth and nail to get her way, while Granny floated free and blissful from issue to issue, gliding above the surface of anger or conviction, thereby keeping the upper hand . . . prodding Emma's rampant Peaviness, not because she cared. Only to get her day started. For fun.

Lucille took a deep breath and, going inside her mind, in effect left the spat for a time.

"Dear LOLLY . . ."

She had written and rewritten it.

"I am sorry to tell you your father is dead. Frank Lasswell was killed in an accident on the job up where he is (*was*, I should say) and is buried there already, in Oklahoma somewhere, where Emma tells me it is cold in winters and the wind never stops. I don't know if it is close to where you live, but the name of the town where he is is Stanton.

Stanton, Oklahoma. In case you ever want to go visit his grave.

"There was nothing left over. He left nothing except naturally the insurance money which he paid for as you know all his life and believed in so, which I should receive a check for any day now. It will be a generous amount I am sure. And you deserve a part of it if you will come and get it. If you want to, then do.

"Emma is fine. She reads a lot. (Unlike her mother and grandmother!) I hope you are well, Lolly, and get this. Love, Your Mother Lucille Lasswell."

It didn't sound right. Why had she put in Frank's whole name, as if he were a stranger? And wasn't "I hope you get this" altogether ridiculous? If she got it, it wouldn't mean anything and if she didn't . . . well, it was gone now, no way to get it back or change it, it was on its way and whatever happened next simply would. Maybe Lolly would never get it. Maybe she'd never come back but would die like Frank, not knowing. Maybe . . . oh Lord who could tell, it was all such a risk, such danger, and she wished this minute she had never sent it. If Lolly came back and Emma and Granny found out she'd asked her to, oh Lord . . .

" . . . *bastard!*"

Lucille dropped her fork and looked up.

Obviously, Granny had said it, but she was still eating. She had crumbled up some bacon and put it inside a buttered and jellied biscuit and was gumming it up with zest. Gleeful. Waiting for Emma's response.

It was a word they never used; otherwise Granny's mouth knew no boundaries of politeness or taste and neither did Emma's, they both said any words at any time and cursed with ease and regularity, particularly during a fight. But the game did have certain unspoken rules and one was that Emma was not called that name ever. She lived there. It was going beyond all bounds to bring up such a bone-deep unalterable fact.

Granny swallowed her bite and grinned.

Emma held on. She didn't flinch noticeably, and yet the word did stop her, it did, it kept her from answering immediately. She pushed away her plate, still full of food. . . .

Knowing what Granny wanted, unable not to provide it: nowhere to go. She would give the old woman what she required in spite of herself.

Lucille was puzzled. The argument had changed. What about the Christmas tree?

Emma spoke.

" . . . a piece of junk and you know it, you just won't admit it to me, to anybody else it'd be different, it only shows what they think of us, giving us such a miserable excuse of a thing while they go around shining their tails in a new one and wouldn't be caught dead in ours. Just let one other Peavey stick a nose inside and . . ."

The car? Had they gotten on to the *car?*

It sat outside, rusted and pitiful. Always had to.

Once Emma re-entered the argument, after that momentary silence, Granny had started to speak too. Now they talked at once, their speeches going on and on without pause or hesitation, drawing little or no fire from one another, each self-perpetuating. Once started, each one went on and on, on the energy of its own natural rhythms and nonstop flow . . . like turkeys with their heads up, they gobbled on and on, Peaveys, never listening, needing no motivation or give and take. Only a word now and then to take off on.

" . . . have you know my *son* gave us that car and you Miss Priss ought to get down on your knees and thank your lucky stars for it and not only the car either . . ."

Lucille's mouth flopped open. *Esker?* Granny had never had a kind word for Esker or his so-called gift, ever.

" . . . no place I want to get to too far or . . ."

" . . . that this family even saw fit to do for you like it has
when we never had to but could have sent you back to your
mother wherever she was or your father, that snake-eyed
Blue, we could have found him if we'd wanted to too, Miss
Miss Blue . . ."

" . . . nothing I have to do bad enough that I have to
stoop to ride in such a . . ."

" . . . but no. We do what's right and take you in. Give
you a roof over your head, three meals a day, a bed to sleep
in, even a car. And what do you do? Miss *Miss? Walk.* Refuse to ride. Too good, are you? Baloney SHIT, Miss high
and mighty chink-lover."

"Wait!" Lucille said, but it got choked out halfway up
and didn't come out strong enough. That about the choice
of taking Emma in or not wasn't true, this was her home.
Emma need show no gratitude, she need not feel rescued, it
was hers. But Granny and Emma brooked no interference,
and gave no notice of Lucille's attempt to enter in but only
went on, leaving Lucille helpless, with one finger in the air
and her breath drawn in, preparing to inject an opinion.

" . . . dare jump on Alice Chow! You ought to see *her*
car . . ."

How did they get on cars?

The fact was, they were already off cars. That topic having worn out its usefulness, Granny had shifted the argument some, with the mention of Alice Chow. They would go
on to that for a while, until either Emma did what Granny
wanted, exploded, or did not. In the second case, Granny
would have to think of something else, but she didn't think
she'd have to, not now, the girl seemed close . . . close. . . .

Lucille did not understand how it went, that there was no
reasoning to this kind of squabble, that you could not figure
it or see from how it went what the pattern or final consequence might be. Nothing counted and everything went.

The spat would go as it would and you could not read it. Lucille kept trying, and that was why nobody wanted to fight with her, because it was boring: Lucille tried to argue a thing out until it made sense, and that wasn't the point, not at all.

But to trace it back: Emma had said she would not even have to be driven because there was a Christmas tree lot less than a quarter mile south on 84, where she had gotten one last year. This was after they had argued whether or not even to get a tree for a while, so that both were warmed up to it, and Emma did not say "car" heedlessly, but knowing full well which car she meant and how each of them felt about it. " . . . don't need to take that stupid car either," she had said and that did it. Granny was bored with Christmas trees anyway and ready to move on, which Emma knew too, they both toyed with one another's feelings in this way, and soon they were off on the car, which then led Granny to say how ungrateful Emma was, especially since she wasn't even an honest member of the family and not even an orphan either but a pure and simple bastard.

Had to.

From that point on Emma not only was losing but had lost: the game was all but done. Getting the card that morning was almost enough to assure it anyway. Granny, if she didn't know exactly why, like a horse sensing a rider's fear, took advantage of something new in the air, a sense of panic about the girl, and leapt on it. Went for her throat.

It turned on the Nash, yet never did, had nothing to do with it or any car or any Christmas tree either. But they didn't like abstractions and never described their feelings; they focused on things. This time the car. Which they burned apart with their blow-torch rage so that it was never the same in either of their minds again. The rage was handy to both of them; they could call it up at will and did.

Poor Nash . . . sitting outside unloved, unused and neglected. Nothing it could do. Or had done. No way to escape it, the argument would have its fill. And to soothe its hunger would eat up whatever came in its way; Lucille did not have a prayer of interrupting it or making it go away with her pacifying phrases, it would go as it would. By the time Emma said "heap of trash" the spat had gone far enough that it was ready to explode. Anything would have sufficed, the car, a chair, the shirt Emma wore, anything. Because the time had come and that was all that counted. That the time was ripe: one of them would either throw something or hit the other or stomp off in a storm; the rhythms were right; the flow required a culmination. It had to go one way or another.

One way only. Set, from the beginning. Unfair from the first, from the time the mail arrived.

Why couldn't she forget? One time? Let it go, not send a card or money or Love, Lolly . . . ?

" . . . at least her engine turns over!" Her face was red, her James Blue eyes blazing. Lucille put a hand on her shoulder; Emma shrugged it off.

Meantime Granny had turned quiet . . . in retreat, as content as a fat purring cat, victory slinking toward her now, easy and sly. The girl would do it to herself now. Granny let her . . . sipping coffee in great noisome slurps.

"I wouldn't take a *dog* for a ride in that Nash. . . ."

No way to go back from it now; too late. Her head felt raked and burning, as if something had been scraped across it, leaving it ragged and cut through in lines.

She picked up her coffee cup and threw it, not at Granny but across the room. Nothing was in it and it didn't break. Only made a loud, dull thump against the kitchen floor.

She left.

Went out the door, headfirst and furious, slamming the door behind her good and hard.

Where . . . ?

Just go. Just go. Don't stop until it's used up. *Go*.

Granny looked up at Lucille, daring her to speak. Her eyes were beaded and drifty, way back in her head, under that overhanging wide Peavey forehead, her face was shriveled to a prune, her head like a shrunken totem. There she sat, exactly where she was, in the precise here-and-now, not off mourning some lost cause . . . some dead husband or some footloose and trashy low-life mother . . . but here, where she sat, reaching across the table to gather Emma's plate to her. Eat the girl's cold eggs and grits.

Lucille rarely defied her mother, but this time she did it without hesitation or consideration of consequence. She would not see it happen again without doing what she could to avoid it.

"You mean, spiteful old woman. You will not drive her away or take away her rightful home."

Lucille scraped back her chair and went to the front door. She held her hands around her eyes to shield them from the light. Emma had just got to the end of the gravel drive and was turning right down 84 in the direction of Eunola, going like always, headfirst, as if a string were tied to her forehead, pulling at her. Lucille took a breath.

"Em-MAH!"

It came out as loud as she hoped for. Emma stopped, turned. . . .

Lucille? Standing at the door screaming?

"Em-MAH!"

Lucille yelled it again, and then again and once again, standing there while people came out their doors all over the trailer camp to see what in the world was happening in the Lasswell trailer to cause Lucille Lasswell who never said anything to anybody to stand in her front door with her face toward the highway screaming.

"Em-Mah. Em-MAH? Em-MAH." Over and over, until the girl was out of sight, when Lucille came back in, hoping she'd just go get a Christmas tree then come home again. Granny had left the table. She was back in bed . . . letting her food digest she would say. Lucille began stacking plates.

Go. Use it up, play it out, to its end.

Where . . . ?

Don't ask or figure or measure, just go. On with it. Have to. Instead of sinking. Having to play it out, not let it go to work inside. Must not turn in, must not think too long or sit too still, have to use up Love Lolly and Miss Emma Blue . . . pushing out. Until the wheel has wound down and Nash is forgotten and the girl in blue coat stepping from horse and carriage at least is put aside. If not forgotten at least playing second fiddle to other demands. For that, you have to move on . . . until the hurt uncoils, that circle of hurt taking up her whole chest, making her feel love and hate at once, making her feel she could eat up the whole world in one gulp and never notice, making her . . . she ran, walked, ran, put her hands to her face, let them go, ran until her side hurt then walked again, when she could, ran once more; it was still there; she was still the knife thrower's target. *Zap*, to the heart. And a blistered finger besides.

Use it up, it up, on with the keeping.

She passed the Christmas-tree lot.

Was Lucille still screaming? Emma thought she could hear her: Em-MAH! She shook her head. Against somebody else calling her, drawing her in, someone not the one, not the Mama, not ever.

She ran.

Run!

Every time Mattie Sue got up it was a trial: had to push hard against the glass-top table with one hand and one

elbow, in the other hand hold whatever light or ornament
she was hooking to the tree. Not easy. The last Christmas for
her, that was certain. Used to be she hung them so carefully,
making colors come out even and lights just so. Not now.
Getting them on at all was difficult enough.

She pushed at the last light until it did not fall and
plugged the string into an extension cord in her lap, puffing
lightly from the exertion. Because she sat as she hung them,
all the yellow lights were on the left and the top of the tree
was practically dark and most of the lights—all the reds and
greens—were at the bottom.

She pulled out the plug but left the lights as they were
and pulled a box across the table toward her.

She had not missed a year getting one; every year a small
black boy came to bring her a tree. Used to be, a big one,
but somewhere along the way she had told Carroll it was
too difficult to reach up and down, just to send one she
could put in the sun porch on the sideboard there. Only, she
had insisted, don't forget. I do want a Christmas tree.

Not for celebration particularly or tribute, not to bring
any sort of holiday spirit to fruition or to worship the birth
of anything, only to fill her needs and keep her schedule set.
Such a fragile thing: she had to keep to it exactly. As long as
you did, and organized time to suit you, you could act like it
was yours, in your care. You could keep it in a box and
change its straw from time to time like a pet. Days in a
square. The week in a line. The year a long rectangle. It
didn't get away from you that way . . . if you watched
which day was which and observed old customs, held to tra-
dition, remembered the significance of particular days. Like
Christmas.

The box in her lap, she lifted the top flap and pulled out
the protective tissue. Like eggs in a carton, they were perfectly placed, ornaments packed in newspaper. Most she
had had forever; others Carroll had dug out of Lady's things

when he refurbished the house. They were old too, some of them having belonged to Lady herself as a girl: like this angel with spun gold hair; she looked like Lady herself. Mattie Sue laid her aside. The angel went at the very top of the tree.

She drew out an old Santa Claus made of glass thin enough to shatter in your hand. Its red suit had flaked off some, and its face was all gone. Only the indentations of eyes, nose, mouth, no color. Like her own face. Pale as skimmilk.

She stood to hook him on the tree. She used only those ornaments with hooks already attached; her hands were too stiff to slip in the wires. Carroll would come tonight; he could hang the rest. She placed the Santa halfway up the tree and sat down.

Stand up, Mattie Sue, stand up, don't give in, not sitting down with a box of perishables in your lap, not like that.

In a minute. She would stand in a minute. Not yet. She could do it, only not quite now.

December was particularly reliable: every year the same thing happened, every year a black boy came, sent by Carroll to set the tree up for her, every year he was scared and anxious to get out of her house, every year a black boy told her with his nervous eyes how old she was and how scary she looked. It seemed like the same boy every year; they always looked alike. Small and dark and bright; antsy; uninterested in Mattie Sue Cunningham.

She held up a snowman. Grainy white sprinkles made his body rough. He wore a black top hat and held a broom. She reached and hung him without getting up.

What you did was what counted, that was why routines mattered so. There had to be containment and ordering, no unmarked sense of loose flow. Had to be schedules to go by: TV programs, holidays, day clothes, night clothes, lunch at noon. It did not matter in what spirit you celebrated a holiday, it only mattered that you *did*, that was what counted and kept a person strong, not how or why a thing was done or in what frame of mind, simply that it was, simply that. Actions, one by one; they might be toted up with the exactness of numbers. The rest . . . reasons, satisfaction . . . was tied up in that, tied *to* it. You had to pay the most attention to what you did.

Otherwise . . .

Otherwise forget it, you lost.

She sat down again. Oh but it did tire her. This was her last time around she was certain; she still had not found anyone or anything to oust the orphanage from her legacy, and she had believed so strongly that she would and now . . . nothing satisfied. Nothing came. To enable her to die in peace, knowing it had been fairly rounded out.

The house was quiet. And dark, even in daytime, except for her small space. The big calico cat had provided some company, dashing about under the house, coming to her back steps for food. But the calico was dead, ten days after giving birth to what the vet said was her only offspring, one black female kitten. Mattie Sue had convinced Carroll to take her home. A mistake, probably. Should have kept it; would have at least made noise . . . hollered when she was hungry or in heat and Carroll was already talking about having her spayed. Oh well.

The angel lay on a yellowed sports page. She wore a silver dress; her hair was pure gold, long and curled under at the end; there was a silver halo around her brow; her hands were together in prayer; her eyes closed.

Mattie Sue smoothed down the angel's hair. Her own hands were gnarled and tough, frozen in certain cramped positions, her fingers thick, blunt on the end, but her fingernails were clean and shaped: what she could keep up with, she did. Bathing however was impossible; she only washed off with a rag now and was aware of a constant, faintly soured smell. Her clothes weren't quite clean either. It wasn't going to happen, it wasn't, she could see a small light at the end of her life, the possibility of nothingness, of no equity, of simply dying blank, like that, no footsteps to take up where hers left off, no nothing behind to round out her life in a satisfying way: a fat blank zero. Might it be? She had not believed it; she had thought the thing had to come to some justification, some rounding-out full circle, the basket of flowers eventually passed on if you waited long enough and concentrated and believed.

Would it? Or not. Maybe just this. This pure dumb silence.

She looked at her hand: her thumb was over the angel's face. It was stone dead-white with spots of brown and veins pushed up like rope under a wet cloth. Never? Yes. Just end. Zip, like that. No flowers, no grace, an open circuit, the last link dangling, no chain.

She moved her thumb. The angel smiled, as if confident her prayers would be answered.

Poised on the outside edge of concentric, graduating circles, Carroll could see the center, but could not get to it. He was on the outside edge and could not move closer in; he was going round and round; any minute he would be flung from the safety of the circle into the air. Or would go the other way. Into the center. Where he wanted to be but could not stay long. Only for an instant.

Then . . . back to the edge again, where the danger was flying off into nothingness again. Rootless, groundless, adrift. No consolation.

His eyes were closed. When he did get there, no one would see; he would take it for himself. He kept his eyes shut and soared at the heart of himself but did not share, ever. Keeping it for himself. Getting what he needed to go on, unable to open up and be totally with whoever he happened to be with, at that moment in the here-and-now. Unable to grant himself that. Unable to admit there were two of them moving together into the same center of the same wheel of graduating circles. Two. One. You and I. Us . . . for an instant if no longer. No. He could not. He kept his eyes closed.

She was not soft, but tall and thin and lean. Athletic. And not young but he didn't care. She was married. She came to him for, in her words, proof positive there was something else besides. Something more. Some dream to go on.

He lifted up off her for a time, to give her a breathing spell, and opened his eyes a little, only to slits. Hers were closed too. She had long, carved-like lids and deep-sunk eyes. Behind the lids she was traveling too no doubt. Off in her own patterns, struggling. In her own fantasy. Possibly involving her husband. In her mind right now perhaps he was there, the one she was escaping, doing things to her, or watching . . . Lord, but weren't people perverse.

That irony cut into his concentration and for a moment he lost it . . . direction, path, reason, the circles . . . and was loose again, drifting.

He closed his eyes and lay back down full weight on top of her and changed his rhythm slightly. To wake himself back up again to the right track. To get back into the circles again.

He had been asleep when she came. The maid had knocked and said testily that someone was there. Carroll had not wakened however until the woman actually came in and shook him. Even Maude helped, by meowing in his ear . . . Maude, his lean black, gold-eyed cat. Who slept with him every night, curled up perfectly round at the foot of his bed.

He slept deep down inside himself, private and tight. Dead weight. Heavy as stone. Yet in his dreams he often flew. Like this morning. When he finally came to, he was in

the sky, hovering, at the peak. That topmost moment, when
you know the next thing to happen will be the crash. There.
He always woke up there.

Women complained. He curled into himself when he
slept, they said, and never shared bed space but seemed to
fight off companionship instead, his hands knotted in tight
fists. He couldn't help it: sleep for him was density and ten-
sion. Only inside, he was flying. To waken was to fear for his
life. To stop before he crashed.

He had it again. He pushed ahead toward it, his eyes shut
tight, fixed on the centermost circle, the tiniest, brightest
one.

He felt Maude at his feet, licking. He kicked her off. She
landed uncomplaining on some covers and instantly curled
back up into her moon shape there. Maude was born under
Mattie Sue's house and suckled in a next-door field; she knew
how to scrap for her survival. Nothing fazed Maude much.

The angel was easiest to place; it had no hook, you simply
set it on the tree's topmost spike. Holding the angel firmly at
the neck, Mattie Sue leaned forward to heave herself up,
knowing it was not right to hang her yet, the angel went on
top and should be held off for last as the crowning, reward-
ing final touch. But she couldn't wait. It seemed important
to see her now. It might help her do the rest.

The angel was in her right hand. With that elbow and her
left palm, she started to push against the glass of the table
then, in position, hesitated. . . .

She turned her head. Did someone knock? Couldn't have
been, who would have. Carroll was coming but later and
anyway he would not knock. Must have been a branch. And
if someone was at the door well, let them, only some sales-
man, some stranger.

She pushed hard with her left hand and, because she had

turned to listen behind her, missed the table altogether and pushed not against the table top but past it. Her weight moved down against nothing, against the air itself, for an instant she was in the air, pushing her weight into nothing.

Until finally her hand came to rest, not on the table but against the seat of a wrought-iron chair. Her feet slid behind her, her right arm went over and across herself to help catch her weight, the knocking came again and yes, someone was at the front door, at the same time that Mattie Sue fell, not to the floor but halfway down with both hands on the seat of the chair.

The angel went flying. Across the doorjamb, into the kitchen. It hit the floor there and broke. Shattered into a thousand shiny splinters, sparkling on the linoleum.

She had not fallen far but she could not get up. Her legs were behind her at a slant, she was in a crazy V, with her feet stretched back and both hands on the chair seat. She could not move; if she did she would collapse altogether. She inched her toes up a bit, but not enough. She was caught. Like meat on a hook. She hung her head; her back complained. Lord. To go this way. To give up and fall on this stupid uncomfortable chair with the tree half-ass and the angel in pieces.

"Shit," she mumbled to herself, and when the knock came again, said not half loud enough to be heard, "Please. Come in. It's not locked." Something was going. In her chest. Some tight high place was loosening, weakening, falling down. "Please."

The front door opened.

"Knock-knock?" somebody said.

Thank God. Was it Carroll?

When she lifted her head toward the door it put her neck in such a strain she could not speak loud enough to be heard.

"Carroll . . . quick."

It came out raspy, barely more than a whisper, but whoever it was did respond. Footsteps came toward the sun
porch, fast and direct. Mattie Sue looked up to see who it
was, her head so heavy she could just manage to lift it.

A girl.

The one with the blue eyes in the window.

"Help me."

The girl with the frizzed-out hair and the cast of intensity
in her eyes.

And wouldn't you know, too late.

He stopped. Did not come free from her but only stopped.
Lay still. He felt her body tense up, asking why, then relax
into it. She would take the hesitation for herself, use it for
her own purposes and then enjoy it. Smart girl.

Something . . .

His whole body felt tense, disconcerted.

The woman was sliding beneath him. Not moving much
but enough. Finding circles herself now. Doing herself herself. Riding him only, using him as he used her.

He buried his face in her neck. Her hair was red and
coarse and smelled faintly metallic. He breathed her in, trying to get to her. To get her to. To get past himself and
closer to her.

He still had not moved, only pushed down in a certain
way, from his lower back, to give her the counterpressure
she needed. He held it, for her. The least he could do. Let
her move on past him whether he found his own center or
not.

Because of her agility, she could move in certain ways
that he found delightful. Could tighten certain muscles

wonderfully. His hands were on her shoulders. He held her hard.

Emma went directly to the old woman, put both arms around her middle and lifted her out of her terrible position. There was a gentle whooshing sound, as if air went out. Emma threaded an arm under hers to help her to a chair, held it stiff to support the old and obviously tired back. But the old woman collapsed then and there. Like a rag doll, she crumpled very delicately in Emma's arms and they went to the floor together, Emma with her all the way, her legs cradling the fall.

She stopped. Slid back and forth with a kind of diagonal twist added, then stopped again. Carroll held on, gave her her thrust to move against. Again back and forth, again a hesitation, only not quite as long, movement again, hesitation now only the briefest breath taken. Her rhythms. She had it. Soon. The back and forth came now without pause, she was close now, close, his head was tight against her neck, he could feel her making her way but she was not quite there yet, she was taking her time, making sure, she would not lose it now, she would not. She slowed up a bit. Women did not like the hard fast insistent beat he sometimes preferred, but took their own sweet time, easy and even, a little, a little lax. Sometimes when he was barely hard, it seemed they liked it best. He lay still. She was going in circles now. He could feel that hard bone there, gritting against him going around. He buried himself deeper.

Too late, too late, she was there but too late.
She tried to say it. Tried to say "Shit" to vent her anger a

bit but it did not come out, she didn't think, she wasn't sure. Thirty years' waiting and finally it does come and too late. The girl held her . . . close, like she knew, with that look in her eyes. She cradled her head in her strong young arms and stroked her face.

"Shh," she said. "Shh . . ."

As if she knew.

Her eyes were pure and fixed, dead-set aimed on what they meant to get to.

It was leaking now, coming out of her, going not fast but steady. She felt something warm slide down her face inside that crease there beside her nose. It reached her mouth; she tasted its salt. A tear. She had never cried, not once during all those disappointments. Not until now. When she knew it was there and too late.

Her eyes rolled up into her head and she saw only darkness. They came back down, opened, took a second or two to focus, found the girl again. The light kept dimming. A narrowing. Deep behind her eyes, to the back of her head . . . like a door closing. It shut out the light completely, then opened again to let some back in, but never as much as the time before, it was going out.

Closing off.

She thought of Carroll when it got dark. When the light came back, the girl was there and she saw only her. Those two bright blue lights to fix on.

Dark: Carroll.

Light: the girl.

Dark . . . dark . . . light . . . like an easing down and a lifting up, both at once. Her body becoming pure light. Pure darkness. Not yet! *Shit.*

Emma felt a sudden dip in her certainty: how would she explain her presence and who would believe she'd never

been here before and just happened to drop by today, when
Mattie Sue Cunningham fell down and died. Who would
believe she was on her way downtown to shop and see the
Christmas lights and visit Alice? No one was who. Not a
soul. Archaeologist with notebook and chisel would never
wash.

She dredged a tear from the crease by the old woman's
mouth and wiped it on her arm. Her eyes were rolling up
then coming back down, her pupils were narrowing. Emma
rubbed her brow. It was cool and damp, and the loose old
skin curled back and forth under her fingers.

She was trying to say something. She raised her left hand.
Pressed two fingers against Emma's lips. Let it drop.

Part of her was lifting up, part going down, both ways at
once; she was helpless to change it. Up into darkness. Not
yet, not yet. No use how often she said it. No way to stop it
now. A coolness came, from the center out, like water in rip-
ples.

Dark. Dark. Light.

Her circles got bigger against him, she was there. She
knew how to hold on, did not go wild like the younger ones
but kept it smooth and flowing and it worked; it went on
longer that way. She crooned. Her mouth was near his ear.
He felt the sound of her voice come into him too and it was
soothing, he felt her there. It thrilled him every time, to feel
them—her or some other—get there. Even if he was only
quiet and observing he was thrilled. Seeing what happened
in their faces, how naked they truly were, at that moment.

This one was strong. She moved not against but with it.
Wanted it. Came for it. Took it when it came, however she
could.

Carroll moved a little, as he felt she needed it, counter to her clockwise. His new movement extended what she had even farther. Kept her going a beat longer. She crooned again.

It was getting him started again. Back in the circles. Back in the right direction.

He could see the center.

The telephone rang. Beside his bed, on the table.

He let it, but it distracted him. It stopped.

He stopped.

There was a knock at his door.

"Telephone. Says it's urgent."

He pulled out, rolled over, lifted the receiver.

"My name is Emma Blue Lasswell," she said. "You don't know me but . . ."

She had considered leaving but could not. It seemed blasphemous somehow, to share in a death and then leave it, witness it and not say so. Also, Mattie Sue looked so lonely lying there with the tree half done and the ornament shattered on the kitchen floor. Seemed an improper death. No, she would not, she would stay. Mattie Sue had reached up before she died and touched Emma's face: it seemed a charge Emma could not simply shrug off and turn away from.

Still sitting on the floor cradling her head, Emma found a red flannel cloth meant to wrap the Christmas tree trunk in and placed it across Mattie Sue's face. Easing her head to the floor, she pulled her legs out from under the dead woman and stood over her, shivered once and then did what she had to: went to the kitchen, found the telephone book, looked up Carroll Cunningham's number and dialed it. She stood with her finger under his number in the book.

"My name is Emma Blue Lasswell. You don't know me

but . . ." Oh well, this would be some adventure, explaining who she was and why she was at his dead great-aunt's house. Exploring?

Special mail trucks ran during the Christmas season. Lucille received the foreman Leonard's box later on in the afternoon that same day. A letter was taped to the top.

Lucille took it and a kitchen knife into the bathroom, locked the door and sat. With the knife she pried off the tape and opened the letter.

Dear Mrs. Lasswell,
Thank you for your kind letter. Mrs. Lasswell, there are some things I left out, like for instance his drinking glasses, which were only the plain A & P kind that jelly comes in, which I didn't think you'd so much care about having. Also his sheets and towels which weren't in such good condition. And his boots which were a fine pair, of high quality leather. They fit one of the men here perfectly, and he was in need of a good pair of boots, so we gave them to him. Anyway, they seemed like clothes too, so since you said we should keep the clothes that seemed all right. Well, you'll be glad to hear I think that that man was more than happy to have them. I hope this squares with your feelings. The rest of his clothes were passed around too, as per your instructions (except for a jacket, which I have enclosed, because it was too old to be of much use to anyone long and looked like something you might want. It seemed personal). Oh, and there is something in one of the pockets I never did take out and look at. Mrs. Lasswell, it is a hard thing to go through a man's last effects. You don't know when to stop looking and when to keep on.

I am also enclosing a check for $750 for the truck. I have

given the certificate of title to the man who wanted to buy it. This man said he appreciated your generosity but he wouldn't think of accepting anything as big as a truck free. He came down on his offer, thinking you might feel better about taking this than the bigger amount. I would like to tell you that your husband Frank Lasswell was a good worker and an honest man. He did his job by the numbers and was well respected by his co-workers as a man you could depend on. Once he saved a man's life from a gas leak none of the rest of us had smelled, and that man about to light a cigarette too. Frank Lasswell didn't talk much or let us much in on his life, but what we knew of him we liked. He never lied. I just wanted to say that. Please let me know if I can be of further service.

Yours truly,

She put the letter aside and opened the box. In it were:

Two curled and yellowed paperback Westerns
His glasses, unbroken, the same ones he'd worn when
    he left, in the same black case, stamped EUNOLA
    OPTICALS, PRECISION EYEWEAR SINCE 1932
A thick brown envelope containing printed papers
His stainless-steel shockproof water-resistant watch,
    the one he'd always worn
A single-edged razor
A high-intensity flashlight
A wallet she recognized
A small coffeepot, the drip kind
Two cups, two plates, one aluminum saucepan, three
    forks, two spoons, two knives
A pocketknife she recognized
Two wool blankets
The jacket.

Carefully, methodically, Lucille crumpled up each sheet of the newspaper he had used for packing, looking for small items she might have overlooked. But that was all, there was nothing more; only filler. Those items were all he left, the sum total of his life.

She knew which jacket it was even before she saw it: the brown leather one he'd worn constantly and had zipped only halfway up no matter how cold the weather was, to accommodate his style, which announced he was not a man easily brought down or yielding. He was never so taken by a cold wind that he had to zip a jacket to the neck to escape its sting; he was tougher than that. Although bleached out by the weather and wear and rubbed free of color altogether at the elbows, the jacket, except for being as limp and lifeless as a dishrag, was in good condition. So soft she could wad it up in her fist. There were a few things he had prided himself on having and this jacket was one of them. It gave him some pride and a feeling of superiority. It, and a good watch, a good flashlight, good tools and boots . . . these were things, he said, a man ought to have.

Slowly she slipped her hand into the right-hand pocket, then quickly drew it out. There was a paper in there, folded neatly, snug down in the point of the slippery triangle. She felt it again . . . a good grade of paper from the feel of it, fine stationery. She rubbed it for a while, as if trying to read it by touch. Why was she so afraid? Finally, gradually, she eased it out and held it before her. The folds were worn down to a fuzzy gray. It had been in there that way for a long time. She unfolded it once, but the paper was still tucked down inside itself. Was this the message? Something for her? No matter if he did not intend it; still, it might be something she could take from and use to live on, even if he had not meant for it to serve such a purpose. Her heart moved close to the surface of her skin. Trembling slightly, she lifted the top half of the page up, then opened the bot-

tom half. There was printing near her thumb, a letterhead
. . . she had it upside down . . . turned it over. . . .

It was a letter from his insurance company, dated the
month after he left Eunola, assuring Frank his payments
from both Eunola and Oklahoma were valid, since the company was covered in every state in America. And that was
all. Thanking him for his inquiry, congratulating him on his
"faithfulness and attention to that which will in the long
run benefit not only you but the lives of your loved ones as
well, your wife Lucille and your daughter Lolly, and make it
possible for you—and them—to maintain in your life a particular system of values and rhythm, that does not ebb and
flow with difficulties and setbacks but only continues, as you
choose for it to, even after you are gone. And this, we feel, is
the truest measure of a man's worth: that he look to the welfare of his survivors, and make certain they are cared for, in
both senses of the word. We congratulate you on your diligence, Mr. Lasswell. It is clients like yourself who make the
life insurance business work to its maximum effectiveness.
Yours sincerely . . ."

Nothing for her. No wonder he kept it. The letter affirmed
his very life.

She felt in the other pocket. Nothing. Some loose tobacco
culls, nothing more.

She slipped the watch on her wrist, set it, wound it,
clamped the band shut. It was stainless steel, with a flat
kind of chain band. When she moved her arm, the watch
slipped loosely across her thin wrist, rubbing the round
globelike bone there, and came to hang finally down over
the lower part of her palm, encircling her thumb joint and
the wide crisscross of veins on the back of her hand.

She put her arms into the jacket. As if waiting, the taffeta
lining embraced her softly, came into her shape and was, that
quickly, hers. She zipped it up.

She held the pocketknife tight in one hand . . . the jacket

cuff hiding the watch and her knuckles . . . trying to imagine in hers was the warmth of his hand, which had worn it almost totally clear of paint. She put the knife in the lefthand pocket.

The dishes were cheap, a dime-store kind with a gold stripe around the rim and a bunch of flowers tied with ribbon in the center. The pots were of the thinnest, easiest to scorch aluminum, and the coffeepot was black inside and out from years of use. Cheap stuff, she put them aside, along with the silverware to be set on a pantry shelf, back where they would neither be in anybody's way nor attract any notice.

In the brown envelope were his valuables, the final affirmative nod, the testimonial his life most required: his insurance papers and will.

"I, Frank Lasswell, being of sound mind and body, do hereby . . ."

Nothing there. Only a form somebody had typed out and had him sign, everything left to his wife Lucille Peavey Lasswell, his body not to be shipped home but buried in the cemetery closest to his death, in a plain cheap casket, sparing as much expense as possible . . . everything saved for afterward, when he was gone and they were left to receive his last crumbs. All for how he was; nothing for his presence. Like Lolly, he had been seduced by style: the way of his life, which cut everyone else out of it, even the girl herself, even Lolly. Something in the back of Lucille's mind twitched. A raw nerve, set to jangling. How little he understood. And how much he spared himself by sealing himself up this way. She, who had spent so few days out and about in the world, had more knowledge of its ways and reasons.

She reached for his wallet . . . hoping. . . .

She remembered it well. It was hand-tooled and laced around the edge with a leather thong; he had had it for years; had bought it at a Western shop. But though it once had bulged with cards and pictures, and receipts and claim checks—whatever he carried, she didn't know what-all—now it was thin, almost flat. She opened it and no wonder. It was a dead man's wallet, telling no tales. He had always carried several pictures of Lolly with him, including one newspaper clipping accompanied by a picture of her in her gold-sequined suit leaning so far back the tips of her hair grazed the ground. And there had been an old, old one, she thought, of herself, a school-day picture taken the first year of their marriage when she had been finishing her senior year in high school. Those were gone now. Empty plastic windows, scratched almost white, testified to their former place. She looked in the leather pockets for a driver's license, hoping for a picture of him, to see if he had changed, but there was none. And yet he had a truck, the foreman said, and Frank had always insisted on following laws and rules to the letter. But no, she finished her search and there was nothing. A gas credit card; a Social Security card; insurance card; several filling-station receipts for gas . . . otherwise, nothing. No messages, no farewell clues to hang on. Nothing. But what she already had. What little she always had had of him.

Lucille gathered the jacket close and let her head hang. There.

At last, something, a single bequest. Not actually handed down, but within her grasp after all. It came back to her with clarity, he could have been standing there it was so exactly him. As much as anything . . . his smell. That dark, rusty odor of leather and clay earth . . . something running in the lines etched on his face and hands . . . faint now but still there, palpable, mixed with the other, the smell of his most constant companion. Tobacco. The cigarette smoke. That endless chain she had hated so but never thought to throw up to him; how weak it was and how contrary to his hard, unfeeling ethic. Now it was all she had left. From him, this one thing, a smell. That from her husband. From her daughter, a flashing signal, that LOLLY. It wasn't much. Lucille took it in, inhaled deeply. And lifted back the jacket cuff to see what time it was, experimenting how it must have felt to be him, to wear this jacket and consult this watch and smell this way.

Rescue: there had never been the least hope of it, not from him or anybody else. The loss was terrible. She would have to manage it on her own or let the idea go . . . live out her life as it was, resign her hopes and energies and decide to stay in the trailer, no Winding Willow or Lazy Lakes Estate ever. Or change it altogether. Like Granny said: one thing or the other, not both at once.

She sat back against the toilet and stared at the white tile across from her.

Emma got home before dark with a tree over her shoulder and a sack full of presents.

She began unpacking Christmas lights and boxes and wrapping paraphernalia, holding them up one by one for Lucille to see.

"How'd you get here with all that?"

Emma grinned.

"Cab."

"All this way? Must have cost a fortune."

Emma wouldn't say.

Granny came out at some point and watched. She didn't care about Christmas trees, one way or another. It wasn't unpleasant, however, to sit and stare at the colored lights until they blurred.

She wondered which of Emma's boxes was hers and what was in it.

Emma said nothing of her day. It was too soon . . . too much had gone on in the pink house; she had to see how it sounded in her mind first, before deciding how much of it to tell.

She and Lucille laughed and talked and hung ornaments;
Granny watched. But it always took too long and became
more tedious than anything after a while, especially the
way Lucille liked to decorate, so carefully and in such
strict order: lights first, exactly so, even all over, no over-
loading on any one side before hanging one ball; big ornaments next, then less big and so on. Then she would stop,
and stand back from it every so often to make sure their
work pleased her and had a balance of color and light. It
happened every year: by the time they were ready to drape
the icicles, Emma had grown bored and wanted simply to
stand back and sling on the silver strips, letting them fall in
clumps, as they would. But Lucille said no, never mind, if
you're tired I'll do it and proceeded, lovingly, to draw one
strip at a time from the cardboard holder, to lay it over a
branch, stand back to look, then draw out another. She still
wore the leather jacket and silver watch, even though the
colored lights after a while made her hot and uncomfortable. When she finished, every bough was bent down, as
if with real ice.

Granny never left the room. When they were entirely
finished, Emma went around turning out the other lights in
the trailer and they all sat, not saying anything, just sitting
looking at the tree lights and thinking whatever came into
their minds, mostly remembering other Christmases and
trees. By that time it was past midnight: Christmas Eve.

When Granny got ready to go to bed she did it. Just up
and went without saying anything to either of them. She
had not spoken one word since the decorating began. Lucille and Emma sat awhile longer, then went to bed themselves.

Worn out from the day's exertions, Lucille fell immediately asleep. But Emma kept seeing him: Carroll Cun-

ningham; those eyes looking up at her. Asking what? Or
maybe not asking. Maybe telling. Like he knew . . .

Kneeling down next to Mattie Sue, with his gray-green
eyes fixed up on Emma, he seemed to know who she was.
With his great-aunt lying dead beside him, he looked up
and, in some way deeper than names, recognized Emma.

But she'd never met him. She went over and over the
scene in her mind and thought she would not be able to go
to sleep from puzzling over it but finally did, though the
next morning she couldn't remember when . . . if it had
been soon after she went to bed or if, like Granny, maybe
she hadn't slept a wink all night.

You never know. Girl, you just never never know.

III

THE FUNERAL

Christmas was a perfect day, mild in every respect, the sky bluer than summer, the air winter fresh and dry, the light a clear yellow that came down like water from a bucket and splashed across the landscape and gave it life. It broke your heart to look at, it was so beautiful and poignant coming when it did, between damp gray winds. Even the trees, bare and black as they were, looked proud. The wind touched down occasionally, soft and harmless as a party kiss, then left for a while . . . then whispered down again and ruffled your hair. Clouds rose up early and stayed all day, white as white, in sharp relief against the sky, like a child's version of clouds, those flower shapes kindergarteners cut from white paper and paste on a blue background to make distinct and apart, cloud as one thing and sky another. Today the child could say, *See:* the innocent version had come true. The temperature was soothing and brisk, calling for scarves and maybe light sweaters. It was cold early on but by noon the sun had warmed up the cold ground and space heaters were switched off and Christmas coats put away. New bicycles and skates were brought out to learn on and neighbors stood in their yards watching, chatting across hedges thinking what a world they had, how safe and pleasant and perfect. At twelve or so when churches let out, worshipers streamed out smiling and radiant . . . smug in fact, nearly . . . looking up into the warm sun as if they had earned it, a Christian day. Christian sky, Christmas gift.

Perfect. Perfect Sunday, made-to-order Christmas.

The grave had been dug on Saturday.

Forty-eight hours after she died she would sink into the ground to stay, her last footstep, deep and cold, marked by a marble sign, pink as her house had been.

He wanted it over with. He would only feel worse if he waited. And by doing it fast, he hoped to keep the services quiet and private, to get her discreetly buried before the whole town found out and made a point of showing up.

But news was slack on Christmas Eve and Mattie Sue's death made the front page. DAUGHTER OF EUNOLA FIRST MAYOR DIES AT HOME, the headline said. They had called Carroll to ask for a picture but he said he had none and none could be found in their files and so they ran one of the pink house instead and down under that a tintype of Sexton and a sidebar about how he had come to Eunola in 1866, been elected mayor, had the first public school and library built and so on.

Emma's name was not mentioned.

Nor were any details of the death. Only that she died at home and was ninety-four and that Carroll and Preston were her only living survivors.

And so everybody in town knew; Carroll could not get her buried fast enough to avoid it. People called and called to offer condolences and the funeral home in that one day was flooded with flowers. Food came to the Cunningham house by the church-carload. Smoked turkey, hams, pies, cakes, fruit, rolls, vegetable casseroles in Pyrex dishes with owners' names taped on the bottom. Who they thought was going to eat all that and how they got organized so fast was a mystery to Carroll.

Still, having services on Christmas Day was a blessing. Most people did their duty by sending something out instead of coming.

Her lawyer was there and her doctor, a friend or two of Carroll's, a former partner on a land deal, a woman who once nursed Mattie Sue through an illness, a few curious strangers, some cottonmen from the old time, out of respect to Preston, a deacon representing the Presbyterian Church . . . Lady's church, which no Cunningham had attended in years . . . some others, not too many, at least not a circus.

If nobody comes it will suit me fine, Carroll thought. If it's only the three of us it will be enough.

Preston didn't seem to connect with what was going on. Carroll had worried he might start to mourn Lady's death again; after all he had not been to a funeral since hers, and Lady's body had rested at the same funeral home. But if Preston made that connection he didn't let on. Only sat quietly between Judge and Carroll, quiet and respectful, nodding when anyone came to shake his hand and offer sympathy. No one ever knew what was happening behind his calm glassy gaze.

But at least the whole town didn't feel called on to show up. At least it wasn't a circus.

Emma came.

When Rose-Laura Peavey Lusk drove out to the trailer to bring Granny her Christmas gift, Emma hitched a ride back into town with her and asked to be dropped off at the cemetery. She got there at one and since the graveside service wasn't scheduled until two, had time to sit and watch what preparations were left to be made.

Used to be a really lush cemetery, with thick heavy trees hanging over the graves and the grass kept up careful as a golf course. Stones always used to be clean and tended to, and flowers brought regularly. Now it seemed on the shabby side. Not run-down exactly, like downtown, but tatty: like a worn dress, dirty at the seams, frayed at the edges. An unseasonable ice storm one year had killed off a good number of the trees and many of the others hadn't seemed to have recuperated and, like the downtown library, the place simply was not valued as much as it once had been. Maybe because it was the oldest cemetery and the descendants of these dead were dying off themselves. Or gone. Hard to say. But cemeteries captured Emma's interest, and this one, being the oldest and the closest in, she had visited now and then over the years and had watched deteriorate as the town's interest moved away from it.

She sat on the marble pedestal at the head of Sexton Cunningham's grave. It was colder here than in the sun; when the breeze blew it had a chill to it that out of the trees you didn't feel.

She pulled her jacket a little tighter and once again ran her hand down it. Frank's jacket: Lucille had given it to her. "I know you like old things," she had said. And she was right: Emma loved it. It looked like something valued and precious, handed down. She dug her hands into the pockets.

A tent had been set up next to the open grave. Underneath it, metal folding chairs were set out in rows. Between the chairs and the grave was the preacher's lectern and between him and the grave was a semicircle of flowers on stands. The lectern was at the center of the semicircle, the main focal point. Men in suits opened up the folding chairs and put them in place. The chairs made a cracking sound. Emma looked toward the cemetery gates for the hearse.

Emma had been sitting waiting on the front steps when he drove up, with her chin on her hands. His big car had bounded fast up into the curving pea-gravel drive and had stopped just there at her feet. He got out in a hurry; she stood; he rushed up to her. They waited a minute together, then went in.

"I couldn't move her. She's on the floor."

He didn't speak.

She followed him in, feeling somehow to blame. Not that she was. But she'd been there and felt called upon to explain. Somebody would call her to account, she was sure. When she'd done nothing but help an old lady, a stranger, die not so lonely.

Hurrying up behind Carroll, though she knew there was nothing to hurry for, Emma felt another panicky flutter. Something. Some need to explain. To give some accounting why in the world she happened to be there in the pink house on Christmas Eve's eve, at that particular time of day; just happened to come in, in time to watch this old old woman die.

Season's Greetings, would that explain it? . . . *Love Lolly,* the girl in blue with the fur muff, Granny, bastard . . . ? No. None of it. She could never tell the truth to anyone, it was nobody's business anyway, they would hear the middle and have to accept it as the start.

Carroll went to the sun porch and found her, stretched out with a red cloth over her face. Lifting it, he knelt beside her and put his hands across her eyes and let his head drop to his chest. He gave in to his grief. "Not yet, Mattie Sue . . ." Emma thought he said, "Not now." Old as she was . . . still, he wasn't ready. Emma knew propriety demanded she leave, that this was private grief she had no right to be witness to and yet didn't she. She had not abandoned a dying woman when she well could have, but had stayed and seen her through and that was something, maybe a lot. Emma stood in the kitchen door, solidly rooted. She would stay for the rest of it too.

Carroll placed the red cloth back over Mattie Sue's face and reached down for her blunt old hands. The left one was on her leg, curled slightly, thumb against fingers. The right one was balled up tight in a fist. He unclenched it. Something was there. He dug his fingers into her palm and pried them straight. A wig fell out. A tiny, gold wig. Like doll's hair, spun gold and shiny, still in her grip.

There was a blank space next to Lady. Sexton was on one side of her and on the other side of Sexton was his wife Corrie Ann. Beside Lady was actually Preston's rightful place but Mattie Sue had had only one request regarding her burial and that was that she not be set in next to her brother Sam. Sam was on the opposite side of the huge stone and statue at Sexton's head, lying perpendicular to the others, with his wife Jewel. There were only two spaces left: one over on that side next to Sam and one beside Lady. Otherwise the family plot was filled up, as was the graveyard itself. No new plots had been sold there for years. When Carroll died he would have to be buried someplace else.

Carroll gave Mattie Sue Preston's place beside Lady. Preston wouldn't know or care. All the Cunningham gravestones were small and discreet, except for Sexton's, that enormous bronze knight in armor statue he had had erected to honor his life.

The hearse turned in at the old brick markers, one of which was half knocked down, butted into by a drunk driver one night and never fixed back. The police escort came first, and pulled over to the side of the road to direct traffic around the funeral procession. The hearse came down the gravel toward the gravesite. The men in suits moved aside, their work done, and went to wait in the cars they had come in. Emma stood, and went behind Sexton's marble stone then, thinking better of it, and before the hearse got there ran to wait beside a mausoleum beyond the Cunningham plot, where she could not be seen. After the service began she would come take a seat on the last row without being noticed.

Finally he had looked up.

His eyes were strange; gray-green and indistinct and yet persistent too: once they fixed on her they did not leave but locked her up into his gaze. Leaning against the kitchen doorframe looking at him, she couldn't look away.

They'd never met and yet he frowned once then cleared his brow and came free enough from his grief to see her and in some suddenly familiar way; as if to say . . . *you!* As if he suddenly understood who she was, beyond her name, which as far as she knew was all he had and then only because she had given it to him. There was no way he could know specifically who she was, unless he had known her mother and of course he might have. Unless he suddenly saw her as that *daughter of* she so strongly resisted.

Whatever happened happened; she couldn't say. But it was clear he had suddenly had some kind of revelation there about her. And Emma still didn't know what it was.

She felt pressed to speak but could not. She cleared her throat, shook her head, tightened her lips to stop them from trembling. He was still staring at her. She began to explain.

"I just happened to come by, just knocked, no reason, thinking I'd like to meet her. I'd wanted to before and one time almost did but got scared and ran. But this time I went ahead and knocked. When she didn't answer I just, I don't know why except that I had already decided ahead of time to do it, just opened the door. It wasn't locked and I heard

her. She called out. To you I think though I can't say for
sure. I think she thought I was you. I came back here and as
soon as I went to her . . . she had fallen, sort of, across that
chair . . . she fell. Like that. Just fell. Or, not *fell*, more like
all the air went out of her, just poof, to the floor. I sat with
her until, the rest of the way. She didn't say anything but
she looked like she wanted to. She reached up and touched
my face, put her fingers against me here and closed her eyes
and well, that was it. I'm sorry."

Carroll kept looking at her. Looking and looking. She
wished he'd say something. She got so tired of his looking at
her that way she thought she'd scream.

He wore a gold bracelet, loose on his wrist. A thin but not
womanly chain connected to a smooth pure gold rod. Like
an identification bracelet only more special. Fancy. It dan-
gled on his arm. She couldn't help noticing it. When she
pictured him now she saw that bracelet, loose and dangling
and beautiful, and his eyes, light gray-green and knowing.

Suddenly everything happened at once. The door flew
open and people came in, a doctor, two ambulance attend-
ants with oxygen, a policeman, bustling in in a rush like there
was something they could do if they got there fast. They
pushed by Emma and diverted Carroll's attention and gave
her her chance to leave. She slipped out behind two more
men carrying a stretcher, went down the long dark hall and
out the front door, pushed through the thicket of vines and
bushes out onto the sidewalk.

Carroll had not been to the cemetery since Lady's funeral
either and for a moment, when the black Cadillac pulled up
to the site, he thought he would not be able to go through
with it, could not get out in front of other people and simply
sit there next to her grave and not give in to the old seduc-

tions her death offered him: to join her. To give up and find
only discouragement in Mattie Sue's example, become separate and lonely for good, leave the world and its bad
choices, choose to die as she did. Lady.

He opened the car door. Sexton's statue was just across
from him, that bronze knight in armor Sexton had built for
himself. The knight's sword was unsheathed but its point
was down, between his feet, and his eyes were low, as if in
contemplation.

He opened the back door and reached in to help Preston.
At that moment someone touched his arm and Carroll
turned. It was Judge. "I'll do it," he said.

Carroll smoothed his tie inside his suit coat, ran one hand
across the hair above his ears and set himself to get through
it. A bland-looking man in a black suit directed him where
to sit and he went there. Other cars came, parked. People
assembled behind him. Judge brought Preston to sit on the
front row then sat there too, as Carroll had asked him to.

The casket was placed behind the preacher's lectern. It
was solid bronze and seamless. A bower of red roses lay atop
it.

A light wind blew through the tent. Colder than it
seemed outside. A core of chilliness when you weren't in the
sun. Carroll looked beyond the open grave to Lady's stone, a
simple pink marble marker, a pink soft as dusk. Sexton's
stone, behind the statue, had been defaced and written on.
All over it names had been scratched, and notices who loved
whom. Carroll made a mental note to have the site seen to.
Better taken care of.

The preacher took his place and said, "Let us pray. . . ."

Emma came quietly from behind the mausoleum, to take
a place on the last row. Two of the men in suits she'd seen
cracking open the folding chairs were there too, perhaps,
she thought, to fill up space, perhaps only to rest awhile as

they waited it out, until time to snap the chairs back together again and take them away.

He knew her immediately as the one Mattie Sue had been waiting for. Come too late but the one. Her wild hair was frizzed out the way Mattie Sue had described it and those blue eyes, that look . . . Mattie Sue had once told him about such a girl, said she had come up to the window of the glass room and did he know anyone who looked like that and Carroll did not and said no. There was no mention that this wild-haired girl was the one she was waiting for, to finish out her circle and make it complete, but Carroll knew. And when he saw her that day he recognized her. She was the one. And wasn't the situation properly ironic and grim too, a joke: that she should finally get there and be too late. He couldn't decide if it was better for Mattie Sue to have recognized her before she died or not.

Payments. One choice: how to die. Not much else, little to do to change it. Die lying on a floor when your life had made as its staying power the will *not* to sit when you could stand or lie down overlong. What is extracted. No way to make a death suit the life it ends but to choose it. Choose how.

Dead. Dead while he fucked a married woman, dying while he closed his eyes and pushed faster. Falling to the floor as she came. Dead as he found his way clear again.

Payments. What is extracted. How to put it in balance. Preston could not, when Lady killed herself. The balance was too out of kilter and so Preston gave it up. In his own way. Dreaming his life out, inside it altogether, not saying not telling, not giving out information at all, rather than doing it wrong again.

He did not want to make too much of where he was and what he was doing when it happened . . . he did not like to think he believed in signs, or in messages he could not understand the origin of . . . yet and yet how could he not, it was too strong. The one life he revered and wished most deeply to honor, going dark as he pressed himself into another, some other, eyes closed, trying to go beyond life, to lift out of it, being all he could be and more. Yet pursuing that was not what he hoped to make out of his life: he had hoped to imitate Mattie Sue, to set his life on a line dead straight for what he wanted, to make it go a different way, his family's energies and strengths, his family's and most of all his own. Meantime, as he flew, meantime at the same time, this. A body gone cold. Her life growing lighter too, and lighter still, too much, drying up like paper in a fire, less heavy than the wind, outside the circles altogether and in the arms of a stranger. A young girl who had been waited for and finally came too late, who . . . did she know? . . . mysteriously had shown up just then and even more strangely did not leave when she saw what was happening.

Signs. Payments. It was too much outside of what Carroll knew. Too much beyond the kind of calculating he understood, adding, making lists, averages, gains against losses, assets and liabilities toted up, net worth figured clear, in numbers.

". . . the soul of our dear sister and neighbor Mattie Sue Cunningham and on this Christmas Day guide her sweetly to your side . . ."

Oh Lord if Mattie Sue could hear it. He hoped she could not. Sweetness was not a word she'd have had put into prayers for her soul.

He did not bow his head. Not when he had not been to church since he was a child, or pray, he would not be that hypocritical. He had however lowered his chin a bit. So that a person sitting behind him didn't quite know if he was or wasn't. Not bowed. But not straight either.

Emma's head was high. Over the bent ones she could see

Carroll's, taller than the rest, half up and half down. She could not quit looking at it, she wondered if he wore the gold bracelet. His hair was curly, and cut to her thinking too short; if he let it grow it would bunch out and make a fine fullness there. Beyond his blond curls was the black blur of the preacher's robe and beyond the black, the garnet fog of the roses.

". . . and we pray too dear Lord that on this magnificent Christmas for which we do thank thee abundantly that you will help us in our grief and bereavement to find in the example of Mattie Sue Cunningham's long long life proof of thy grace, thy plan, thy . . ."

Every time he said Mattie Sue Cunningham, Carroll imagined him rehearsing his prayer at night, saying instead of her name, "Fill-in-the-Blank": pray for the soul of fill-in-the-blank. Now he was talking about her sweetness again. Carroll did say one small prayer. To Mattie Sue. Asking her to forgive him this.

He hadn't known however what preacher to ask for and this one had simply shown up, said he had been "your mother's minister," and would be honored to conduct services and so he'd become the one. Only because he asked.

He was a jolly-looking man, gray and rather stout, with an innocent, childlike sparkle in his eyes.

"Amen."

There was a general coughing and shuffling about.

Before the bowed heads had time to straighten altogether, Carroll, sensing something, turned around suddenly and as quickly switched back in place. He thought so. Thought she would come, felt her there, knew it was like her, like anyone with such intensity, to see a thing all the way through to its end. She looked surprised that he had discovered her. She was not old enough to sense he was as fixed and as intense as

she. Her marblelike eyes widened in that one quick second
and he turned back, and felt lifted up a little. He heard little
else that was said.

The preacher turned to Scripture. When he got to a part
about a woman making raiment for her husband so that he
may go to the marketplace and she will feel proud, Carroll
tuned out altogether.

He was saying too much and she knew it, but what could
she do except listen. She sat abnormally prim, with her hands
in her lap; watching him; fascinated. Mattie Sue's house was
dark and smelled musty. Sheets were thrown over some of
the furniture.

"I knew it was happening," he said. "She had been letting
things slip she was ordinarily so careful about. Like her
clothes and her hair. The floor wouldn't be swept. I'd come
and she'd be in bed."

"Well. But she was old." What else could she say?

"You know it's coming but you never really are ready.
You know? You never are, no matter what."

He sat in a wine-colored overstuffed plush chair. No lights
were on. He was slouched down in the chair so that his
lower back was on the far edge of its cushion, his legs
sprawled in a wide V. Not like he had appeared at the cemetery . . . stiff and correct and unyielding . . . but sad; and
lonely; and wide-open scared. He was drinking. A bottle
was beside him. Every now and then he poured some of it
into a glass and sipped it.

"I don't drink usually," he had said emphatically and re-
peated several times over, then poured himself some more.
"But this is different," he said before drinking any, every
time.

He talked to her and yet did not. If she had left he'd have
noticed, she provided some kind of counterpoint for him to

bounce his grief off of, and yet what he was saying had little
to do with *her*, with the person Emma Blue Lasswell sitting
there across from. He said what he had to, let it roll out in a
way she thought was not natural to him and somehow it became so, because of her. Something about that moment of
recognition on the sun porch. Some reason he felt called
upon particularly to seek her out after the funeral, bring her
here, sit her down and begin to talk.

"Every day she got fully dressed. You know? She waited
here in this house they stashed her in for thirty years, thirty,
four years fewer than I have lived, more by far than you've
known, and got dressed every morning, shoes, stockings, the
works. Her way, you see. Of keeping it together, of not giving
in. All the time concentrating. Thinking it would come.
Thinking it had to. 'The circle rounded out full,' she used to
say to me. 'The thing passed on.'"

He let his head flop back against the chair and was quiet.
She thought he was asleep but no, he raised his head and
took a drink. Every time he lifted the glass, the gold bracelet went down into his sleeve, then came back again to his
wrist.

"You were it, you know. *Are*."

His eyes were full on her; her hands came unfolded and
found the chair arms . . . what was it about him. She could
not deal with his gaze and the way he made her feel, not in
any of the ways she had come to rely on to protect herself.

She laughed. It sounded foolish.

"Me . . . what?"

"The rounding out of her circle. The one to pass her life
on to. She wanted an heir. Somebody she could tell her life
to and die knowing it would stand for something. 'Footsteps'
she used to say. 'New feet to retrace my old footsteps.'"

Emma refolded her hands more tightly. Bunched together,
they might gain strength one from the other.

"But you came too late. Orphans will get this house. They

don't even know. She got a flyer once from an orphanage, asking for funds. It sounded worthy, she had me check on it, and then signed the whole thing over to them, this house and her ten acres. The house of course is worthless but the lot is not and the ten acres is prime real estate, out from town near where the new school is."

"Eunola Christian?"

"Eunola Christian." He had not recognized her scorn.

"But the orphans weren't what she wanted, not really. What she wanted was you. Not by name. Only . . . what you are." He looked over at her once again. There was little light in the room, the sun was going down and winter was coming back, soon the house would be like ice. They still had on their coats, for even before the sky turned gray the house had felt cold. Wrapped up in bushes that way, Carroll had told her, it never really warms up. Emma drew her new leather jacket close. This was not what she had expected when he asked her to go with him. She had thought he wanted to thank her, and she had her speeches made: she would turn down any offer he made, gifts or reward or favors. But he had driven her here instead, they had come in avoiding the kitchen and sun porch where she had died, had turned beside the stairs instead of going on beyond them, to come into the living room, which from the looks of it hadn't been sat in in years. It was cold and musty; cobwebs and dirt were everywhere.

"Listen, I don't know what you're talking about . . ."

She felt a quick urge to get out. What was she doing there? Something strange was going on. She'd heard funny stories about Carroll Cunningham.

"I know . . ." But he had this way of talking that nearly hypnotized her. It was very precise and careful. He enunciated so clearly. His lips went around every word as if it were something precious. As if he were that concerned that you understand not approximately what he meant but exactly. His gestures were the same. Sparing but clear and precise: when he drew a circle with his hand it was for a particular purpose and you watched it, those fingers long and thin and agile making that circle exactly as he meant them to with no exaggeration or excess, and the bracelet going up and down. He looked at her intently as he spoke, in a way no one in her life ever had, as if he was afraid she might break or be hurt, or suddenly go up in smoke. If she fell, he would be there before she hit, to cushion her fall. Not because she was who she was: because he was that particular, a person able to carry through what he believed in. He locked eyes with her and would not release her, as if by force of will he meant to keep her. As if he wanted her here that badly.

"It has nothing to do with you Emma Blue, nothing. You didn't know. I'm only saying . . . too much. More than you want to hear."

As if to stop himself, he stood.

He was thirty-four, the same age as her mother. Old enough to be her father.

And?

So?

Voices rumbled back and forth in her brain, saying yes, saying no, saying old enough to, saying so what. She stood. Her lips felt thick. She had not. Had never. And if he refused her? So what. Risk, consequence, protectiveness, loss . . . suddenly it all went out the window, every calculation, all odds and caution. Behind her eyes there was a kind of quietness, as if the darkness of the room had moved inside. One thing or the other, do it or not, time to get on with it. He did not lift his arms or offer help; she did it all. It was time and she would, did, it felt like something you couldn't quit on once it started, like once you've decided to walk not backing out, like when something in your stomach needs to come up: you have to let it, no choice anymore.

Suddenly she was beyond choice and one-by-one deciding.

No signs about her. No voices in her mind going back and forth. Only herself in the darkness, becoming darkness too, a blind rush. Lifting up.

He looked surprised.

Those blue-stone eyes, that urgent no-holds-barred look about her. Something about her. Going for what she wanted no matter what. She came at him. He had heard about these new young girls, how they were, but was not prepared. She nearly smothered him. His married friend, with her expertise and litheness, could not have given him more.

It was late when he took her home. When she opened the car door she was particularly aware of the interior light coming on, and the sight of him there in front of the trailer. They had eaten at a drive-in hamburger joint; she had gobbled hers as if she'd had nothing to eat in a week.

"Emma," he had said, "it's up to you. You're young and I never would have. Give it some time."

"I know" was all she could manage to reply. But she did give him a look so he knew how she felt, and laughed with him when he explained in detail about Mattie Sue's will and how she had wanted an heir and how he thought she had been the one all the time but only got there too late.

A circle rounded out.

He invited her to come to his house anytime, but she didn't have a way. He said maybe he could help her out on that, but she said actually she liked the pink house better, until it was turned over to the orphans, they could meet there sometime again maybe and not to worry, she did not go out with boys from school at all, ever; he was not keeping her from anyone or thing.

She hardly dared look at him then after such boldness,

but finally found his eyes and knew there was no maybe: she would, again. Be with him. Wherever.

The blankness came back, behind her eyes, and the warm thickening of her mouth. Lord.

You never know. Girl, you just never never know.

He waited until she was safely inside, like a parent.

Lucille was asleep in the living room. The Christmas-tree lights were still on. Emma tiptoed into her room, closed the door, undressed and went to bed. She lay with her hands behind her head thinking back over what had happened and what he said. Her stomach growled. The fried onion rings . . . she'd had too many. Something happened in the other room, a door, some footsteps. Most likely Lucille had not been asleep but was lying in the dark waiting for her to get home. The footsteps came to Emma's door, the door opened a crack, but no one came in. The Christmas lights sent a red-orange glow into her room.

"Lucille?"

She started to speak.

Granny.

"When I was a little girl not even five years old I went to the fields, out there thinking it wouldn't be so bad if the others had done it so could I. But it was bad. Worse than I ever could have dreamed. We just had to go at it and go at it and never stop and the children kept coming, fourteen in all, so the work could get done. Went to school three years. Then there was a bad year. I came home. Worked like the rest. Everything I learned I had to learn late. From your great-grandfather. He was nineteen years older than me you know. Matthew. Matthew Peavey. He was a carpenter, used to, they tell me, come by and swing me when I was little. He was a grown boy even then and he would come by our house and see me sitting in the tree swing and come give me a push. Matthew was quiet, he used to go off in the woods and write poetry and I don't know whether he waited for me from the time he was swinging me on, or whether he just never found nerve enough to ask anybody else. At any rate when I was fifteen, barely fifteen, he was waiting for that day, he asked Mama if he could marry me and Lord I was so happy to get out of that house, you can't imagine. They never gave us a minute's peace not a minute but were after us all the time to do more and do more and if we weren't working we were going to church. Primitive Baptists we were, you know, went to church all the time, said anybody who wasn't one of us was going to hell, like the Church-of-Christers, like Pauline's church. Everybody else but me stayed in that church but I saw what was what early on and said no thank you and got out. Church and work was all we did, work and church, church and work. When I got married well I vowed then to rest: if I never did another day's work until the day I died, well I still would have done more than my share. You just can't imagine. Nobody can anymore. Nobody works like that anymore, nobody gets hands anymore like my brothers got, nobody gets that bone tired when they're five years old and needing to be skipping rope not picking weevils off stalks. That's what the little ones did, the close work. Closer to the ground, we were told, do the closer work. Now I know what Zhena and the rest say about me, I know what you think, I know what every one of them says when I'm not in the room and that'll do, it's fine by me, let them. Things work out in a funny way, not ever like you expect: soon as you think you know, you wait and see, it will go in a different direction. Soon as you think you got it wrapped up, the ribbon will bust and the box come apart in your hands, you wait. Things go I don't know how sometimes they get so tormented but they do and sometimes it takes a long time to figure out what gets you up and what, that seems friendly, will weight you down and drag you to the bottom. But anyway. Sometimes you can figure out a thing or two. They say I nagged Matthew, that I know. And maybe I did. Matthew was soft, he let people run over him, whenever he got blue he flat up and left, went down to the cemetery and wrote poems. Poems. I still got them, you can have them when I go, I wrote that down. Nothing to them. A man lonely, wishing for better is all. But we did laugh some, I had not laughed in I don't know when until Matthew came along, there didn't seem to be laughing matters in my house, only sins and payment and work and suffering. And I tell you, I have lifted myself out of that. Whatever you and the rest may think of me. And it was not easy just to go away from it. The old habits were there and sometimes even though I knew how bad they were I'd get homesick for them, especially with me having all my babies then too, just like my own mama, one after the other in the bedroom all those years until your grandmother Lucille the baby. Then I said that is it Matthew, no more. Well he was old then anyway, Matthew was in his fifties when Lucille was born—and ready to give it up I suppose though I am not sure he did. But I did. No more I said to him, if you need to, do it somewhere else. And that was it. And I mean it. When I said so I meant it and he knew it and rolled over and never rolled back onto my side of the bed again. Happy, I hear people talking about now, who's happy, how to be, what to do to be. We never thought of it. Just went on. Did what had to be done, what seemed the next thing to get to. But now that I think of it I tell you: the best time for me was, the time when if I had to say what was a happy time for me, if somebody said you got to say some time or another I would have to say it was before I came here, when I was out by myself living in that shack at the end of that dirt road planting my flowers and sitting on that front porch watching the cotton come up, bloom, get picked, shrivel up and die, start over. Now that was a good time when I think of it. Electric company's there now, the time's gone by. Wouldn't have done me any good to try to stay, anyway I was getting past it and the winters were too hard. But when I think of it that was it. Matthew got so bent over by the end that I couldn't hardly stand to look at him and that was too bad, for him it was worse I know even though I do think he had his comforts even then, you couldn't tell, he never seemed regretful and always looked at me kindly no matter how hard I was on him. He was a good man and believe you me he cared for me, the last person I guess who did. Really. So.

"You remember where you come from, little miss. Do you? Know who you are? You should. This is it, what I'm telling you. After that it got watered down. You better stick to my part of it, the early stuff, and leave the rest go, Blue and those, it won't help you. Stick up for me. For my part of it. Or anyway remember it. Do what you have to to make it keep going. Round it out and roll it. Don't forget. I am going to bed now. Good night."

Emma pulled the covers up to her chin.
Don't shake the tree. I'm still in it.

IV

THE
COLLECTOR

A brown and white car, brown on bottom with a white vinyl top and one slim white stripe down the side, is waxed, oiled, vacuumed, serviced, ready to go. The wife is taking it south for a three-day trip; it is her car; her husband stands in the drive and tells her good-bye . . . to drive careful. She will be back in three days, after the sale and show in Memphis are over.

She drives south, from craggy bluff-type terrain to rolling hills in a straight line south, lower and lower in altitude; the trees get fatter the closer she comes. She arrives in Memphis; stops for lunch; gases the car; continues south. At the Memphis city limits, she drives over the last hill she will see for a while: the road in front of her now is perfectly straight, the land around her perfectly flat, she can see from sky to sky all around her, the whole sky like a bowl turned upside-down over her head. The trees are fat now, and deeply rooted: tap roots that go down and down, impossible to find the end of, in ground so rich and fertile her father used to quote his own father as having said: "Stand there long enough and your feet take root."

Exactly what she meant to leave. Had left. Had escaped from.

Nothing had changed: that was the biggest surprise. After all the so-called shifts in the winds of things, things were still the same. The highway the brown and white car went on was as bumpy as ever, with the same cracks in it she remembered from her childhood. And beside it were the same tar-paper shacks with the same corrugated-type tin roofs and washing machines on the front porch . . . the same front yards with no grass and dogs asleep beside the steps. The same dusty black children playing there.

It was a poor state with backward ideas; she was glad to be out of it.

She lit another cigarette, kept her speed within ten miles of the limit, aimed the nose of her brand-new car directly south, on and on, with the keeping on, directly set to get there once she'd decided to do it. No going back now; she'd made up her mind to go there and see; do it and leave. Settle up with her father's death then leave it behind once again. Go back home again, free and clear as before.

She passed the city limits of the town of Sunflower, ten miles north of Eunola. Sunflower kept up its streets and traffic lights by issuing speeding tickets to out-of-state cars traveling through it. Which she should have remembered; she'd lived nearby. There is no warning sign indicating a speed zone ahead; they give you no chance to slow down. Just past the city limits marker, there is one sign: 30 MPH it says. So that even if you are going at a legal speed of 55 MPH before hitting Sunflower, there is no way to slow down that fast, suddenly gear from 55 to 30 that fast, in seconds.

So if they want to get you in Sunflower, they get you.

The next thing you may see after that city limits marker

and the speed sign may be the deputy sheriff chasing you, and he may even have his children in his car with him; his wife works as a nurse; it depends on what shift she's on.

The brown and white car was doing 68 according to the sheriff's radar. Was she in some kind of hurry? he asked. Didn't she *like* Sunflower?

It was the day after New Year's, a holiday since New Year's fell on Sunday; the courthouse was closed. They went directly to the jailhouse so she could pay her fifty-eight dollars: twenty dollars for the insult plus a dollar a mile for each over thirty she was doing.

After that interruption, the brown and white car came on again, south down 84 toward Eunola but slower now, staying 55 and below for those last perfectly straight, perfectly flat miles.

When the knock came they didn't hear it, they were too busy yelling, wrapped up in football games and bets, the three of them arranged in front of two portable TV sets in a semicircle, like stuffed birds: glued there, for the day. They had watched the parades that morning and would stick with the football games until the last gun was shot signaling the end of the last game of the day, which wouldn't be until well after midnight when the second day of the new year had rolled over.

One of the sets was up full blast; the other one ran a soundless picture. The three women's attention pretty much stayed with the game they could hear; the other one was almost over and seemed pretty well settled by now. That TV stayed on too, however, in case some crazy thing happened—which still might—to change the outcome. If not, Lucille had won the first twenty-five-cent bet of the day. Lucille was the luckiest gambler Emma knew. Every year they did this and every year Emma tried to figure a way to beat her out. Lucille let Emma choose first; sometimes Emma went with the points and took the underdog, other years she stuck with the favorites and sometimes she did both and mixed them. Didn't seem to matter what she tried though, if she picked all favorites it turned out to be the very year the underdogs had their day.

Emma had hopes for this game however. Lucille's team, in orange, was ahead at the moment, but only by seven and the momentum seemed to be changing. The only thing was, Lucille had three points as well, so that Emma in fact was down by ten.

". . . way to *go!*"

But her team was moving and looking good. And with five minutes or more left to play, well, as Lucille often said, you never know. Girl, you just never never know. Or as the broadcaster would have it: this game's not over *yet*.

Granny grunted once. She was looking at the silent set.

Granny professed to hate all sports, especially any that Emma and Lucille so obviously enjoyed, but she would not leave the sets either; she would be there when the last gun sounded just like the other two except she would be complaining. Granny would spend her day saying over and over how stupid it was for near-grown men to go out in funny suits and hats and beat up on one another for the sake of a ball and how much even *more* stupid anybody had to be to sit and watch it.

The brown car is there now, just at the edge of the trailer's front steps, dead still sitting there. The driver is staring at the front door.

Like a meat locker door, Lucille used to say.

It was metal. The trailer looked exactly the same. The drapes were shut. Beside the trailer was a beat-up old Nash.

The car door handle was recessed, a flat, plate-like piece of chrome you had to reach your fingers inside of, to open the door. Her fingers were light, agile, and thin. She curled them around the flat chrome plate and pulled it toward her, keeping her eyes on the metal trailer door.

It was more scratched up now, was all; otherwise it looked the same, exactly exactly the same: Frank could have stepped out of it, in his silver hardhat and metal-toed working boots and she would not have been surprised. She herself could have skipped down those stairs, idly turning her rubber-tipped baton in a casual four-finger twirl and the woman in the two-tone vinyl-roofed car would not have been shocked. She was that far away from her own childhood.

When she was out of the car, she closed its door softly. Inside, its clasps caught securely, in a reassuring way; it was a fine car. Her husband saw to it she got the best. What good did it do for him to be in the business, he always said, if he couldn't get the best first for his wife.

She pushed her purse farther back on her arm, tossed her hair back over one shoulder and set her chin up in a high, confident tilt. She had checked her make-up on the highway, past Sunflower: everything was in order, she was fixed up satisfactorily, if ever she was ready it was now, she might as well go on and do it. One thing or the other, sit or stand, walk or don't but something, go *on*. Who used to say that. Granny no doubt.

She knocked once, lightly, and at the sound of her knuckles against the hollow metal door drew her hand back.

Nothing had changed, nothing had changed, nothing had.

Lucille actually preferred pro games; the Super Bowl was still ahead and that would be her special day. College seemed too chancy, too flash-in-the-pan. You never could

tell how well the young boys would do or how many bad
mistakes they'd make, and anyway she particularly enjoyed
fancy passing and a good quarterback sack now and then
and you got very little of either in college football.

But Emma loved the bowl games and this all-day watching was a ritual she ardently looked forward to. They had
spent much of the day before reading the sports pages,
figuring out their bets and calculating point spreads with
the seriousness of professional gamblers laying down thou-
sands, risking house payments and babies' shoes; they were
that careful and serious about their twenty-five-cent bets.

Emma stood, waving her arms.

"Get it, get it . . . yeah . . . now take it on home, boy,
take it . . . aw shit. Just *shit*, why can't they read defense."

An alert cornerback for the orange team had picked up
the play and set Emma's team's star running back, in green,
on his behind.

". . . might have reached the line of scrimmage . . ." the
announcer said.

Emma scooped up a handful of popcorn and sat back
down, grumbling about dumb offensive linemen.

As her bottom hit the chair pillow, she felt Granny, next
to her, tense up and lean toward her.

"Girl, you sure got some mouth on you," she said.

But Emma did not respond, she would not anymore, it
was her New Year's resolution: to be calm and passively un-
attached, to be outside the reach of this old woman's gall
and vituperation altogether. Granny could not touch her
anymore; she could say bastard every other breath and
Emma would not be moved, Emma had something of her
own now, her own secret, and whatever it took to protect it
from Granny, she would do. She was inside her own safe
chalk circle now. It was drawn about her feet and there was
no room for a crabby old lady inside it at all.

"Mother," Lucille said sweetly, doing what she could as

well to preserve good natures, "would you like me to move
a TV back into your room so you can watch something else?
You don't have to watch football if you don't want to. We
don't need two sets. . . ."

But Granny only grunted and squinted one eye at the TV,
as if to see a certain play better . . . not on the set Emma
and Lucille were watching but on the other one, the silent
set. She'd be quiet again for a while now. Every so often she
just liked to be scratched, was all. Like a dog needing a pat.
Every now and then Granny just up and said something irri-
tating like that, then once somebody gave her something
back she was happy for a while. Until the itch got raw
again.

No one could have heard the first knock, she had barely
tapped the metal surface of the door, and she could hear a
television set going inside, and the sound of voices. She
would have to do it again, harder. She pushed her favorite
wave of hair—over her left eye—closer to the middle of her
forehead where she liked it, then knocked again. More decid-
edly.

Nothing like her own front door: white wood, Colonial
style with a solid brass knocker in the shape of a hand. Nothing like anything she had now was anywhere within sight.
She waited.

"Yes, yes, YES!"

Emma was on her feet again, yelling.

She didn't hear the knock and neither did Granny, whose
hearing wasn't so good, but Lucille did. Lucille had ears like
a cat. The knock was prim, distinct, sharp; Lucille knew
who it was. She pulled up and away from the back of her
chair and raised her hand from its arm as if to get up or

make some statement but could not move any farther than that and sat frozen that way for a second or two.

Emma's man had broken through the defensive line, straight through a hole that seemed to have opened up especially for him, and had gone all the way, twenty yards into the end zone; six points for Emma's—the green—team.

Granny didn't hear the knock because Granny was watching the game just like Emma. She wouldn't admit it but she was. And the next day Emma and Lucille might hear her on the phone with somebody or talking to them in person, and she would be telling them play by play what had happened during the games today, complete with football terminology and exact statistics, describing game plan goof-ups and alternative strategies as knowledgeably as a TV broadcaster. Emma and Lucille would just roll their eyes at one another then, knowing that was simply how and what Granny was. Knowing Granny didn't miss much but kept whatever she could lay her hands and mind and time on stored up, like a pack rat for future use in the event of no-telling what.

"Marker on the field."

Granny was the one to notice it first, a yellow handkerchief thrown by a referee back at the twenty-yard line. The touchdown was being called back.

"No *way!*" Emma was screaming, while Lucille was sitting in her chair still but jabbing at Emma with her finger and saying over and over again, "Emma . . . Emma . . . Emma . . ."

"He's in the tank. No *way!* What *is* it, Lucille?"

She reached down to the knob and turned it slightly. Locked of course; it locked on closing.

Like the door of a meat locker, her mother always said. *Everything inside it shut up for good, good and locked and airtight, like sides of beef in a freezer.*

Clunch. That awful sound it made. She remembered the last time she had heard it, when she left that morning before anybody got up or could notice. Emma had been sound asleep in her bed . . . not in her child's bed, in her mother's, not in Emma's bed but Lolly's, the one Lolly slept in as a child. As a teen-ager. Emma would be almost seventeen now, seventeen the middle of this month in fact. Did she sleep in it now?

She would give it one more minute, then leave. She counted to a hundred by fives.

"Emma. Quick. Somebody's at the door."

"Oh all right. But, shit, why'd they have to do that. A clip my hind foot . . ."

Emma went backwards to the door, keeping her eyes the whole time glued on the television set so as not to miss anything. Third and eighteen now, three and a half minutes to go. The play was crucial.

Lucille had lowered her hand, and she now gripped the arms of her chair as if it was about to run out from under her. She watched Emma. It was her, she knew it was, it was Lolly. Lucille was never wrong about such things, she could just tell when certain things were about to happen, that was why she had been up so early that other time, in time to watch Lolly leave: because when trouble was coming she could see it ahead of time in her mind, like pictures flashed on that screen there. It wasn't intuition, she could actually *see* it. And she could see who it was knocking on their beat-up metal front door in that prim, sharp way, it was Lolly. She'd gotten Lucille's letter and come home and now, oh now what? Oh Lord, she had caused it and the others didn't know and now what were they going to do and say . . . oh you never know, do you, you never do. Lord.

Emma opened the door with her back to it and her hand behind her, then went with it as she opened it but never

looked: she and the door moved aside together, so that
Emma was against its inside rim, leaning against it, her attention still on the game, when the door was opened wide
enough for the person knocking to be clearly revealed. And
Emma didn't hear Lucille gasp as she saw who it was, so she
still didn't look yet . . . this was all a matter of seconds . . .
and Emma was so wrapped up in the game it seemed more
important to stay with it. At least until the crucial play was
through.

This time they made it. The quarterback lobbed a short
lateral pass to a flashy wide receiver known for his high-
flying footwork, the receiver found a hole and went for
the first. This time there was no penalty; Emma's team got
her eighteen yards and a few more. The referee held up his
right arm and slanted it toward the goal line. First down.

"Hot dog!" As Emma said that she realized where she was
and then turned from Lucille and Granny's upturned, still
and very surprised faces to see who it was at the door making them look that way. Emma was standing with the door
there right next to her and turned her head toward the outside to see but not in time. The woman at that moment
swept into the trailer without being greeted or asked in. A
wash of perfume swirled by; a flash of red; a clicking; a long
flowing mane of soft curling long hair. And she was inside.
Without being asked. As if she belonged there too. As if it
were her trailer as much as theirs.

And did not stop until she got to the far end of the room,
next to the door to Emma's—once her—bedroom. There she
stopped, threw back her hair and turned around.

It was her. The Mama. Telling stories in the night.
Me. You should have seen it. Me.
Come back. All that rush and shine and fancy perfume,

those clicking red shoes and slim pale tightly stockinged white legs. She set down her wooden boxlike little purse on a table and clicked it open.

Emma looked outside, to see if anyone was with her. There was a brown and white car there. On the front bumper the license plate said LOLLY. The front bumper was practically on top of the bottom step of the front stoop. Emma looked back at her; no one was in the car; no one spoke.

Emma put one hand against the door and shoved it.

Clunch.

Lolly's head snapped up and she looked toward the door, quickly, then turned back away, to some business she had there with her purse, one hand fumbling about in its interior.

She was not pretty, the story sometimes went, *but she was special: somebody you just can't help noticing,* and she still was. She was thin and small; wearing a red swirling dress and make-up just so. She was not somebody you would pass lightly by without looking at if you saw her as a stranger on a street. Something about her.

And thin too, when Emma was so square. Thin and contained: everything pulled in and controlled, just so, neat and pliable. Even her feet: her arch lifted high inside her red T-strap shoes and looked compatible there. Emma's feet were square and boxy; a pointy-toe design cramped her toes and her feet were always running out the back and sides of whatever kind of shoes she bought, except sandals. She was barefoot now. She wore jeans and a blue work shirt, nothing more. Emma plain.

Lolly found what she was looking for. She drew out one cigarette and a small silver lighter and lit up.

"Missed." Granny announced.

In that one silent packed flash, Emma's team had scored and she had missed it. But the kicker botched the extra

point, leaving the orange team still ahead. By one point on
the scoreboard, by four in the point spread.

That fact was not lost on Emma, though she never turned
to acknowledge it to Granny, or looked in the direction of
the TV, or said a word. Her eyes were on her mother.

One Lolly; three. Three women might as well have
walked into the trailer that day: one for each of the women
sitting in it watching bowl games all day, they saw her that
differently, interpreted her reasons for coming that differently. That night, Emma, Lucille and Granny would
lie in their beds and entertain reruns of what had happened
that afternoon and who it was exactly had marched so
abruptly into the middle of their TV watching during that
third-down-eighteen-to-go play, and each would keep so
implacably to her own version of it that there would be no
constants to go by, if they ever tried to get together and
bring the three Lollys together and merge them into one.

No grounds for a true-false rendering and no desire on
any of their parts to square the incongruities . . . no recognition in fact that there were any: dead straight ahead, each
one, seeing what she saw all over in her mind again, seeing
what she saw as fact and true without compromise as the
only truth.

No other way to tell it.

Each believed Lolly had come for a particular reason and
from that belief followed the rest. Like a Peavey spat: yes-I-
am, no-you're-not, it-will-too, no-it-won't: no possibility of
resolution or culmination and no other way to tell it.

Even if Lolly had stood there and told them why she
came and what she wanted one-two-three, they would not
only not have believed her; she would have, in their minds
as they rethought and retold the incident, spoken different

words. They would have made it go to fit their needs, no matter what.

"You got my letter!"

Lucille was the first to speak. The other two turned immediately to her: what letter?

Lucille saw honor in her daughter's return; the need to square up old wrongs. Frank's death had triggered regret in the girl and she had come back to make amends: she would take Emma back with her. She was not raised to go off and leave a daughter she had given birth to, she simply had not, she had come home to reunite with her own flesh-and-blood daughter and take her off to make her a new life. Lucille never once doubted this rendition of her daughter's return and never would. That Lolly did not take Emma, did not even ask to, or give any indication that was why she had come was no proof to Lucille: they had never given Lolly the chance, that was all. Or she would have. She would have done it.

She had come to rescue Emma, Lucille could see it written all over her face: rescue.

Emma looked at Lucille. What letter? She had never seen Lucille so radiant. Her eyes were wet and shining and the skin on her face was as pink as a young girl's blush.

Granny cocked her head in that direction.

"Lucille," she said, "you're a fool."

The insurance check had been for $50,000; Granny had no doubt but that Lucille had it in her mind to give it to Lolly to take Emma home on. No doubt Lucille had written Lolly telling her all that. No doubt Lucille was a fool, but Granny had always known that. Lucille never had the sense God gave a midget piss-ant.

For the money. Lolly had come for the money, that was what Granny saw. Lucille was a fool to think otherwise:

Lolly was no different now from what she always had been, a high-and-mighty, chin-in-the-air piece of fluff. A leftover shred of cotton boll, one ragged piece on a defoliated stalk: it would blow in the wind and fly away, of no account to anybody or anything in the world ever. Never had her feet on the ground to start with; no use to think she did now. And anyway she had no right to come back expecting soft considerations, she had made her bed, now she could just lie in it, was how Granny felt. When a dog left home to go chase wild meat, it could not come home hungry and expect to get gravy, it would have to take what it was thrown and be grateful.

Granny turned back to the silent set, noticing on the other one that Emma's team had recovered a fumble and was back in the running again. The announcer was going wild. Emma didn't even know.

People were too soft. You had to know what a thing was and call it by its name, not beat around the bush and give in to fuzzy maybe-thises or maybe-thats or possibly in some cases, some others. You had to know. And say. You had to call a spade a spade and not butter up your seeing with wishes or dreams, you had to keep to what your eyes could clearly see and then speak out about it. Then everybody knew what was what. A person knew where he stood. Lolly had no right to claim grief over Frank's death and there were no buts about that in the world, not a one, she'd left and that was that. She had cast her bread upon the waters: let her eat the moldy crusts that came back to her now, it was all she deserved.

Granny waited. Pretending to have no interest in Lolly. Feigning interest now only in the game.

Money. That was the cutting edge. The cutting edge was money.

Lolly drew on her cigarette and walked to the bedroom

door. It was shut. She turned from it and went to a side table next to the couch, to tap off some ashes into an ashtray there, a blue one, and shaped like an upside-down top hat. Sun from a nearby window shone through it and left a blue flutter of itself beside the glass ashtray.

What's this? the young Emma had asked that last time, turning it over. *Why's this shaped like a hat? What's this? This? This?*

Panic shook inside her chest. It felt like her ribs were coming unglued. She had to get out. She could not stay. It was not doing what she had thought or hoped it would. Nothing had changed. She felt like something perched on the razor-sharp edge of a knife blade. If she bore down at all, or relaxed into it, the blade would slice into the tenderest part of her feet. She had to get out.

She had not come to stay, that was clear. The way she flew in announced it; she might as well have said as she came in the door—the way Aunt Pauline did when she came to visit—NOW I CAN'T STAY LONG, before anybody had a chance to say whether they wanted her to stay a long time or not. Now she was pacing. Back and forth across the width of the living room, smoking that cigarette, blowing smoke up over her head in a dramatic movie-star style that looked practiced. Like she'd stood before mirrors doing it. To see how it looked best . . . her lips, her eyes, the curl of the smoke.

Emma only wanted her to speak, to look at her and say something. She wouldn't be there long, that was clear. Emma only needed her to finish out *her* circle . . . say the magic word so she could find out if the voice she kept hearing in her head was truly the real one, truly the Mama's, in the mountains telling stories to a young girl in her bed.

Nothing had changed, nothing was here to be gained, she would simply turn around and go, back north the hundred and fifty miles to Memphis, to the antiques show, like she had said she was. She put her cigarette out in the top hat.

"Touchdown!"

Granny looked up to see if anyone heard. But Emma's clear blue eyes and all her attention it seemed were exactly where they had been since the woman came in, on her mother.

Granny grinned. She was keeping every detail of the game back in her mind, for future use. Later on they would want to know what happened, and would have to turn to her to find out.

"Lolly," Lucille begged, seeing the drift of how things were about to go, "come, sit down, please."

Her eyes were heavily made up. Almonds of a sea-ish tint like thumbed bruises were between her eyes and brows, and her lashes were blackened and thick. Her hair however had not changed, it was as spectacular as ever and fell exactly as the stories would have it, as natural as water in a color like no other, like mud and rust with sunlight inside it. When Lolly lifted a hand to draw a curl aside, a long red daggerish nail trailed down her temple and tracked the curve of her ear. Like the girl on the Christmas card she was perfect: no curl escaped that had not been calculated to. Her lips were pale pink. She licked them often to keep them moist, and set them in movie-star poses.

The Mama. Blue velvet and ermine, foot poised over the snow.

Listen! she had said.

She was thin but not just. Lucille was shocked how slight she was. More than thin it seemed. Like something was eating at her. Down to bones and beyond.

To Memphis. The show was supposed to be a good one and there were bound to be choice things to buy. Quality things she certainly hoped, otherwise she would keep her money in her purse. Her mind moved on: she would get out of here and go, to where her expertise was valued and her presence always welcome. Where she was admired. Looked up to. Respected.

Here was nothing.

Here was the past.

Was nothing.

Suddenly all three women spoke at once and it was to Lolly as if three giant birds had suddenly descended on her, to hound her into corners and peck out her eyes.

". . . can't tell you how happy . . ."

". . . do you *want?*"

"Lucille, did you write her about . . ."

Like the green team's wide receiver Lolly looked for daylight, found a hole and went for it. Her head was high, her purse was snapped shut on her arm and she was heading out. Headed home. Back to Memphis, then home. Free and clear again, where nobody knew she'd lived in a trailer. Where nobody knew even who Emma Blue Lasswell was, not her husband, not his two sons, not anybody. She had said she was an orphan, loose in the world with no family. And had become, practically, that too, to herself as well. Had lifted herself out of this as well as if she had flown away from it. Was free and clear in her own kind of life, or had been until Lucille's letter. Frank's death had moved her some. Enough to come here to see, but enough was enough . . . she was dead-aimed for the front door.

Which Emma was dead-flat leaning against.

". . . WHERE DID HE COME FROM?" the TV announcer was screaming. "Goal line to goal line, a kick-off return touchdown. I tell you, it's pandemonium here. . . ."

Emma's awareness dipped down to the game for a sec-

ond. . . . Who had scored? Who was ahead? . . . then returned as quickly to the woman coming toward her.

She was a collector now. She said to herself: some people
are this, some that, some the other; I myself once called myself a baton twirler, and I was that too. Now I collect. I am a
collector. It's what I *do*. What I know. What I am. And am
good at it too, the best.

Cups and saucers. That she knew about. If they had asked
her about cups and saucers or even what her new interest in
life might be, she might not have left; because she dearly
loved to talk about what she knew. Which was cups and
saucers now: ask her about cups and saucers, she can tell
you all you need to know and more.

Me, the Mama had said: *Me!*
Emma stood stolidly; she would not be moved, not now.

The sons were not Lolly's but her husband's from a previ-
ous marriage, which he had dissolved in order to marry
Lolly. They lived in a large brick house on five acres; it had
a man-made lake beside it and faced westward, toward sun-
sets.

Inside were hints and clues and indications of Lolly's new
passion. It was Lolly's house in fact. Her husband said: I'm
second to the collection. And laughed. Chuckled to his
friends how crazy his wife was for antiques and cups and
saucers.

Cups and saucers were on tables in the living room, cups
and saucers on a corner shelf behind the piano and even
scattered about on the piano itself as well, so that they jan-
gled slightly whenever it was played or tuned which was

rare, because no one in the family played. Some were in the
dining room on the buffet; some on a bric-a-brac shelf; some
inside a china cabinet. Cups and saucers were all over the
place, daring a footstep to fall too heavily or a child to trip
or tussle.

The maid did not handle the collection; Lolly took the
sets down herself to be dusted. Twice a year they were
washed, on schedule. She went from room to room, taking
down one set at a time in order, then took them to the
kitchen to wash carefully in a plastic dishpan and dry by
hand.

They were not just beautiful however but an investment:
worth a great deal in the antique market. When she said this
to people they looked at her curiously, waiting it seemed for
her to cover over her seriousness with a trace of irony or
humor. But she hadn't a trace of it to give. She only cata-
logued her new acquisitions in a dry and calculated number-
ing, this one and this one and that, as if the truth, the value,
the seriousness of what she said could not be challenged or
laughed at, ever.

This one you see . . . she said.

Notice on this set, she said. . . .

Her husband was proud of her. He told his friends how
good she was at her collecting. Lolly can't get enough of
cups and saucers, he said. As for their investment value he
wasn't sure, but he indulged her, even though to him they
were only dishes you couldn't drink out of. To a car dealer,
no prize.

She was the prize.

Simply, he adored her.

Even though she showed little feeling for his sons and
lately seemed to be drifting even from him.

Not simply thin, Lucille thought. Drawn. Something used
up. Little was left, she'd used up too much.

"A little late aren't you?" Granny growled as Lolly passed
her. One tiny eye twitching with pleasure, Granny then
looked back down, as if at the TV set, but kept the thin, com-
posed woman well in her sights.

She had gotten past Lucille and Granny without
difficulty, now . . . but Emma stood against the door, leaning
back on the thick metal, daring her to approach it.

Not a pretty girl, not even attractive: square, messy, her
hair wild and frizzy . . . Peavey hair it was . . . her blue
blue eyes . . . Lord. Another one Lolly had willed herself to
forget. James Blue. There he was, in his daughter's eyes, her
daddy's eyes exactly there on Lolly.

Emma Blue Lasswell. Lord what a name to have chosen.
What a girl for her to have given birth to. Ordinary, just as
she had thought.

Afterwards Emma didn't know where she got the courage
or the notion, except that, after all, the Mama was leaving
and certainly was not coming back and so what did she have
to lose? Nothing to lose, everything to gain: like Granny
said, don't measure, don't look back, just do it.

First she grinned; that stopped her. Lolly Ray Lasswell
Turnage Mama on the way out was stopped dead in her
tracks.

His smile too. When he took off his silver mirrored sun-
glasses, his eyes stayed serious like that. So you couldn't tell
what he was up to, or calculate correctly which way he was
going to go, it gave him that power.

Lolly drew in her breath. She could not let that stop her
either, she had to go.

"Lolly, *wait*." Lucille was standing now too, though her legs seemed hardly able to hold her up.

Emma spoke.

With her wild frizzy head still against the bescratched metal door, she said, "How you been . . . *Mom?*" And grinned again, her eyes still dead set stone serious and set, fixed that way, like marbles.

She could do anything now, she was ready: Emma had assumed her very best bluff-tough stance and from now on she could handle whatever came. Now that she knew what the risks and advantages were; now that she had scoped out possible odds, probable consequences, inevitable endings. Now she could choose. Had. Chosen.

"Good girl," Granny mumbled.

The game was over. Lucille had won in that final kick-off return touchdown. Granny kept it all filed in her head. Later she would use it.

Lolly was so close Emma could hear her breathe. The greeting had worked; she stood motionless there, forced to confront her daughter, unable to get past her until Emma allowed her to.

Emma looked deep in her eyes. There was some life there. When she said Mom, it came up, small points of life, flecks of anger surfacing, like shredded bits of paper floating on water.

Lolly drew back her arm. The eyes lit up.

The arm came back before she knew it. She had never before slapped anybody in her life. But the girl was standing there smiling in her James Blue way, threatening her with that remark, challenging her. . . .

The hand stayed behind her in the air, out of control, she

could not bring it down or go one way or the other but kept it there, or it stayed there, on its own it almost seemed, trembling with indecision. Which way, which way . . . it didn't matter; only don't come back; whatever would get her out the fastest and make it most certain she would never be back.

As Emma braced herself for the slap, she looked deeper, beyond the life she had seen, for what sustained her, beneath those flecks of anger. But there was nothing. No life, no hope, no vision: Mattie Sue's black eyes at ninety-four were younger as she died, and more spirited, than these. Beneath the paper flecks of anger was a flat still endless plane of nothing. She was dry. She had discarded too much and, having kept too little of substance and nourishment too soon, she now lived on a diet of fancy nothing. She was used up and empty. The Mama was a pumped-up dead woman. More alive in the voice Emma heard than in reality; her sparkle only make-up, her control merely passiveness. She was a stopped person, bottled and capped.

Emma knew she would not carry through the slap, and moved aside.

That quickly . . . like that . . . the anger was gone. Her hand came down and when Emma moved aside she went to the metal door, turned the knob, walked out.

"Shit," Emma murmured. She had hoped for the slap; it would have served.

Lolly went down the steps toward her car. Emma moved to close the door behind her.

But a great whizzing movement brushed by Emma too, all arms and desperation, a screaming and running, a great jazzy wind of determination.

"No!" Lucille screamed, coming to the door, gesturing to the woman in the brown and white car with LOLLY on the front bumper. "Wait! Wait!"

Lolly got in the car and started it but did not leave. She would give it one more chance and that was all.

Lucille ran to the kitchen pantry, picked out something of his, went to her bureau—in the living room beside the couch she slept on—dug madly for something else and ran out the front door to catch her before she left.

Lolly sat calmly behind the wheel, engine running, as her mother ran out the door, arms flailing, a package in one hand, her long arms flapping crazily, flinging something back and forth. Lolly rolled down the window.

"Here," her mother said, gulping for breath, "you ought to have something at least."

It was Frank's flashlight, a good one with a strong beam. Lolly remembered it. It was silver, with ridges of silver the length of it.

Lucille's eyes held steadily onto her daughter's. It was the first time Lolly could remember her mother not looking off the minute she found eyes on her. Lucille's long chin was firm, her mouth was pulled down tight, and her forehead was smooth as a baby's, without a wrinkle. She looked strong. Saying nothing, Lolly took the flashlight and laid it beside her. In her mother's face she saw familiar traces, something she had seen before. Herself. Her own face. A resemblance. She hadn't known. It was Lolly who looked away first.

"And here . . ." She poked a package into the car decisively, as if to keep her from returning it. "We don't need this and you might find reason to, in case there's a girl up there you might want to hand it on to."

No. No daughters in her house. Only men. And none from her own flesh. Not ever again.

She could not look at Lucille again; it would only weaken her resolve.

Lolly took the package, put it on the seat beside the flashlight and, without looking back, left . . . drove to 84, flipped down the left-turn blinker, wheeled north in her brand-new LOLLY-tagged car and went toward home, going fast.

Lucille watched as the brown car turned left then moved out of sight . . . like him, not likely to come back. This time she knew ahead of time and could accept it: Lolly was not coming back. This time it was clear to Lucille and as real as something she might be standing there holding in her hand. Only it was the absence of a thing she was holding. The absence of her daughter in her world now, and from now on. Lucille let her hands drop. The watch hit her knuckles.

She had not come home to get Emma. Had never acknowledged any responsibility or owned up to any commitment. As always her chin was high and she was marching. Her knees were popping high, her hair was shining loose and free and she was jumping and jiving over and across streets and football fields, as much now as ever, she would never change, she hadn't anything else to go on.

Lucille looked at the place where she saw her last, at the end of the trailer road where the red blinker flashed and the LOLLY tag disappeared. She let go of her but kept her too. *Mother of* still: she would not imitate her and Frank and let it all run from her grasp.

She went back into the trailer expecting a fight, but Granny and Emma did not look up at her or say a thing. They were seated as before, in front of the two TVs. They had changed their watching however, and had turned up the sound on the left-side TV while the post-game wrap-up show was on on the right one.

Lucille came and sat in her chair, on the near side of Granny.

She had finished her sink rug, but couldn't bear to lay it on the floor to stand on and get wet. It hung on the couch, across the back of it. Granny sat against it now, her head against the branch the eagle's talons clasped. Lucille won-

dered if Lolly had noticed. Or if she had, if she had any notion who had hooked it.

"Here . . . you win."

Emma held out a quarter. Lucille's team had won by one
point, giving her four over Emma.

The games went on all day. They watched until past midnight, Granny barely griping at all now, all three of them
abstracted somewhat, dreamy, remembering . . . that remembering taking them to other and other remembering.
Emma paid as much attention as she could to the games but
her mind kept wandering, as she tried to think what she
might do next, to get out of this terrible new hurt and move
on. Whenever that happened, she would clear her throat
and make some comment about a player, or ask about a
play, to get herself back into it, and watch what she was
watching while she was about it. She went to bed that night
feeling loose, freed. It was while she lay there rerunning her
version of the day that she came to understand about her
forward-leaning walk. It was not pulled ahead as Lucille
thought, but reacting against. Against the rope trying to
hold her back.

On the road . . . she would go to Memphis now, and attend the auction . . . Lolly fondled the package, certain she
knew what was inside.

Just this side of Sunflower she pulled over to a roadside
park and took off the yellowed tissue paper tied with string.
There. Yes. Preserved like a wedding gown. She held it up.

Every sequin had been sewn tight—most looked new—the
zipper had been replaced, the elastic was fresh. It looked
brand new. Her homecoming gift. But why? The suit glittered in the sunlight, and as the sequins shifted, they shim-

mered and argued with the sun, and sparks of color bounced
from window to window and made her close her eyes. But
even then it did not leave, even with her eyes shut. Arcs of
red and green and gold danced on, inside her lids there, and
pictures came by in a grim parade. Sometimes memories
held on in spite of everything, and held on and on, and like
shards of a broken mirror sprinkled over the surface of the
mind, hurt. Sending messages and reflections back and forth
in endless recognitions and reversals, cruelly making her recall what she had let go of: where she had been, who had
gone beside her then. But why? Why would Lucille bother?
She was crazy, always had been. To spend time and effort
on something from a time dead and buried was crazy. Lolly
folded the gold suit carefully, bringing the neck and elas-
ticized legs to the middle like a letter folded in three,
and after rewrapping the package went on again—slowly
through Sunflower this time, nodding to the sheriff and his
brood when she passed them—and spent the rest of the trip
thinking of Lucille and how she had looked handing her
Frank's flashlight through the window and then the yellowed package, and shook her head thinking how crazy it
was to do such a thing.

Thought of this and thought of it, and of Emma and how
she had looked, and of Granny, and remembered what had
seemed long dead and buried until she got close to the
Memphis city limits—that hill that came just before the sign
marking it and the next saying WELCOME TO MEMPHIS,
QUEEN CITY OF THE SOUTH—when she stopped. From
then on she didn't think of it anymore, but directed her attention away and set it back where it would stay for the rest
of the trip, on the show ahead, the cups and saucers there.
An expert buyer, not easily fooled, she would go from one
display to another tapping cups with her long fingernails,
holding saucers to the light, peering carefully at trademarks,
brushstrokes, signatures. Seeing her, dealers would put away

their near-undetectable imitations and go for the real thing. Lolly Turnage knew what she wanted and bought accordingly, with money to spare for authenticity.

But she found nothing to interest her at this particular show and went home the next day empty-handed, to find life normal, and greetings warm but not exaggeratedly, suspicions in no way evident. She had risked nothing after all. Nothing had changed . . . only sometimes, her sleep. Otherwise, it was the same. Love still seemed unnecessary and beyond reach; responsibility was drudgery disguised; connections, merely restraints. She would be a twirler still, in her way; free high-stepping with an eye on flash and style. In mountains now, where the climate was cooler and less dense and more unfamiliar to her past. Where demands were gentler, and explanations . . . guilt . . . those Peavey-type confrontations not called for. Where feet were less likely to sink, the earth being solider there.

She packed her gold suit carefully in a drawer and left the silver flashlight in the glove compartment of her car.

Believing whatever she had left would always be there to go back to if she wanted to. And was it so much? Believing it would stay preserved for her in the trailer, wrapped up in tissue and string like the bright uniform of her youth.

And—after all—was it so much?

Was it? She was gone.

The farther she had got from them, the thinner the trees became. From the fat-trunked ash and pecan and oak with their spreading limbs to sit under, to thin birch and dogwood and cottonwood and firs. Scrubby pines meant she was home. Home. Her collection. Her new family, who asked so little of her that she never felt pressed, never engaged.

Lucille had changed. She was letting her hair grow and had new glasses and was stronger. Lucille. Of all people. Who'd have thought Lucille would be the one.

In the spring she planned to take down her collection piece by piece and wash it; inspect it for damage; rub the frames with lemon oil.

In the spring. She looked forward to that.

Her picture was scheduled to be in the March issue of *The Collector;* she wished there was some way they would see it. She might think of a way.

V

GRADUATION

Six o'clock. Two hours yet. Emma drove over the railroad tracks, felt its bumps beneath her, went down Main half a block and when she got even with the pink house, stopped.

The vines had been cut down and the house repaired. The circular window between floors had four intact panes and the drive had been restored, the windows cleaned, curtains replaced by shades and blinds. She could see, past the trimmed pyracantha, someone working in the backyard. Planting most likely; it was May, time to be planting or thinning or rooting out weeds.

Mattie Sue would have been proud. The house provided a home for teen-agers without parents. They lived with a couple there, who were in charge. The high school was nearby, and they had some semblance of home life in the pink house. On the ten acres, which it turned out were not only close to Eunola Christian School but backing up to it, against its rear barbed-wire fencing, a new orphanage was being built.

At the curb, Emma stayed parked for a while, seeing how

beautiful the pink house was, just sitting there, all by itself
on that bare empty block.

The car was hers, a gift from Lucille out of the insurance
money. It was small and red, an American economy car, not
powerful or fancy, but Emma loved it, loved it; from the
minute she sat in it she loved it. Closed up inside it she felt
like she finally had something. Some freedom. The way to
go was hers: how to get there. She could ride when she
chose to, go *as* she liked. Such comfort, closed up and tight-
surrounded with the radio going, her own space, wrapped
up in metal.

Carroll had offered her a car as well, Lady's old Thunder-
bird, which was still in his garage. A wonderful car, it was
white with a black removable hard top and red leather interior, and Emma longed to take it. Carroll said he would
have it fixed up, put on new tires and get it in top running
shape. But she could not, not after being with him the way
she had, those times in the pink house, not after he had told
her what he wanted. Not yet at least. Later . . . maybe, she
wasn't sure.

She put the car in gear and drove on.

The sun was nearly down behind the levee. A rosy darkness had crept down Main. Emma drove into the sun.

The radio was on, playing rock music loudly. Downtown
was quiet, business traffic having left for the day and Fri-
day-night drunks not yet far gone enough to be out yet. At
Jesse's Cafe she turned left, went a block down River Road
and at Court turned right, in the direction of the levee and
the water.

Wishing as she went she had not thought of Carroll.

The levee was paved for that one block between Court
and the next street, Jefferson, and you could drive on it right
down to the water's edge if you wanted to. This paved block
was divided into two distinct parts. The older, larger section, built just after the flood in the twenties, was made of

concrete blocks. These came from deep under the water's
surface to its edge then sloped up in a wide and gentle incline. The crest of this section was the same as that behind
the monument and that of the levee all up and down the
river. The second part—built since the monument's war-in-
question—was simply a hump of smooth pavement, set on
top of the older levee as reinforced protection and to give
the ship people access to land in times of high water.

The car was clean and waxed; Emma kept it impeccably
fit. She drove up the lower incline of the levee's town side,
then shifted the car down for the steep ascent. She went
left, up to the newer part of the levee, high over the street
below. Midway between Court and Jefferson, the car
stopped on the hump, its nose pointed slightly down and toward the water. Emma pulled the emergency brake, got out
of the car and climbed up on its hood, looking west, toward
the water and the sun, and thought again of Carroll.

At first it had made him uncomfortable, the way she kept
her eyes open and watched, but because of what he wanted
—the change his life required—he did it too, in imitation of
her; learned to keep his open too as he yielded to her and
from the tight hard fist of himself let it flow out. And the
blank space behind his leveled-out eyes filled to overflowing,
with her and this loving need and, exchanging life, one for
one, they not only gave to one another, with eyes wide open
watching, but shared in what came between, what was
created by the sharing . . . each taking a portion of the
other, meshing self with self, trading back and forth and
back and forth until one seemed actually to melt into the
other, all the while maintaining the rhythm, keeping steady
the rolling, the rolling rolling flow.

Because the car was pointed toward the water, Emma
didn't see Alice Chow leave the library and lock it for the
night, then carefully pick her way down the steps and across
the jagged, broken sidewalk, taking prim, sure steps, as cau-

tious as a well-mannered child. Alice went to her car and there, looked back at the sunset—gaudy, inimitable—outlining the levee, but also did not see a sign of Emma or her car, which was parked too far down the other side. Alice carried a wrapped package. She planned to go home before the ceremony. She had not seen Emma much lately and wanted to give her a graduation gift.

Emma did not see Alice pull away from the curb in her car, after looking both ways for traffic, then—to be doubly certain—checking once again. Emma was looking at the water, in the other direction.

The sun was almost gone. It was May, and setting late now, but soon it would resist going for even longer, not until past eight, when lawns were all mowed and golfers and farmers finished with their work and families fed; when the nightly TV movie had begun and people thought they could not stand one more half second of the terrible heat, when mosquitoes were fat and the long day was glutted and had spent its energy for a while. Only then would it let go and, for a few hours, disappear. Now, the sun's bottom arc was flattened like a bitten candy wafer, as it dropped into the water into an island in the middle of it, a flotilla of mud and trees. The sky was streaked with trailing smears of color, and the water took on those hues as well and, glamorized, smoothed and preened itself, stretching langorously, preparing for its rendezvous with its more compatible and less urgent lover, the moon.

Emma lay back against the windshield, her arms pillowing her head.

The last time they were together was in his office, but not so close then: sitting on either side of the marble slab like strangers, as if the other had not happened. His body had resumed its old inflexibility for the occasion—his head once again set like a tulip on a stem—but in his eyes if she forced it she could still find that private self; he could never take it from her altogether anymore . . . the part she knew fluttered up occasionally, whenever he took her gaze on fully. But when that happened he would lower his eyes and take it from her, keeping a portion of himself in check, something in reserve, to go on in case she said no.

He made his offer.

Shocked, she was the one who then looked away, down at her feet. She had been unable to respond for several minutes.

And didn't things come in funny bunches. Like Lucille always said, you just never know. What Lolly had wanted so desperately and had worked so hard to get, her daughter could have without turning a hand, or almost. Just by saying yes. Marriage, he said, or not; now or later . . . however she wanted it; he didn't care. As he put it, she could call the shots as far as formal arrangements went. Only one thing: he needed a definite answer, her word on the commitment: yes or no. So that he would know what to expect and be able to make his plans accordingly.

I would like very much to make a life with you. Those had been his exact words. He had ended his small speech with that bare simple statement. And then waited. It took a long time for her to answer and when she did, she said only that she could not say. She would have to have some time. Thinking: Lord. You never know.

He said he understood and then sat waiting again, hitting a pencil on the table, first on the point end and then the eraser. His gold bracelet went up and down with the tapping; he was waiting . . . for what? Were they going to . . . ? Like they always . . . ? She waited too, not quite sure whether to approach him or not. And then she understood: he couldn't risk it, not now. Not again. Not until she said, one way or the other. This was as far as he went. He would give her the rest and wanted to, but only if he knew what to expect, where she was when she was there with him and how long it would be for. Finally, she got up and very quietly left. She hadn't seen him since. And she missed him terribly, him and what they had shared, lust, love, sex, skin . . . whatever it was. Could still share, she supposed, but she wasn't certain if it had changed or not, she didn't know enough about it yet.

She looked to her left to the southwest and squinted, to see if she might catch a glimpse of the bridge down there. It was too late. The air was not clear enough now. You could see it only when the sun was high and the silver beams and girders sparkled between it and the water, and even then it was the shine you saw and not the thing itself; the water's reflection in place of the actual river.

Another car whined up the steep incline from Jefferson Street. When it reached the top of the hump it went straight down the river side then turned sharply and screamed back up it again then zigzagged back down again. Inside the car, a girl held her face in her hands and shrieked, as two boys laughed, watching her. Passing Emma, they neither waved nor acknowledged her presence but went on with their roller-coaster weave then left down the Court exit, the girl still singing her gleeful fear.

Emma had never participated in that kind of easy thrills. She hadn't even the vocabulary for it, could not spit out slang with ease the way others did, the way you had to, to join up with them. She would not have freely chosen her outsider's stance of her own accord, and would not have spent her youth in the company of old people, if it hadn't seemed the only option that left her with any dignity. Like anyone, she would have enjoyed approval; it would have warmed and supported her and she could have been comfortable in its safe and blankety circle . . . no matter where, in the trailer, in the pink house, at Carroll's, school, wherever: approval went with you once you had it and then you didn't have to match wits constantly for it or fight the need to want it either. Now she was independent, but alone, without loving arms for refuge, or a glib, offhand manner to shield her.

But acceptance was a slippery thing, and she was clumsy, with little talent for manners or flattery. And so instead of making a fool of herself, she had removed herself from that contest and had opted for their attention instead, going where and as she would, into unexpected places at inconvenient times, an adventurer scouting territory, investigating means and manners and how decisions got made.

Lolly, she thought, wanted both. Attention *and* approval. And in the long run she hadn't done much better than Emma. As for the loneliness—she hadn't seen a trace of it inside those blank-wall, mascaraed eyes. And she didn't know how it would be to start over that way, on new ground, leaving so much behind. If she did—left all the Peaveys behind, Lucille and Granny and all the rest—what then? All the family she'd ever had? She wasn't sure. Even with Cunningham possibilities in her future.

Emma Blue Lasswell Cunningham? It was a mouthful. Being what Lolly wanted . . . having to do nothing or next-to, in order to maintain her position and keep her acceptance, not twirl or turn or shine, not bow or nod or flash, only be who she was, herself with her name . . . could she do it?

The prospect was more inviting than Emma would ever have expected.

Because it was spring the river was high, with more thaws and rains yet to come. And so the lake before her, fed by the river, was high too. Only half as many concrete blocks as usual were in sight and the boats seemed about to come out of the water, like turtles reaching shore, to move into the town itself.

Close enough to walk to.

The water seemed endless. As if it were the rest of the

world. As if there was nothing beyond, only the water, there, all the way to the sun and past.

She stared into the blood-red half circle until it blurred in her eyes and became part of the sky, indistinguishable from it.

Lolly she would not forget. She kept pieces of her pasted in her memory, like the last petals of a corsage. Something Lolly could have given her, she had chosen not to, from the first; some piece of herself, if only the tiniest, had been denied her daughter. And for what? A new car? A home? Rich perfume and blue-green eye shade? A nagging pain still haunted Emma, one empty place in her heart, saved for its nesting. She would not close it up or let it disappear. She would nourish whatever Lolly had left her, even pain, to visit with from time to time. A reminder, to keep her mind set outside itself instead of turning in, as Lolly's had, devouring its own resources, not setting enough aside to live on. Like Granny said, you got to know who you are and hold on to it. Don't leave it.

The reedy treetops had captured the sun and now nibbled away at its bottom. In its loss, the air turned a sudden and faint blue-gray, shot through with an almost silver light, giving a false semblance of coming light instead of darkness. The day's last stand.

A cabin cruiser roared up for docking and the water lapped gently from its intrusion, making soft licking sounds against the concrete blocks. Then it was peaceful again, except for the mosquitoes, which had begun to swarm.

And her stomach. Lunch had been hours before, and hunger was not something Emma could tolerate; when she felt it, she had to assuage it or she became irritable and nervous. That, Lucille had often said with some pride, was exactly how Frank had been. She got that from Frank, Lucille said.

Now only a sliver was left. The treetops tugged and bit by bit won their prize. Slowly it joined them, rested for a minute in their joints and knuckles and then was gone. The shot of light had disappeared; the air was a dark gun-metal gray.

Frank was still one of the mysteries. She could not imagine going off that way forever. Dying there with no people, no home. Something in her would not allow it, the Peavey part perhaps. Peaveys had a habit of staying, not only to the end of a thing but way past it too. What they had to learn was when to leave.

Emma sat straight up and scratched a bite, killing the mosquito perched there, smearing her own blood across her arm. The sun was altogether gone now, or they, the earth, had moved around from it, though she never could quite accept that in her solid mind, that motion itself was the root of it all. It made things too undefined, too indistinguishable, one from the other. Only the sun's bright trail remained. Instantly, the air grew cooler and up there on the levee's hump it was even chilly and made Emma draw her arms in close. Behind her, streetlamps automatically turned on, and she could see them lined up for the length of Court, all the way to the railroad tracks. On the other side of which, after a jog to the right, was the high school. Graduation. Her stomach roared.

As Emma turned the ignition, the radio came on.

She aimed the car straight down the hump and without turning on its lights took off the emergency brake and let it coast down. The hump was steep; the car rolled swiftly down and took her breath; she felt her stomach drop and catch itself. On the concrete blocks, the car began to rumble slightly but still moved on as quickly as before, down. The water was so high. . . .

At its edge she heard the tires slap against its gentle lapping, then felt them give somewhat, losing traction in the wetness. She turned the steering wheel to the right, switched on the headlights, turned back up the levee then at its crest went down again, onto Court Street.

Through town, Emma crossed the railroad tracks, passed
the high school—the auditorium of which was already lit up
in preparation for graduation ceremonies—and at the intersection of Highway 84, turned left onto it.

On the edge of town, at the Dairy Delite, Emma pulled in
and ordered a fresh banana sundae and, when it came,
promptly ate the bananas and sauce before touching the ice
cream. Every time, she promised herself to save the sauce
until last, or at least to eat it gradually, along with the ice
cream, but it was no use, she couldn't help herself and ate
the best first, as always, scraping the sides of the paper cup
with her plastic spoon to get it all, before starting in on the
curlicue peak of the soft custardlike ice cream.

She sat on the left front bumper, swinging her legs against
the tire, enjoying her feast. And just happened to turn her
head then or she might have missed them; looked to the
right as they approached, in time to see them coming from
the north, down 84 toward Eunola, a small yellowish light
heading south.

Cup in hand, she slid off the bumper and walked away
from her car toward the highway.

No mistaking what car it was, that was for sure. Not the
slightest doubt. There wasn't another car in the world even
close to looking like that one. But who was daring to drive
it? Who was coming toward her? Emma moved a bit closer
to the highway, but not so close that she could be seen, and
squinted to see better as it approached. They had said they
weren't going.

Now and then the car made a slight squeaking sound on
the concrete, as its bald tires rubbed back and forth against
it and the car bucked slightly . . . not violently, only a gentle tug backward, an occasional resistance to staying in gear.
Emma knew the habit, she had had the problem herself
with the car. Sometimes it bucked in that back-and-forth
lunge-squat pattern for miles. But it was still coming, not

fast but coming, the ochre awful Nash, its cockeyed headlights and window-screening grille nosing a cautious way
into the night. They said it was too much trouble and they
were too old. They said she could tell them about it when
she got home.

Lucille was driving. When they got closer, Emma could
see her plainly, her chin so close to the top of the steering
wheel she seemed about to push through it; her hands close
together right under her chin, gripping the wheel. Both
women peered out the front windshield with great diligence, their heads so near the glass their breaths must be
fogging it, as if they were driving through a terrible storm
and could barely make out the way . . . on guard. But not
afraid; there was nothing of fear in the way Lucille drove or
held herself. Nothing about her drew back or flinched in her
usual way . . . all her attention was on the road, on the way
to get there, bucking or not. Had they changed their minds?
Or was it a planned surprise?

She could see them so plainly because they were so well
lit: the interior lights were on, another problem Emma was
familiar with. It was tricky to turn on the headlights without
including the interior lights too; you had to cock the button
to the left a little, just so, to do one without the other. Obviously they had not been able to hold their wrists just so. And
so Emma could see them as clear as anything, her grandmother and great-grandmother, driving to her graduation,
wearing the new spring-colored pantsuits—their first—which
Lucille had without warning made them for Easter, buck-
bucking into the darkness toward Eunola, going on and
dead-straight on, lit up inside where they were. The car
looked like a friendly little room, moving through the night.
And the two of them were, like explorers, on the look-out,
finding out for themselves where they were going, on their
own. They passed her by.

Emma watched until the car was out of sight. As Wymer

had said, Lucille drove well; she kept the car in an exactly straight line on her side of the highway, veering hardly more than inches one way or the other. And when the rounded hind end of the ochre tube Nash had disappeared, Emma returned to her car and finished her melted ice cream. She would give them time to get into town before leaving, so that she wouldn't pass them by or in any way fluster their new dignity.

Carroll had not thought he would go either. After all, she had given him no answer, he was only leaving himself open to the curiosity and stare of friends and strangers; nonetheless, he was dressing. Going in spite of the risk, in spite of the offer left hanging, in spite of his own resolve. He had not told her so and hardly knew the feeling well enough to recognize it himself, it was so alien to his life and experience, but . . . only part of what he wanted was her spirit and her energy. That was what had piqued his interest in the beginning, but now it went further. It came like a slice in his heart to think it, but there it was, he loved her. Going to her graduation was his own statement—to himself—of that fact: that he loved her life and how she embraced it, that he wanted her near him and would take of what she had whatever he could get, however much she could give and in whatever manner. With or without commitment. However she responded to his offer, with yes or no, he would not let her go.

Sometimes, once in your life anyway, you had to just do it. Take whatever risk you had to and make the leap. Without hesitation, in face of whatever odds. And he was. Eyes wide open, giving it his best shot.

He stood before the bathroom mirror turning his head from side to side, inspecting the blond waves he had let grow to please her. They came out from his head and made

him look top-heavy, he thought, too full around the ears.
But he expected he would get used to them. His sideburns
now came past his earlobe.

This was as far as he had ever gone; to go yet another
step, to think past it, into what else might be required of
him or how he might be hurt was too terrifying. He would
not give in to the terror of too much openness or too wide a
field of possibilities the way Preston had. He would only try
to keep it going. Move ahead with it as it went, at whatever
pace, with as much trust as he could manage. The way
Emma did. He checked his watch. Forty-five minutes yet.
He did not want to get there too early. He would wait
twenty, and then go.

For the first time in the history of EHS the seniors were
wearing caps and gowns of a color other than the traditional
black and gold, the school's colors. But then this was also
the first graduation class from EHS to be comprised more
than half of black students too, and so when the vote was
taken on what color caps and gowns to order, the new majority had stood together and voted to change. Not that maroon and white meant so much to any of them. But that the
power to change did. They wanted something new, to mark
their presence and its permanence.

Now the students milled about outside the auditorium as
the senior counselor tore around herding them together, trying to break up cliques and arguments to get everybody
lined up as they had practiced, in alternating alphabetical
order back and forth across two rows. When the strains of
"Pomp and Circumstance" began and they still weren't
properly arranged, she almost fell apart with anxiety, so
disorderly did the mass of different colored students seem.

But they did get lined up in time, and marched with dignity down the two aisles of the auditorium. Seeing them,

you wouldn't have guessed what a giggling, hysterical crew they had been only minutes before.

Alice sat about halfway down with the present in her lap, a dictionary. It was to be a symbol of what she hoped would be Emma's direction now. She wanted to see her leave. Get away from the Peaveys and go to school, find a profession that interested her and would give her the freedom she needed. Alice sat very still and calm and did not turn around as others did to see the seniors come marching in from the rear, but looked patiently ahead at the stage, waiting for them to file onto it.

Three rows from the rear in the center section, on the aisle, Granny Peavey craned her neck around and leaned out into the aisle looking for Emma, her mouth working away as she eyed each graduate.

But Emma never came; Emma was on the opposite side, with her hair coming out from under the cap in that terrible madwoman frizz so that from the rear you could hardly tell her from one of the new darker-skinned majority. The seniors who did come down Granny's aisle, however, saw the old woman. She stared back at them as if about to take their heads off, that wrinkled and shriveled old lady with the topknot of white hair, wearing a lime-colored pantsuit and tennis shoes, muttering under her breath "Now where the hell is Emma."

Beside her, tall and happy, was Lucille.

When Emma got to the stage and took her seat, she looked out to find them, her eyes going up and down rows in the audience from side to side until she came upon the brown-spattered old milky-white face with the cottony hair, straining to overreach the heads in front of her. And beside her, in yellow, Lucille. Serene and proud. She had driven to town. Sitting tall and correct, she was what she was and where she was, in time at last in the plain here-and-now, now. As she listened to the introductory remarks and invocation with diligence, her face seemed to shine, lit up with pride. She had finally done it; had driven herself into town. Now anything was possible, now she could go where she pleased, now she could save herself, herself. Her hair curled softly about her face like an ornate frame; setting off her wonderfully high cheekbones and deep-lidded eyes. She was beautiful. Deep in Emma's throat was a victorious cry, for Lucille. She could just barely restrain herself from releasing it.

Then she spotted Alice, sitting prim and sweet and cool as ever, a package in her lap. For her, Emma expected; a graduation gift, something to help her square out the rest of her life. She meant well, Alice, but there was something missing from what she offered, something of skin-to-skin immediacy, something Alice's professionalism left out, that Emma craved.

She had almost given up on Carroll when at last she found him. He was sitting where she should have known he would be, in the very last row of the outside section, as near an exit as he could get. It seemed only the wildest dream that he would come, but there he was, sitting with his neck stiff and his head pushed back as if in recoil, at an oblique angle; tilted to one side . . . a fuller head now, since he gave in and let his hair grow, but still, in public, a rigid fearful head, keeping himself contained, behaving as he had learned to, to get by without losing too much. He even slept that way. Curled up in a tight knot, his chin set just so, as if fighting the loss of consciousness instead of enjoying it. She grinned, thinking of how she had known him, lying, sitting, standing, squatting, in the chair, on the bed, wherever; his head moving up toward her as he felt it, his mouth moving down at the corners . . . how he had looked those times, those private times they took each other's eyes full-on. Knowing what was deep inside the rigidity others assumed was his entire self, knowing what was feeding that staunch, unyielding tightness, she had to smile.

The speeches went on, the audience grew restless, the air conditioning was up so high people began grabbing for sweaters or rubbing their arms up and down if they hadn't brought one. Crazy town. Where you froze in the summertime and in the winter burned up: just because they had newly installed units in the school didn't mean they had to show them off by freezing everybody half to death.

The counselor had worked out the process of receiving diplomas down to split-second timing. Each student was to get up from his or her seat the minute the name of the person immediately preceding was called, according to alphabetical arrangement, thereby assuring that the flow of seniors would be nonstop and that the rhythm, the solid, steady beat of students, would be maintained, and not drag on or be too staccato either. And so when Emma heard the name of DONIHUE SIMS LANCASTER called, she got up and headed toward the front of the stage.

Donihue however, a tall black boy, was not ready for her yet and brushed his elbow by her head as they exchanged places, and knocked her mortar board askew. Intent on getting where she was going, Emma didn't notice, and so when she got down to the podium where the principal was and he called her name, EMMA BLUE LASSWELL, loud and clear, her cap was at a flirtatious and jaunty angle, down over her left eye like a wink.

The principal sighed. There was always something undignified about that girl. She could never get the hang of how to behave.

That was how she looked as, smiling broadly, she accepted the diploma, shook the principal's hand, then, as she flipped her white tassel to the other side, cast an illicit, strictly prohibited look out into the audience. She stood there longer than she was supposed to, down on the apron of the stage, when she had been given strict instructions not to, so long that the counselor's stomach began to flutter. Emma smiled broadly at them. It would work out. Somehow.

The name of EDWARD LUNSOM LOU had already been called and Edward was there waiting for her to move out of the way by the time Emma finally turned from her family and went back to her place.